BRENDA ASHWORTH BARRY

Finding My *Heart*

Sweet Valley River #1

Satin Romance
an imprint of Melange Books, LLC

SatinRomance.com

I dedicate this book to my husband and his on-going support through all late nights and early mornings.

To my wonderful loving parents who always gave me their love and support.

My Melange Family. I feel blessed to be a part of the family.

SOME DAYS WERE JUST MEANT TO BE ROTTEN AND TODAY WAS ONE OF them. Starla sat in her Honda Fit, on the side of some godforsaken road outside Bardstown, Kentucky, watching the steam fly from her vehicle. What in tarnation had she been thinking, taking a road she didn't know, just because a wooden sign said Highway to Heaven? Now, she was up shit creek without a paddle. One would think the light on her dash turning orange would have given her a clue. Most people had knowledge of such basic information. She could blame it on being upset after meeting with the doctor, but that would be a lie.

It had taken eight days to find out the lab results. So, the whole week had stunk to high heaven.

As far as car issues, this sure as heck wasn't her first rodeo with being stranded. She was always forgetting to check things. How often had she ran out of gas and had to call someone for help? Too often to count.

Glancing in the mirror left no doubt—her brown eyes were filled with pure foolishness.

Maybe it wasn't a brilliant idea to leave on the first of May, it was always busy, but the walls had been closing in on her. The memory of Dr. Langley's words, yesterday, kept smoldering in her brain, no matter how often she tried to push it away. Her thoughts wouldn't turn off.

This was supposed to be a vacation. A time to put all worries away and try to relax, but that was something else she wasn't any good at.

After she left the doctor and went to work, she flew off the handle at two of her employees. That was the minute she knew it was time to take a break. However, being at home only made her feel worse. Since it was Friday, she packed up her bag and left for Bardstown, it was one of the most beautiful cities in Kentucky. All of America, for that matter.

No map, no plan, just the grand idea of an adventure and vacation. She picked up her cell, dialed information, and got them to connect her to the nearest towing company. The connection sucked, but all that mattered was getting someone out on this road to help her. It hadn't been on the map she had studied before she left. And of course, she hadn't brought it with her, so she hoped and prayed someone knew where it was. The phone pinged with the number from the operator. It was hard to hear, but at least she got the text. Why didn't they put the name too, instead of just the number? She looked down at her phone and dialed.

"Hello…" Static-static. ".. Ed's Company."

"I've broken down and was wondering if you could tow me into town?"

"Where are…?" Static-buzz. Just like with the operator, she couldn't hear much.

"I saw a sign before I broke down that said Valley Freeway, but there was this other sign that said Highway to Heaven." She heard more crackling. "Hello?"

Static. "I'll be right there."

Then, there was nothing. No sound and no connection. What kind of town was he coming from and why was the connection so bad?

"Heavens to Betsy." This was a pain in the... she had to wait and hope he showed up soon. She scolded herself mentally and continued complaining.

Why in God's name would she leave Interstate-64 in the first place, then take a road she'd never been on? Which now seemed like a highway to hell, not heaven. Wasn't there a song about that? She tried to remember the words.

She stepped out of the car and the air fanned its way around her. At least the temperature was nice, she mused, scanning the horizon. The place presented beautiful pink trees with lush greenery and a gentle breeze. A large bird of some type caught her attention as it squawked and landed on an evergreen. Dear Lord, it was staring right at her. She shuddered—it was a little bit creepy, the way it stared at her.

She slipped back inside her car. What was going on in her life? Why was everything going wrong? Had she brought this on herself? A tear trailed down her cheek, but she brushed it away. No way was she going to sit here and have a pity party.

Glancing down at her watch, she sighed, it had been fifteen minutes. Just great. She tapped her steering wheel. "Where the hell is the guy?"

❦

CONNOR OPENED THE FOLDER ON HIS DESK AND WONDERED HOW they'd fallen two weeks behind. His stomach took a dive thinking about his clients being jammed in that small trailer for an additional two weeks. The Owens were not thrilled, to put it mildly. Nobody could blame them. Being stuck with three children in such a tight space had to be tough.

Wait—he knew one thing he could offer. Nobody was in the office on the weekends. He glanced around at the beige walls and Berber carpet. The waiting room had two couches and a TV. The kitchen was small, but it had everything they'd need.

Better yet—why couldn't he just move the paperwork into his home office, so they could stay here? After all, his house was right next door and he had remote forward on his phone. There wasn't a bed, but there was a bathroom with a shower and commode. Plus, he had two air mattresses, or they could use their trailer as their bedroom. He had plenty of outside plugs. The little backyard was fenced and would give their dog a chance to play outdoors. He'd stop by and talk to them today.

Whelan Construction had a reputation to maintain. In a small town like Secret Valley River, where the population was less than twenty thousand, word of mistakes seemed to travel fast. Although, nobody was ever mean about it, he still wanted to do great work and in a timely matter. Most important was to keep his customers happy.

They'd push extra hard to get done, and he'd throw in some extra upgrades. Like carpeting and the refrigerator, they wanted. He could use some of his own money and surprise them. With a deep, lingering breath, he pushed the stress out of his mind. It was early, and he needed to relax and chill. Even though that was easier said than done. At least he'd planned on a small ride today. He needed to feel the wind against his face and enjoy all the nature around him.

Truth be told, age thirty-six was telling on him. He was plum tuckered out from working his ass off at the gym at o-dark-thirty, this morning. The day before, he'd been out in the field, helping his crew. Tommy hadn't been feeling well this last week, and that was one reason he was behind. Although, Connor suspected the guy had been burning the candle at both ends with his new girlfriend.

Damn. Connor felt his muscles tighten. He got up, stretched his arms over his head, and moved his shoulders. That was when his stomach reminded him that he'd skipped breakfast. It rumbled and practically shook the entire office. It was past time and he was starving for a good home-cooked meal. He had a great idea. He'd head out to Logan's Grill and order some of those biscuits and gravy with bacon and eggs. Hell, he'd just order the biggest meal on the menu. Just thinking about it made his mouth water.

He pulled his jacket off the hanger and slipped it on, then grabbed his helmet. It was a nice day, but in May, the breeze could get a little chilly, especially before noon.

The minute he stepped outside, he saw Megan heading in his direction. By the look on her face, she wasn't happy.

"Uncle Connor." She ran and threw herself in his arms. "Can you talk to my daddy, please?" She burst into tears. "I got asked out to the prom by Eli, but Daddy said I can't go. I'm fifteen, and all my friends are going with boys. I'm going to be the laughing stock of the entire town."

He stuffed back a laugh. "I'm sorry, sweet pea, but you know none of your friends would do that. That's not how the people around here act." One thing he loved most about Secret Valley River was that they had zero tolerance for bullying.

"I'm not sure if I can change your daddy's mind, but I reckon I could try. Why aren't you in school?" He brushed the blonde curls out of her face and watched more tears fill her pale blue eyes.

"Teachers' day or some nonsense like that. It's just an excuse for them to get the day off."

"Is there something about this Eli boy that your daddy doesn't like?"

"No," she said. "Eli is wonderful. He makes good grades and runs track." She sniffed. "Oh, Uncle Connor, Daddy says I'm too young to go to a dance with any boy. That I can only go with my girlfriends." She swallowed hard. "Please talk to him."

"All right, I'll give it my best shot." He winked and watched a tiny smile appear in the corners of her lips.

Yep, this girl was already a master charmer. Her daddy did not understand how much gray hair he would have by the time she was eighteen. Or maybe he did, and that was why he didn't want her to start dating.

"Thank you, Uncle Connor. Not only are you the most handsome uncle in the world, but you are also the best uncle ever."

He touched her nose. "I see." He laughed. "I'm fixing' to go over to Logan's Grill. I'll call your daddy and see if he'll join me. How's that sound?"

"Awesomeness." She gave him a giant-sized hug and released him, then walked away, but turned around after a few steps. "Thank you again, Uncle Connor." She met his gaze. "I love you." She also signed the words, and his heart melted like an ice cream bar in July under the summer sun.

"I love you, too." He blew her a kiss, put his helmet on, and climbed onto his Harley. She sure reminded him of his baby sister at that age.

"Oh hell, what have I gotten myself into?" He shook off the worry and headed on down the road. It was a gorgeous morning, perfect for a bike ride. After he ate, he would take one.

Once he rounded the corner, he had to pull over and get a glimpse of Secret Lake. He cut the engine and watched a flock of ducks skimming gracefully until they touched down. The lake was flanked by an avenue of cedar trees, casting reflections across the water. The way the wind blew its breath from corner to corner made the ripples glimmer.

Connor observed people paddling their canoes and could hear the laughter. Mr. and Mrs. Pauls had on their hats and gave him a wave. He nodded and watched as they used the oars in perfect harmony.

"Hey, Connor!" someone yelled, so he turned, and saw Gary Cox honking and waving.

He waved back and realized how lucky he was. Not everyone had a connection of friends they'd known since childhood. Growing up here had been great. All the secrets and whispers of unusual happenings had always seemed mysterious.

Local legend was that the water out near the hot springs carried healing powers. One time, he'd hiked out there after dark and seen fireflies. Before he could get a closer look, they had flown up toward the nighttime sky. Truth be told, he hadn't had much time to think about it. He'd seen the Indian woman and her wolf but didn't feel much like a conversation. He'd never gotten to know her, but his parents said she was a wonderful woman and a medicine one at that. The whole thing had sure as hell blown his mind, mainly because lightning bugs weren't supposed to be around in the winter.

Rumors also said that the waters not only held powers to heal you physically, but also emotionally. He wondered if that would have helped with depression.

Two bees buzzed around his shoulder, he waved them away. "Okay, y'all need to take off and leave my shoulder alone." And just like that, they were gone.

There was no pushing away the pain of the memories. These last six years, he'd dated a lot of women, if you called what he'd done dating. He had nothing to offer, except a night of fun.

He stared out at the lake and thought about his childhood sweetheart. When he first asked her to be his girl, it was on the banks of this water. She was only sixteen, not much older than Megan was, but at the time, she'd seemed all grown up, at least to him.

Connor had been the quarterback, a total jock, and she had been a drop-dead gorgeous cheerleader who kept her nose in books most days. They were in love and became inseparable. Everyone in town knew they belonged together. And the simple truth was they did. He thought he had his future all mapped out, but sometimes, things don't work out the way they are mapped.

All the reminders still brought up a fury of emotions, which left a nasty taste in his mouth.

He reined in his thoughts, got off his bike, and pulled the cell phone from his pocket and dialed.

"Hello," Duncan answered.

"Hey big brother, wondered if you had time to have breakfast with me at Logan's?"

"I ate hours ago, but I could go for a piece of pie. Everything okay?"

"Yes, brother. I'm out here by the lake, just remembering things. How about we meet there? I'm starving." He glanced out at the water one more time, and then climbed back on his Harley, still talking to Duncan.

"You sure you're okay?" his brother asked again.

"I'm good, just wanted to see the lake. So, can you meet me?"

"Sure, sounds good. See you soon," Duncan said.

Ten minutes later, Connor walked into the restaurant. The aroma of sautéed onions and garlic made his stomach rumble. There was also a hint of maple and cinnamon, which made his mouth water. The place was always busy for breakfast and the sound of clanking plates and light chatter filled the room. Ever since he could remember, Logan's Grill had never changed its décor, even when it was named Lakeside Grill. It still had the same old knotty pine walls and hardwood floors. The glass case still revealed some of the best desserts in the world. Logan had won many contests with his various pies.

"Hey, Connor. Nice to see you here."

He turned to see Logan and noticed Earl Rogers, the mayor, sitting at a booth talking to some young woman. He nodded, and Connor gave a short nod back.

"I know; it's good to be here. I've been so doggone busy lately. Running around like a chicken with my head cut off."

"Well, put your head back on and let's get you some grub."

"Duncan is headed this way too. I'd bet my Harley, he's going to ask for a piece of your sweet pecan pie." Connor laughed. "He always did love it for breakfast."

"We can certainly accommodate that." Logan picked up two menus, leading him to a booth close to the front door. That was perfect because he could see who came in and out.

"Thanks, Logan. This is great."

"Let me get you and Duncan a good cup of brew. I'll be right back."

The buzz in the restaurant increased as the mayor got up and strolled out with the attractive lady. Something was being talked about, but since Connor didn't keep up with the local gossip, he hadn't a clue or maybe he did. He'd venture to guess it had something to do with the bleached-blonde woman holding Earl's arm as they exited. The ink from his divorce paper hadn't even dried yet, and the people of the town loved his ex-wife Georgia. From the look on some of the faces, he'd have to say they were downright disgusted.

His brother walked in and waved just before he stopped to talk to Logan. Connor had missed the last couple family suppers and knew darn well he'd better make the next one, or his mama would have his hide. She always said, supper is not just for feeding, it's for nurturing her family.

Looking at his brother left no doubt in Connor's mind how much they looked alike. Both had sandy-colored hair with steel-blue eyes. Only Duncan was a lazy-bones who never worked out and sat behind a desk instead of performing hard labor. He had always been good with numbers and opened his own accounting firm. He was a CPA and had many local business accounts.

Connor, on the other hand, didn't like sitting around all day, and took pride in building up his body. His other brothers combined his mama and daddy. None looked like anyone other than themselves and everyone did their own thing.

But his only baby sister was a whole other story. Like their mama, she was tiny with long, blonde hair and deep green eyes. She was a southern belle, full of spice and trouble. Paige was living in Stanford California, going to medical school, and doing some type of residency program. Ten long years, she'd been gone. She didn't get home often and said it was because of her schedule. Sometimes he thought she had escaped to get away from six big brothers. Looking back, he knew they were all overprotective. Boy, had there been drama growing up.

She would get madder than a wet hen and had come after each of them more times than he could count. The funny thing was, she'd always threatened to beat the tar out of all six of them. One time, she'd cut off Hunter's ponytail when he was asleep. He chuckled, thinking back to that morning and how pissed Hunter got over the whole situation. Now, he was in the marines and kept his hair short anyway.

He still felt bad for the one guy who had tried to date her. Even today, when her old boyfriend, Spencer saw any of them, he went in the other direction. The truth was clear, Spencer had been crazy for his baby sister, but they had made his life hell. Even now, he blamed himself for what happened on prom night. He had never found out the truth, it wasn't his place. But his baby sister had been hurt and someday he hoped to find out why. His mother had warned all of them, to butt out, and they listened. You just don't mess with his mama.

Spencer seemed like a good guy, drove a Harley, and held a good job. They'd wave to each other. But, Spencer steered clear.

Duncan arrived and sat down. "Okay, I know why you called me here. Megan confessed she came crying to you. So, don't waste your breath, little brother, she's not going out to some dance with a boy. She's too young."

"But…"

"No buts. I'm not changing my mind on this one."

2

AFTER A WHILE, STARLA GOT OUT OF HER CAR AND PADDED AROUND IN circles. It didn't take long for her to jump back inside when she heard rustling in the bushes. Maybe she should just try walking and see if she would run into something. Right, with her luck, she'd meet a big, hungry bear.

It had almost been an hour since she called. She glared at her dashboard and noticed how dusty it was. "For heaven's sake." She picked up a rag and wiped it away. "There, that's better." Lord forbid, she had dust in her car.

Hadn't Oliver said—"Starla, the problem is, you're a perfectionist to a fault. If you want to get married someday, you must ease up."

He was right too, she rarely took a day off work, because everything had to be perfect in her life. Her car, at least the cleanliness of it, her home, hair, and clothing. Nobody would ever want to live with her, so why pretend the reason was anything other than her ways and not because of her health? That was a fabrication or a fiction story she'd made up.

Well, here she was again. Having a pity party. The good news was she had brought sweet tea in her thermos. Mama had always said, if life gives you lemons, put 'em in your sweet tea and drink the whole damn glass. After taking a sip, she climbed out of the car, wondering again if she should walk.

Another half hour passed. She was about ready to scream until she heard something approaching. It was some guy on a motorbike. Good heavens, was that the towing method? She hadn't seen one vehicle on the road until now, and it wasn't even a car.

She moved closer to the driver's door. He'd more than likely be a madman with an ax or a hammer hidden under his jacket.

Just as she started to climb into her car, he pulled up to the driver's side and took off his helmet. Well, he was certainly normal looking. If you had to be murdered by someone, at least you'd get to enjoy the final view.

How insane had she gone? She answered her own question—three gallons of crazy in a two-gallon bucket.

"Hi there, ma'am." He smiled. "Looks like you've broken down." His voice was low, sexy, and vibrated through her.

"No, I just thought I'd hang out on the side of the road for a few hours and drink a whole glass of sweet tea with lemons."

He climbed off his bike and chuckled before running his eyes across her car. The way he strolled wasn't like a man would, but with a capital M, capital A, and capital N. Every single inch of him.

Even the way he checked out her car suggested sex appeal. He was gorgeous, with cobalt-blue eyes and a body that was solid muscle.

Looking back at her, he ran his hand through his thick, sandy hair. "What happened?" He waited for her to speak and stepped closer, then stared at her.

The way he cocked his head and captured her eyes made her feel like he was reading her thoughts. She'd better think of something else before it was too late.

Oh mercy, a slow grin spread across his rugged face, and heavens above, he was even more amazing. You have to be kidding!

Okay, get a grip and breathe. If she looked close enough, he wasn't all that perfect. His nose was a little big and his strong jaw had stubble on it. Plus, he had extremely muscular legs with wide shoulders. She noticed how he filled out his shirt that was tucked into his, snug… Goodness gracious, this man was a tall drink of deliciousness in tight fitting jeans with narrow hips. She'd bet he had a great butt too. Did she just think that or was someone else living in her brain?

If he weren't standing right there, she would have slapped her own face. But, instead, she was determined to use her professional voice. Although, it seemed lodged behind the lump in her throat.

She pointed toward the hood of the car. "I was driving, and it started smoking. When I pulled over, steam came flying out and it practically exploded, like a volcano."

"Ah, it overheated. Could be the radiator or the thermostat. Not that I know much about cars." He reached in his pocket. "I have a cell phone. Would you like me to call a tow truck?"

"I did, forever ago, but they never showed."

"Who did you call and just how long is forever ago?" The corner of his lips twitched upward.

"I don't know, over an hour or so. I'm not sure whom I spoke with. There was a bad connection and the operator sent me a text. The guy said he was coming."

"Do you think it was Fred's towing?" he asked.

"Yes," she said. "That could have been what he said and the operator. He did say he'd be right here." She twisted her hands.

He frowned. "Sometimes, Fred doesn't always know what right here means. Look, why don't I give you a lift into town? We can get him to pull his head out of his comic books and get out here."

"I have on a skirt and what about a helmet?" She wondered if it was safe to get on his bike.

"You can use mine. Helmet, I mean." He raised his eyebrows. "However, I can't help you with the skirt. All I have are my jeans. I don't think driving around without my pants on is a good idea. My mama raised me with good southern standards and would have my hide." His laugh was rich and warm. "Do you have any pants in your car?" he asked.

"I do, but no place to change." She looked around and tried to shake off the thought of his pants being off.

"I'll turn my head. I'm a gentleman." He grinned.

"Okay, thank you. I'll change." She went to her trunk and pulled out her overnight bag. At least she'd brought enough stuff for a few days.

While she changed into her jeans, she took notice. He stayed true to his word. He kept his back to her and stood by his bike the entire time. What was with his knuckle cracking? Oh, well, most important, he was a gentleman—or seemed like it anyway.

He handed her his helmet and jacket, then helped her onto the bike. "This is a nice motorbike," she said, smiling excitedly.

"Well, my motorbike," he said and chuckled, "is a Harley. What's your name, by the way?"

"Oh, of course, my name is Starla."

"Nice to meet you, Starla, I'm Connor."

Hearing him say her name was better than chocolate-filled caramel with glazed salt. He stuck out his hand, and she took it. The touch of his skin made her heart turn over like a capsized boat.

"Thank you, Connor. I appreciate this." She pulled her fingers away and ignored the shiver that ran down her spine.

"You're welcome."

"Do you have a pen and paper?" Starla asked.

"I do. Why?"

"I thought we should leave Fred a note in case we miss him."

"No worries about that. There is only one way in and one way out of Secret Valley River. Unless you take the back route, which nobody ever does. It's pretty isolated."

"Oh, okay." What kind of place was this town? To have only one main road to get there. What about fires and stuff? Well, she wouldn't be here long enough to find out.

Had she ever been on a motorbike in her whole life? No. She sure hoped they didn't crash. He climbed on and asked her to wrap her arms around him and hold on tight. She needed to focus on something else, besides crashing. There were much scarier things in life.

When Connor took off, the memories came back from the doctor's office.

The minute Dr. Langley finished telling her the news, the room spun, and the floor shook beneath her as his words echoed in her mind. How could this be happening again? What about her business? It wasn't like five years ago. Now, they were booked solid, and Oliver couldn't do it all.

"Miss Holloway, is there someone you'd like to call or have us contact to be here with you?" the doctor had asked.

"No." She shook her head. "Oliver, my best friend and business partner, is on his honeymoon. I'm not going to call him." She inhaled and wiped the sweat off her forehead as her pulse quickened.

"What about family? Boyfriend?" He spoke softly.

"There is no family and no boyfriend. Unless you call three dates with the same guy in the last year a boyfriend. I did take him home and have sex. I suppose that might count. The sex wasn't that great though. Obviously, it was a mutual feeling, since we haven't had another date." She watched the doctor's cheeks turn pink.

"I'm really sorry, Miss Holloway."

"For the bad sex or the test results?" She leveled a look at him and wondered if doctors got used to telling patients bad news.

"Ah, well, both, I suppose." He looked down at his file, fumbling with paperwork. "No relatives at all?" he asked again.

"None that would understand anything going on. My Grandma has dementia and didn't even recognize me last time I went to see her in the nursing home."

§⋯

CONNOR COULD FEEL TENSION COMING FROM HIS LOVELY PASSENGER, so he slowed down and thought that might help. From his side mirror, he could see she seemed lost in a daydream as she gazed off at the trees. It almost seemed as though she was sad.

He couldn't help but notice her hair whipping out of the helmet. The color was pretty and reminded him of cocoa beans, which matched her hot chocolate eyes.

It had been a long time since he had a female on the back of his motorbike. He chuckled inside. He could remember no one, male or female, calling his Harley that.

With her pocketbook tucked under her arm, she squeezed him tighter. He tried like hell to ignore the wallop in his chest. The problem was, she was a small bowl of sugar and spice and he couldn't close his eyes to that fact. Although, he should have closed his eyes while she changed. Instead, he had kept his back to her just like he promised. However, when he glanced into his mirror, there were no missing her curves and those lacy blue panties. Jesus, they had held his eyes prisoner.

He had thought she'd change in the car, but she stood on the edge of the road by her door. Unknowingly undressing right in front of his side mirror. Even if she had opened the door and stood behind it, it would have saved him from being a peeping tom.

Was that what he was turning into? Maybe it was time to take one of those trips out of town.

Because having her warm hands around his waist, with just his thin T-shirt on, was doing things he didn't want to think about. Plus, she had nervous fingers, which didn't help matters.

As they pulled up to the towing company, Fred was just walking to his truck, sure enough with those damn comic books in his hands. He glanced at Connor and smiled.

"Hey, Connor, I'm fixin' to run out to Old Valley Freeway. Someone broke down. What can I do for y'all?"

"This here is the lady who broke down." He lifted a brow and helped Starla off the bike. "Her car is about fifteen miles from here, and she'd been waiting a long time." He gave him a pointed look.

Starla stepped up and explained. "When my car started spewing and sputtering, I pulled over and steam shot out from under my hood. Do you know where we should take it to get it fixed?" she asked.

"Well, there are no automotive repair places opened on the weekends, and they left early today. But, Monday, they will be back," Fred explained.

"Nothing open?" Her voice went up. "I have to be back to work on Monday. This is the busy season."

Connor glanced at her. "Can you call your boss and explain?"

"No," she said. "I am the boss."

Fred nodded, and then said, "Well, that's good because you can't fire yourself." He chuckled at his own words. "I better go fetch your car. Do you have the keys?"

"Yes." She handed them to him. "Is there a car rental place in town? I could leave my car and come back to pick it up."

Fred shook his head. "Nope, no car rental places, yet. I'll take your car on over to Blue Sky Auto. What kind of car is it?" Connor didn't miss the way Fred's gaze drifted up and down her body.

"It's a Honda Fit, EX-L, and it's white. Although, I don't think you'll miss it. The whole time I was there, I didn't see one soul on the road, until Connor."

He nodded, "That road ain't on any map."

"Oh. No wonder, I didn't see it on my map. How do people find this town?"

"We hope they don't," Fred snickered just before he climbed in his tow truck and took off.

Connor would talk to him later about how he treated women. There was no doubt he had made Starla uncomfortable, not just from his ogling her, but also from leaving her stranded for so long and his snide remarks. Fred was harmless. Everyone had nicknamed him Fred Flintstone because of his comic books, also, he was the spitting image of the cartoon character.

Connor looked over at Starla. "There's a great place to stay just down the road, right on the edge of Secret Lake. It's a bed and breakfast and truly nice, with all the comforts of home. There are little cabins with full kitchens if that's what you want. It also has a trail that goes out to some waterfalls and hot springs. Takes about an hour or so of hiking. The hot spring is cool in both places. You can enjoy watching the waterfalls while soaking in the warm water."

"That sounds lovely and well, that's what I was looking for. A place to relax."

"Well, then, you might as well enjoy yourself. The Native Trail goes out that way too. It has the best hot springs and the Grand waterfall, but it's completely remote and about another hour. It's a well-kept secret. There is an Indian woman who lives out there somewhere with a wolf. She's nice from what I've heard. I have said hi to her throughout the years. My parents like her a lot. She's some kind of medicine woman, someone told me. Not that I know what that means." They both laughed. He wondered if Starla would like him to go with her.

"Is there a river?" Starla asked. "I only saw the lake. The town is called Secret Valley River."

"The river runs on the edge of town, but as you saw, the lake runs right through the heart of our city." He gestured around. "We don't have a big tourist season, but it's not bad. We do have our regulars who come back every year to get a dose of our area. Some people have managed just like you to find us, despite us not being on the map."

"It sounds lovely and from what I saw, the town is as sweet as it can be. I'll need to get my stuff out of the car. I should have grabbed my overnight bag, but I wasn't sure if I could carry it." She sighed. "I don't want to impose on you anymore, so if you tell me where he's taking my car, I can walk and get it later."

"You're not imposing." He grinned. "I'd like to take you down to Dragon Fly Inn, and you can see a lot more of our little city as we pass through it. It's a beautiful place and most people fall in love with the area. Plus, you can meet Ria and she will get you all set up. She's a great host. I can grab your bag for you and bring it back. If you are okay with that."

"Thank you so much. That would be great." Her eyes filled with warmth, and he was melting inside. Plus, his heart was beating extra hard.

He noticed her cheeks turned rosy and wondered if she knew the effect she was having on him. They moved over to his Harley and once again, he assisted her. This time, she tucked her pocketbook under his jacket she was wearing, and then tightened her arms around him.

The trip down the street was quick, and of course, he saw more than a few people he knew. He also noticed their eyeballs widen when they glanced at the lovely lady he had with him. Great. He rode smack by where Ivy stood who waved him over.

"Hi, Connor, are you still coming by later to look at my washer?"

"I'll stop by in a couple of hours."

She smiled at Starla. "Okay, sounds really good. See y'all later."

He couldn't take off fast enough. What was wrong with him? He should have introduced them. But her being connected to everything from his past made it uncomfortable. It wasn't every day he had a female on the back of his bike, and never one as gorgeous as Starla. There were great things about living in a small town, but some things were a tad bit annoying. Everybody knew everyone else's business.

STARLA WAS IN AWE OF THE PICTURESQUE TOWN. THE LAKE RAN parallel with all the storefronts, which meant you could see it from every business, along with a beautiful park. Everything was spotless and had colorful flowers, signs, and some even had little ferns out front. They passed a bakery and coffeehouse next door to each other, and even from the back of the bike, the aroma perfumed the air.

People sat at small tables and seemed to gaze out toward the lake, until they turned their attention to her. Obviously, most seemed surprised. There had to be a story or something going on. Why would anyone be stunned to see a girl on the back of his bike? Maybe he had a girlfriend. Oh Jesus, that might not look so good. No wonder that chick was shooting daggers while she glued on that fake smile. However, he didn't seem to be married. There was no wedding band. Or could he be?

Once Connor left the heart of town, he made a right turn down a private road, heading toward the lake. As he slowed down, her gaze meandered toward the wildflowers. The entire area was surrounded with Indian paintbrush, black-eyed Susans, and Bluebonnets. Next, they passed by a restaurant called A Taste of Heaven, it looked lovely and sat right by the lake. People were coming and going. Then as they drove a little further, a massive, white, Victorian house came into view. She couldn't believe the charm. It reminded her of the home in Gone with the Wind. Two weeping willows sat in the yard around the garden areas. The little waterfall flowed right into a pebble stone pond.

"Wow," she whispered. "I feel like I've stepped back in time."

Connor pulled up to the circular driveway and cut his engine. "Did I hear you say something?" He helped her off his bike.

She placed her hand over her heart. "What year is this?" She inhaled.

"It's always been like turning back the years." He looked around and once again cracked his knuckles.

"Yes, it is." She stared into his eyes, but there was a look she wasn't sure about, almost like a wince. "I was planning on staying away for two nights and having some peace and quiet, but I never imagined this. I love it."

"Wait until you see the inside and the little cabins that sit right next to the lake. Ria has done a wonderful job making this a dream location. She has people that book a year in advance."

"I hope she has room for me."

"She will. May starts to pick up a little, mostly with a few newlyweds. However, June gets busy because of graduation parties and lots of people getting married. That's four weeks away. Then from there, most of the summer is crazy."

They walked up to the door. Connor knocked before opening it, then stuck his head inside. "Ria, are you around?" he called out.

The minute they stepped in the entry, Starla froze in place and stared at the loveliness. "Goodness gracious."

Before she could absorb everything, a gorgeous, dark-haired lady looking to be in her early forties walked in the room. Her skin was a dark olive tone and her hair was jet black with white streaks, which made her incredibly attractive and sexy. Even the scar across her cheek made her more alluring.

"Connor, nice to see you." Her eyebrows arched, and she looked between the two.

"Ria, I'd like to introduce you to Starla. She broke down outside of town and needs a place to stay until her car gets repaired."

"Ah, I'm sorry to hear about your car, but happy to meet you." She stuck out her hand and greeted Starla with a gentle squeeze.

"Nice to meet you too. This place is beautiful." She sighed. "Do you happen to have any places open?" Starla asked, meeting Ria's warm brown eyes.

"I sure do." She nodded. "I have rooms upstairs and two cabins open. I'll give you the family discount since your car broke down."

"Well, thank you so much." She breathed a sigh of relief and tried not to show her concern. Connor's chiseled jaw tensed. "Well, I'm going to go wait for Fred and fetch your bag while Ria shows you around." He seemed to smile, but it faded, and he left in a hurry.

Starla watched him and turned to Ria. "He's been just as sweet as he could be. He saved me from being stranded."

Ria's face appeared sad.

"Is something wrong?" Starla asked.

"Connor doesn't usually come out here much. I see him in town, but this place..." She paused. "Brings up too many memories, I'd guess."

"Oh, I'm sorry." Starla wasn't sure if she should ask why.

Ria blew out a breath and moved up to the wooden counter. She pulled out a guestbook, and then picked up the phone. "Hi Jennifer, could you please get cabin ten all ready? I'm getting ready to check in someone. Yes, please. Thank you, sugar. You're just as sweet as a candy apple." Ria hung up. "Well, they are getting it all ready for you."

"Thank you," Starla said. I know it's none of my business, but do you think he'll be okay getting my bag and coming back?" Starla didn't want to cause him any trouble.

"The one thing I know about Connor, he wouldn't do it if he didn't want to."

Starla glimpsed toward the door. Her heart hurt for a man she barely knew, and it sure looked like pain from what she saw in his eyes.

Ria shook her head. "He doesn't talk about the past from what I've heard." She picked up a pen. "How about I fill this out and we get you to your cabin?"

Starla gave her all the information, except her car license, which she didn't know.

"We can get that later," Ria said and continued. "Supper is at six. Tonight, we are having lasagna with green salad and fresh garlic bread."

"That sounds wonderful. Do you want to take my credit card?" Starla went to grab it.

"No," Ria said. "I gave you the family discount." She smiled.

"So, how much do I owe you?"

"Free." She laughed. "Come on, let's get you to your room."

Starla shook her head. "I can't let you do that." She felt awful. Did she look poor or something?

"I'll tell you what. Just tip housekeeping. They love tips."

"I will. Thank you again. I don't even know what to say."

Ria waved her off. "Let's get you settled. On the way, we'll get you a bundle of wood. Even though it's May, it gets cool at night."

Ria led her down a stone path, revealing vine trees that twisted into every shape and looked mystical. She paused and watched the leaves stir across the lawn from the Kentucky Coffee Tree.

"Oh, my." Starla pointed and noticed a type of tree she'd didn't recognize. "What kind of tree is that? It's breathtaking."

"It's the Ginkgo tree, and it's rare. It's been a blessing that we were able to get it to flourish."

"That's really something." Starla paused. "This place seems magical."

They resumed walking, and Starla's eyes widened in surprise at all the flowers. There was, most definitely, something delightful in the air.

There were purple Irises and roses with Poukhanense, Korean Azaleas. Her grandmother had taught her a lot about flowers and plants. From all the time they spent together in the gardens. Those moments were precious memories.

Little benches sat between the trees forming an archway. The view gave way to the lake with small islands. The sounds of croaking frogs and crickets made the early afternoon whisper with a soothing harmony. The sky was blue with sheer white clouds, allowing the sun to shine down its glory on everything.

"This is exquisite." Starla gazed out at the lake. There was nothing she'd ever experienced like the scent in the air, of lavender and gardenia with a hint of honeysuckle.

Starla paused again. "Wow." She inhaled deeply and let out a soft breath. "This is truly incredible."

"I never get tired of it." Ria smiled and stopped with her. "Most mornings, it still takes my breath away. Evenings are even more entrancing."

They both stood staring at the birds skimming across the water. While off in the distance, the song of geese made its way through the sky. This was paradise.

A few minutes later, Ria picked up a bundle of wood just before they arrived at number ten. "This is the Lakeside Cabin, and I promise you won't be disappointed. It's one of the best, and nobody has any reservations until June fifteenth. So, it's yours to stay as long as you want." She took out her key, unlocked the door and waved Starla inside.

Starla had to be in a fairy tale, she stumbled over her words. "Oh heavens, so lovely." She gazed around. "This is sweet and look at that view." The windows that lined the back brought the outdoor sights right into the room.

"This does have one of the best views." Ria walked over and opened the French doors. "Look at the deck. It's small but wonderful and right over the water."

"I love it." Starla leaned over the veranda and looked into the beautiful clear waters. This time, a set of Canadian Honkers, flew their way above them. The sound was like an elegant melody and made the place even more enthralling.

A few minutes later, they moved back inside, giving Starla time to study the tiny cabin. The ivory sofa sat in front of the fireplace, decorated with colorful mauve and peach pillows, with a large throw. It had a small dining table for two with fresh flowers. "Oh, this is just lovely." She liked the hardwood floors throughout. The walls were flanked with oil paintings of the forest and trees. Some appeared to be of waterfalls and long trails.

"So, you like?" Ria asked with a soft grin.

"No," Starla corrected. "I adore it and could live here." They both chuckled.

"Will I see you at supper? I was thinking we could chat and get to know each other better," Ria offered.

"I would be delighted."

"There is a robe in the bathroom if you want to soak in the tub. It has jets too, and that bubble bath is made from all natural and organic products, from a local lady. And, do you want me to send Connor down with your overnight bag?"

"If he doesn't mind," Starla said, her tone light. "I don't want him to do anything that might hurt him."

"I will mention that. There is coffee or tea. The kitchen is fully stocked, and your bedroom has a queen-sized bed with a handmade comforter and extra blankets in the closet. Also, there are some muffins and fruit on the counter next to the refrigerator. The grapes are locally grown, and everything is certified organic."

"That's wonderful. I think I'll just get freshened up. I look forward to seeing you tonight at supper."

"See you then," Ria said and left the cottage.

"This is a dream," she whispered, talking to herself again. "Just what the doctor ordered." She moved across the room to the French doors and stepped onto the deck. The minute she stood alone, she focused on the scenery. There was no missing how the sun left little sparkles dancing across the water.

After a few minutes, she sank down into the overstuffed lounge. "Ah." She was exhausted from no sleep the night before. Her phone rang, so she scrambled to pick it up.

"Hello?"

"Hey, baby cakes! I was calling to see how everything is going."

"Oliver, why are you calling?" She blew out a breath, got up and moved into the living room. "You're on your honeymoon."

"Because we'll be heading home soon, and I wanted to make sure I wasn't walking into any kind of catastrophe."

"Darn, I didn't want to tell you the building fell down. No biggie though, we've been barbecuing outside at the nearby park." She chuckled.

He laughed. "I miss you and so does Thea. We wanted to make plans for dinner as soon as we get back."

"Sure, that sounds nice so long as I can get back home."

"Where are you?"

"I'm in a little town called Secret Valley River. My car overheated, and they don't have anyone to fix it until Monday. I was trying to take a mini vacation."

"No, you're kidding. You—a vacation?" He chuckled. "Hold on, I have to go pass out."

"I've been feeling a little stressed, but I was coming back on Monday. Now, I'm worried if they'll get it done that soon." She sighed.

"Starla Moon Holloway. I've been gone for weeks. Why don't you take some time and try to relax? Everything will be fine. I'll be back at work on Tuesday morning."

"But…"

"No, buts. Take this time. My lovely wife can help out. She's been wanting to learn the ropes."

"Are you sure?" Starla had never left the business for more than a day.

"Yes, I'm more than sure. Now, tell me you'll take at least two weeks."

"Two weeks?"

"Yes. We could drive on over to this Secret place and maybe spend a night with you. Have dinner and you could show us around."

"That would be fun. I would like that." She meant it.

"Wonder-pal." He always used that term. "Starla…" He paused. "Is everything okay?"

"Yes. Why?" There was no way she would tell him anything, while he was on his honeymoon.

"I don't know. You sound funny, and well, since we've known each other, you've never taken a vacation."

"Well, there is always a first, and besides, I've had to slave for weeks. All so you could be alone with your wife, doing obscene things to her." She tried to make her voice sound playful.

He cracked up. "And, boy, has it been obscene."

"Oliver, don't tell her all our secrets." Thea laughed in the background. "We love you, Starla," she called out.

"I love you guys too. Now get off this dang phone and go back to your honeymoon. I'll see you next weekend."

"Okay, we do love you." He sounded way too serious.

"Get off the phone. Now!" She giggled and heard him laugh too.

After they hung up, she let the wind out of her lungs. It wasn't until that moment she realized she'd been holding her breath.

After she went back outside, she whispered, "Two weeks off work." She had to call and reschedule her doctor's appointment and he wouldn't be happy. But she had that right. She needed time to process everything. It was a lot to take in.

Some time, between hearing the chirping of a sparrow and the sound of children's laughter, she drifted off.

3

CONNOR WAS ON HIS WAY BACK TO GIVE STARLA HER OVERNIGHT BAG. He wanted so bad to snoop and see what she had inside, but he refrained. That would be a rude thing to do, even if there was a story there. Why was she traveling alone? Plus, he couldn't miss how tense she was? Somehow, she seemed more lost than just driving directions. Maybe she was just getting out of a relationship and needed to get away. He hadn't missed what she said about needing peace and quiet.

He pulled down the dirt road and memories surrounded him. Stopping, he took off his helmet and felt tears burning his eyes. How in the hell could he still be suffering like this when it had been so many years? How long did it take for the pain to stop? He hated coming to this place, it reminded him of all he'd lost. Staying here with his childhood sweetheart had been the happiest days of his life. He stared over at the weeping willow tree. Holly had loved those trees, saying they shouldn't be called weeping willows. His mind traveled back, and he took a trip down memory lane.

June 13, 2010

"CONNOR LOOK, THEY ARE PRAYING WILLOWS, NOT WEEPING." HOLLY moved toward them.

Connor laughed. "What are they praying for?"

"For love, of course. They want everyone to have the kind of happiness we do." Running, she threw her arms around the base of the tree. She gave it a giant kiss, moaning like she was making love to the damn thing. "I love you, praying willow," she sang. "You make me feel like love is in the air."

"Damn it, Holly. That makes me jealous!" He ran after her, and she tried her best to outrun him. However, a football player couldn't be beat by a tiny little brunette. He was faster and caught her. Carrying her out to the lake, he dropped her in with a splash.

He laughed. "Don't ever let me see your lips on that tree again."

"Connor Zachary Whelan." She stood up, drenched to the bone. "I'm furious." She placed her hands on her wet hips. "Just look at my hair and my new shirt," she scolded in that sweet southern drawl which got stronger when she was angry. "And my new shoes! You have ruined them!"

"They'll have plenty of time to dry. I'm fixing to take you into the room and let you make up to me. You'll need to spend time kissing me and proving you like me better than that dumb old tree." He crossed his arms across his chest. "How many other things, or guys, have you kissed like that?"

"Are you serious? I think you have things confused, or maybe you're just backward." She stomped out of the water and shot him a look. "You'll need to make it up to me, unless you want to spend the night sleeping on that couch." She stormed off, but she stopped and glared at him before she got too far. "I've kissed plenty of other boys before you, so it's none of your business."

"Is that so?" He was really pissed. Why the hell was he acting jealous over a stupid tree? Well, she threw her arms around it and acted like it was a person. Had she kissed other guys like that? He was twisted and knew it. But the thought of her kissing someone else made him downright angry. And he'd just sleep on the couch until she made up to him.

It had been a cold and lonely night, sleeping on that hard-ass-rock couch. So, by the next morning, he caved and climbed in bed.

"Holly, sweetheart, I want you to know, I'll forever be your love, and when it's raining, I'll always bring the sunshine to your life. I love you more than I can put into words."

The minute her Irish green eyes clung to his, he knew all was forgiven.

❧

THE SOUND OF A LAWN MOWER PULLED HIM AWAY FROM THE PAINFUL memory. He slipped back on his helmet and took off. Once he pulled into the parking spot, he noticed a tear had trailed down his cheek, so he knuckled it away. He took in a long, refreshing breath and grabbed Starla's overnight bag.

After taking a minute to collect his emotions, he walked inside and saw Ria at the front desk on the phone. He could hear her talking.

"We do allow well-behaved pets in certain rooms and cabins," she said.

She waved him over. "No, not in all the rooms because some people are allergic. So, we reserve some no-pet rooms."

He noticed she seemed frustrated. "After June fifteenth, I have no openings again until September twelfth. I'm so sorry, but if someone cancels, I could call and let you know. I have your number."

After a few more minutes, she hung up and smiled. Ria was a beautiful woman inside and out. The fact was, she was a good friend. Holly had loved her, and they had come to the inn for supper at least once a month. He had always wondered how Ria got that scar on her face, but nobody seemed to know. It didn't matter; she was still stunning.

"Starla is out in cabin ten. She's a sweet lady, and she really liked the room. She said you can come on down if you want."

He paused, not sure if he could face any of those cabins. They had stayed in number five, but still.

"Connor, if you can't go down there, I'll be happy to take it to her." She gave him a warm smile.

He thought about that for a minute. Maybe it was time for him to walk through the valley of memories and not fall apart. It had been six years. "No, I can do this."

She met his gaze. "Okay, if you're sure."

"I am. Thanks, Ria." He turned and left.

Once he stepped out on the path, he tried like hell to focus on the small suitcase in his hand and not on any of his surroundings, but every sound battered him. If he could turn off the music from the birds and the far-off sounds of laughter from the children, he might be okay. Memories assaulted him again.

"CONNOR, COME ON. LET'S GO SKINNY DIPPING." HOLLY GLANCED around and slipped off her bathing suit as the moon traced her amazing body.

"Holly, what if we get caught?"

"Then we go to jail and become the town jail birds." She laughed harder. "Come on. Don't be an old fuddy duddy."

HE JERKED HIS HEAD OUT OF THE REVERIE AND STEPPED UP TO THE

door. "Knock-knock." Nobody answered. A few seconds went by and he knocked again. Still no answer.

He twisted the knob and stuck his head inside. "Hello." No sounds. "Starla." Still no answer.

He went into the cottage and checked all the rooms. Maybe she went for a walk. When he stepped onto the deck, she was sleeping soundly in the lounge chair. Jesus, she was so doggone pretty. He stood gazing down, clinging to the sight of her dark curls and her soft, ivory skin and rose-colored cheeks. Hold your horses, pal, and stop whatever it is you're thinking.

She must be tired after being stranded and waiting for so long. Plus, he had a feeling she was running away. He had no clue what it was from, but something told him it wasn't good. He'd hang out in the living room and wait for her to wake up. No way would he leave her sleeping outside alone. He fetched the throw off the couch and covered her, then for some reason he didn't fully understand, he wrapped a stray strand of her hair around his finger. He wanted to breathe in her scent but made himself stop. What in God's name was wrong with him? he backed away.

Just as he stepped inside, she called out. "No, no, this can't happen again." Her voice trembled, and she cried.

His chest tightened. Shit, he needed to wake her up. He leaned down, and this time pushed the hair away from her face. "Starla." More sobs.

"Starla." He touched her shoulder.

"What?" Her eyes opened and found his. "Oh, goodness, I must have dozed off. I'm sorry." She brushed the rest of the hair out of her face and subtly wiped away the tears.

Damn, she was gorgeous. She moved the comforter off, and he could see things he shouldn't be looking at. Must be from the chill in the air. For God's sake, he needed to stop staring. Things were waking up south of the border.

He yanked his mind back. "You were crying and talking in your sleep. Otherwise, I would have waited in the living room. I wouldn't have wanted to leave you alone out here for too long. It's getting chilly. That's why I covered you."

"Oh, thank you, Connor. That was very nice. What was I saying?"

"You were crying and saying, no, not again." He tilted his head. "Is everything okay?"

"Yes." She nodded. "Just bad dreams. I don't remember what it was about. Thank you again."

"No problem. I guess I'll be heading out. I'm sure I'll see you before you leave."

"Wait." She stood. "Please let me take you to supper. Or at least buy you lunch, since I can't take you anywhere without a car. I don't know the area, so you can tell me where the best places are. I want to repay your generosity."

"That's not necessary. I didn't do much." He wished she'd at least wrap herself up in that blanket, so he could concentrate on her face.

"Yes, you did. Please, let me repay you somehow." She placed her hand on his arm and a shiver ran down to his feet.

He paused. "Okay, how about this? What do you have planned for tomorrow morning?"

"Nothing. Just maybe taking in the sights."

"How about we go on a picnic? I'd like to hike with you down the Native trail and make our way out to Secret Lake. As I mentioned earlier, there are swimming holes and beautiful things to see, although it might still be too cold for that. But the hot springs feel like bathwater. The Grand waterfall is something else to see and hear."

"Okay, it's a date," she blurted out. "I mean, you can show me the area."

"Sounds good. See you tomorrow morning." Turning, he walked to the front door. He was glad to have bumped into her. He hadn't been looking forward to the weekend in a long time, but now he was.

"Starla." He turned around. "It's been nice to meet you."

She nodded. "You too."

As he went out the door, he wondered what the hell he had just done. He could turn around and tell her he had forgotten about a job. That would be stupid. Maybe he'd just show up in the morning and apologize—tell her something came up.

4

STARLA COULDN'T SEEM TO MOVE. HAD SHE ACTUALLY BLURTED OUT, it was a date? How lame was that? Why didn't she learn not to say everything in her brain? She crossed the room and lifted her overnight bag and took it into the bathroom. It was hard to remember what she had brought because she left so fast.

Oh good, there were two pairs of dress slacks, and two pretty shirts. The great news was she'd packed her bathing suit and it was the whole piece, not too revealing.

"What, no shoes?" How could she forget that? All she had was the ones she had on. Well, at least they'd work for the hike tomorrow and she had everything else she needed. They had cost a fortune and were great walking shoes, so she'd be set for one day. She remembered seeing a boutique in town. Maybe they would have shoes. When she went to supper, she'd ask Ria.

The tub was large and looked wonderful with all kinds of bubble bath lined on the side. She had brought her own, but the aroma of the peach smelled divine. Once she turned the water on and let it fill the tub, she slipped off her clothes and climbed inside. "Ah." The warm water embraced her as it flowed over her chilled skin.

After an hour of soaking in the peach scented bubble bath and enjoying the peace and quiet, she ran her fingers across the two scars on her breast. Reminders of the past and all she'd been through. Maybe she needed to forget everything and for once, be like everyone else. Nobody here knew anything about her life or what she was going through.

People were always asking her, *how are you Starla*, with undertones of worry. And the truth was, she had actually stopped fretting over it. Everyone had treated her fragile, like a delicate glass that would shatter from a single touch. Well, she just wanted to be treated normal, like a regular woman.

There was no damn sign that said feel sorry for Starla. For the next two weeks, she'd be Starla Moon Holloway and nothing more. She had left home to take a small vacation and that's what she was going to do. She'd need to talk to Ria about it. There was no way she'd stay for free for two weeks.

Later that evening, Starla arrived at the main house and entered the dining area. The scent of garlic, basil, and oregano, made her stomach growl. Ria was behind an oak counter, setting things up. Several young couples sat around with different drinks and smiles on their faces.

Ria glanced up and gave a wave. "Hi Starla, welcome." She pointed to a table set for two. "I hope you don't mind. I thought we could eat together."

"That sounds lovely," Starla said as she sat down. She was glad not to be eating alone since they were surrounded by couples.

The room was filled with enchantment and candles flickered, casting a glow across the wall. White, sheer tablecloths with little star vases were filled with multicolored flowers. Synchronicity flowed through the place. The floor-to-ceiling windows gave way to a beautiful scenic view, bringing the charm of the outside gardens and pond into the room.

Starla took a deep breath and allowed tranquility to course through her veins. When was the last time she experienced this serenity? Maybe never.

The crystal pitcher before her held water with lemons and limes floating around. She poured a glass, hearing the ice cubes clink inside. Raising it to her lips and taking a long, slow drink, she closed her eyes. The flavor was nothing like she'd ever tasted. The ice grazed her teeth and flavor burst inside her mouth.

Ria set down two plates for a younger couple, and then went back and gathered the ones for them. Once she placed dinner on the table, she also poured herself a glass of water.

"Whew." She took a long sip. "What a day. Ended up being busier than I thought. Tamera didn't show up for work because she broke her wrist skateboarding. My other kitchen helper is out of town and won't be back until Wednesday."

"That's awful. I'm so sorry." Starla said, and then took a bite of lasagna. "Oh, Ria. This is out of this world. You added fennel seeds and there are at least three cheeses. Perfection."

Not until that moment did Starla know how ravenous she was. She took another bite, which melted in her mouth.

Ria stared at her, perplexed. "A woman who knows her spices is a woman after my own heart. Now I *know* we will be the best of friends." She laughed.

"Well, I should. I own a catering business." Starla winked. "And, I'll help you clean up tonight. I'm fast in the kitchen and do a thorough job."

Ria shook her head, but Starla raised her hand. "I'm also stubborn and will not take no for an answer. Besides, I want to talk to you about booking a room for two weeks. I've decided I need a vacation, and I will pay you."

"How about this? You can help me with dinners this week until Wednesday, and that will serve as payment, but that's not much of a vacation is it?"

They stared at each other for a minute, and then chuckled. "Yes, I would love to help you. Being here surrounded by all this beauty, is a vacation in itself." Starla took a sip of her flavored water. "I can help with breakfast, too." She had a feeling she'd met a kindred spirit.

"That sounds wonderful. If you're sure."

"I would love to help as much as you need while I'm here, and I'd like to explore the area."

"I don't need help until Monday's dinner—I have everything prepared for the next two days." Ria took a bite and nodded. "The lasagna turned out well."

"It sure did." Starla said between mouthfuls. She couldn't seem to stop eating.

"Is there a guy in your life?" Ria asked, catching Starla's attention.

"No." She picked up her napkin and dabbed the corners of her mouth. "Why, is there a dark-haired man hiding around here somewhere? And what about you?"

Ria leaned over the table while looking around to make sure no one was listening. "As a matter of fact, there is."

Starla arched a brow. "Do tell."

Ria gave an impish grin. "Joe Manganiello. I have his pictures set as my computer's screen saver in my bedroom. And, *ooh la la,* he is my boyfriend, and I see him every night."

They both burst out laughing.

"Well," Starla said, "Tell me one more secret." Ria stared at her, her eyes dark and curious. "What is your last name?"

Ria smiled. "My whole name is Ria Celestino Machado. My mother and father are from Spain and most of our ancestors came from Portugal. *Sua' muito nice para atender você.*"

"I have no idea what you just said, but it sounds interesting with a southern accent." Starla smiled. "But it was elegant. You have a beautiful name."

"I said, it's very nice to meet you.'"

"I'm happy we met as well." Starla reached across the table and squeezed Ria's hand. "Now I understand why you have such lovely skin."

"Well, I do have one blemish." She ran her fingers across the right side of her face.

"We all have some type of scarring. Some that show and others that don't. However, yours is extremely sexy."

"Sexy?" Ria tilted her head. "How so?"

"It makes you look mysterious and even more dazzling." Starla stared.

"Did you say you were single?" Ria asked, and they both laughed again.

The night ended up being one of the most playful, fun nights Starla had experienced in a long time. They finished the rest of the lasagna and cleaned the kitchen while singing and dancing to tunes from the stereo, acting like two schoolgirls. Their constant laughter spilled into the dining room.

Around midnight, Starla made her way back to her cabin and walked down the isolated trail. The moon hung in the dark sky, playing peek-a-boo behind the soft clouds, and reflecting across the water. When she climbed into bed, she remembered she had a date tomorrow, reminding her how glad she was that she broke down and came to this town. Although, she knew her doctor would not be happy when she told him she was putting off her procedure.

Maybe she should get a second opinion.

CONNOR WOKE UP TO THE SOUND OF THE ROOSTER CROWING RIGHT outside his bedroom window. "Gosh darn Rooster." It was just after six, and he must have escaped out of the pen. What had he been thinking when he'd gotten the chickens and a Rooster? He'd let his brother talk him into it, but now he'd have to fix that chicken coop again.

Well, daddy always said that success wasn't for the lazy. Connor threw the covers off, and as soon as his feet touched the floor, he shivered. There was still a chill in the air, and he'd forgotten to turn on the heat, so he rushed down the hallway and turned it up. Afterward, he made a pot of coffee. He glanced around his large, country kitchen, knowing he needed to redecorate everything. He'd taken down some things a few years ago, but Holly's fingerprints were still everywhere. She loved pigs and cows. One pig was even wearing a bonnet, but he didn't want them on his walls. The dried flowers everywhere were hard enough to deal with, plus the white-and-pink lace tablecloth. He knew it all needed to go, soon, but he would do it later. Right now, he had things to take care of and people to see.

Just the thought of spending time with Starla filled him with excitement. Plus, he needed to run over to Ivy's to make sure the washer was still working. It seemed fixed last night, but the machine was getting old and he had been rushed.

It had been a much later night than he'd planned, but he also emptied files from his workplace and moved them to his home office. But seeing Mr. and Mrs. Owens so surprised had been worth it. They must have thanked him five or six times. He was glad to offer them some place to stay besides that tiny motor home. Now, he just needed to make sure they got their house finished fast.

Connor turned on the water and, as usual, it was cold as hell—so cold he feared freezing to death. The fact was he needed to take time to finish remodeling his own home. The house was older and although he'd done a lot—like putting in hardwood floors and Corian countertops—the heating and cooling unit needed to be replaced. The thing is, if you looked around, everything looked brand new. The white siding and crown molding had cost a pretty penny. The bathrooms had been the hardest part. Everything had to be removed and replaced.

Nevertheless, this had been Holly's dream house. He felt his throat tighten, he needed to redirect his thoughts.

Finally, after about five minutes, the water warmed. He slipped off his boxers and stepped in the shower, washing away the sadness and weariness. The heat steamed the chill away. After finishing up, he turned the knobs to off, and a pang of guilt ran through him. He was going to meet Starla and take her to the falls, but he hadn't been out there since Holly. The painful memory tore through him.

Holly had struggled with depression after their loss. She'd hardly spoken during the last trip and didn't want to stay. So, a few weeks later after they'd gotten some great news, he'd rented a place at the Dragonfly Inn to celebrate. She had been so hopeful that day, laughter had come into their world again.

Tears gathered in his eyes. "Holly, I wish I knew what happened that night. I know you wouldn't have wanted to leave me." He whispered to nobody, just wanting to stop feeling the pain. Was he supposed to be sad the rest of his life?

Connor stepped out of the shower and grabbed a towel. Once he was dressed, he fixed the coop for his chickens and fed his old ornery cat, Spanky. He stood outside thinking about taking his truck, but the morning was full of sunshine and he wanted to feel the wind.

Driving by trees and little dandelions lifted his spirit. Maybe the beautiful day would not only help him feel better, but Ivy too. She had been a little quiet last night, and he wondered if she was going through another bad time. They had both been through such horrible tragedies. One year after his loss, Ivy lost Larry from a heart attack. She'd suffered so much, and he felt he still needed to be there for her when he could.

Nobody had seen Larry's death coming. Even though he'd had a little Arrhythmia, it wasn't so bad that the doctors thought he'd die from it. Not at age thirty-three. His passing stunned everyone, including Ivy, who had fallen apart. Connor had done his best to step up to the plate and was there for her through the whole ordeal.

Some people had started whispering they might get together, but Connor didn't have feelings for Ivy, and he wasn't ready for any commitment. Ivy had always been like a sister to him—she and Holly had been best friends—and Ivy didn't have those feelings toward him, either. She was a beautiful lady. Her blonde hair and full figure had caused many men to trip over their cowboy boots. And he hoped, someday, she'd find love again. She deserved it.

The minute he pulled up and cut the engine, Austin, Ivy's son came running out. "Uncle Connor, you're here."

"I am." He climbed off the Harley and lifted his godson into his arms. "What are you doing up and about so early?"

"Mama and I are going downtown for breakfast and then to the park. Do you want to come?"

"I can't, but I was thinking maybe tomorrow afternoon, you could come and hang out with me while I do yard work. I've got some ideas I need your advice on."

He watched Austin's face light up. "Okay, I can help you."

"Why don't you go tell your mama I'm here and make sure she's ready for me," Connor said as he set him down.

"All right." He took off while yelling for Ivy.

He sure as heck didn't want to go inside the way he had last night. Nobody had answered the door, so he'd walked into the laundry room since Ivy had said the washer was making loud banging noises. It had surprised the hell out of him when she'd come walking in wearing only a towel while carrying a basket of clothes. He almost fell from shock, but she hadn't thought it a big deal and stood there asking questions. He didn't feel good about the situation at all. Being around one of his best female friends, who was almost naked, didn't sit well with him.

"Connor, come on in. I'll be right out. I'm on the phone," Ivy called out as he stood at the door.

As he stepped in, he saw her go down the hallway, more than likely to her bedroom. Austin stood with his eyes frozen to the TV.

Some cartoon with three little kids was on. Connor noticed how nice their home was. Dog-gone good size. They had off white-carpets throughout the house and brown leather furniture. The tan walls went well with all the décor.

However, Ivy was not the world's best housekeeper. He looked around at the magazines, soda cans, and clothes strewn all around the living room. She didn't work, so there was no excuse for such a mess in his opinion. When he walked into the kitchen, his frown deepened. The place looked like a pigpen. No wonder they went out to eat so much. The sink and counters were lined with dirty dishes. The house had never looked like this when Larry was alive, but he'd hired a cleaning service to come in once a week.

Connor glanced up to the clock. He wasn't meeting Starla until ten, so he took off his jacket, rolled up his sleeves, and went to work. At least the dishwasher was empty.

He could hear Ivy laughing with someone on the phone. Must be one of her friends from high school. The dishwasher wouldn't hold all the dirty dishes, so he gathered up the rest and soaked them in suds and hot water. God almighty, could this woman be any messier?

Austin came walking in and looked around. "The kitchen is all-the-way clean. Our kitchen is never this clean."

"It's not all-the-way finished, pal. Where's the broom?" he asked as he glanced around.

Austin left the room and came back with a large broom. "Here it is, Uncle Connor. You want me to hold the dustpan?" He went under the sink and grabbed it.

"Sure, that would be a big help." Connor swept up all the breadcrumbs, bread ties, and just plain old dirt into the dustpan while Austin held it.

"Thanks, buddy. Want to help me carry some of these bags out to the garbage? They are almost overflowing."

"We can't. Mama forgot to take out the garbage cans and they're plumb full."

"I see." Connor laughed despite the mess.

"Well, let's get these in the garage and I'll come by next week and pick up the garbage and make a run to the dump."

"Okay," Austin said. Together, they carried six bags of trash out to the garage and stuck them neatly in a corner.

When they walked back into the kitchen, Ivy was there looking around. "Oh Connor, look what you've done. Thank you, hun."

She moved across the room and hugged him tightly. "I know I live like a pig." She pulled away, her eyes closed and her head down.

He gave her a half shrug. What could he say? She did. "Well, it's pretty clean now." He did his best to smile and help her do the same.

"Connor, we love you." She sniffed, and tears filled her eyes.

"I love you both, bunches." He picked up Austin and kissed his neck.

He giggled and squirmed, so Connor set him down. "Well, I'm fixin' to leave, but I need to look at that washer."

"Oh, it's fine." She waved her hand. "I used it this morning, and it worked like a champ. I was so afraid I'd have to get a new one. It's not the cost..." She paused. "It's just... Larry bought that for me." She rubbed her brow.

"Ivy."

"Yes?" She held his gaze.

"Smile, sweetie. Everything is going to be fine." He kissed her cheek and grinned.

She nodded and swallowed hard.

Damn, he hated to see her so sad, but he remembered it was Saturday, and when Larry was alive, that was family day. They sure had been happy back then. Even though Ivy could be overbearing. Larry had once mentioned her tantrums when she didn't get her way, but he loved her, and she adored him. They'd dated off and on in high school.

Knowing this, Connor had reserved Saturday for her and Austin for the first few years after Larry had died. Larry had been one of his best friends, and Connor had been his best man at his wedding.

However, he realized Ivy would meet no one else if he were always around. He wanted Austin to at least have a step-daddy again. She was young enough to find someone and start over. Nobody could ever replace Austin's daddy, but he could have a nice step-dad and a fun-filled home, which is what they both deserved.

Connor climbed on his bike and had one more thing to do, but it would have to be quick. He had about forty minutes left until he met up with Starla. His errand was the same thing he did every Saturday— he stopped in town and picked up the usual bouquet of flowers, which they always had ready for him. After six years, they knew he'd be picking them up.

On his way, a rush of guilt ran through him. He'd started sleeping with women again a year ago, but he never gave them a second thought. Yet, ever since he'd met Starla, she was all he could think about. What kind of spell had she put on him?

Once he arrived and parked in his normal spot, he climbed off his Harley. The sounds of birds chirping were all he heard as he pulled the flowers from his bag. The air was crisp, and a slight breeze fluttered through the trees, making the leaves dance across the manicured grass.

The minute he arrived at her headstone, he sunk to the ground on one knee and replaced the dead flowers. With ease, he ran his fingers across her engraved name and whispered, "Hi, Holly Jo Whelan. I've been dreaming of you again. I miss you every day." He swallowed back the burning tears. "It's close to the day you left six years ago, and I still hurt so badly—sometimes I feel as though I can't breathe. I know I'm never going to get any answers, but something about that night still haunts me. How did it happen?" He inhaled deeply. "I wish you could give me a sign or help guide me to the answer." He wiped a tear away with a clenched knuckle and reeled in his emotions.

With shaky legs, he stood. "I have to be going, but I love you, Holly. Always." As he walked away, he felt the breeze drying the tears that traveled down his jaw. He knew it wasn't only Holly who was buried there. His heart was right there with her.

§&

STARLA HAD HER SWIMSUIT UNDER HER CLOTHES AND HAD PACKED everything they would need for a picnic.

Earlier, Ria had invited her to do whatever she wanted in the kitchen, and she took her up on her offer. It had been fun helping her cook breakfast and serve it to the guests. After she had helped clean up and put away any remaining food and appliances, she had made her and Connor some sandwiches and deviled eggs. She'd also found wonderful potato salad and a few slices of pie. There was no way they'd eat everything, but that wasn't a big deal. She'd filled the thermos with water and taken utensils and plates from the cabin and put them in the basket Ria had let her use.

Ria had teased her about Connor, and Starla blushed pretty darn hard. It was impossible to pretend he wasn't a hot-looking guy. There was just something about his swagger that threw her for a loop. He had it going on, and there was no missing that.

Before she could form another thought, there was a knock at her door. She swung it open.

"Hi, Connor."

"Good morning, Starla." He scanned her with what appeared to be approval and gave her that mind-blowing smile, which pushed away her nervousness. However, there seemed to be a sadness surrounding him this morning. She hoped nothing was wrong.

Pushing the worry aside, she waved for him to come in. "I've got everything for the picnic all set and ready. I figure we could carry these blankets." She turned back to face him and held them up.

"I brought my backpack, it's filled with some stuff we might need, along with sunscreen, and a tiny tent, just in case the place is swarming with mosquitoes or we need a place to change." He pointed outside. "I'll fetch it from my bike."

"Are the mosquitos bad?" She clutched her hands, feeling an onset of anxiety. Being allergic to mosquitos made her fear them.

"Not normally, even in August, it's not too bad."

"Good." She blew out a breath.

"Are you afraid of bugs?" Connor grinned.

"No, but mosquitos affect me a little more than most people." She sighed. "I'm bringing my needle, though"

"Maybe you should put on bug repellant before we go," he said with a serious tone. "We have to hike pretty far."

"Okay." She applied the spray and made sure she'd covered herself from head to toe. She hadn't thought of getting bit, but she'd be okay if she had her medication with her. Hopefully, it wouldn't be a problem.

After they got everything ready to go, Connor held out his hand. "We have two paths to choose from. We can either take the peaceful trail, which is to the right side of the lake and starts from the back side of the cabins, it's nice. Or, we can take the Native Trail, the one I told you about, which I think you might like better. It starts out by the gardens, near the swimming pool. There's a lot of trees, places to rest, and more mountains to see, and of course, the hot springs that overlook the Grand Waterfall."

"That sounds just like what the doctor ordered." Starla put her hand in his and noticed how they fit together perfectly.

"What doctor would that be?" Connor gave her a questioning look.

"Just a saying." Starla kicked herself mentally, then pasted on a smile. "Lead the way."

As they made their way down the trail, nature presented them with several pleasures. The birds chirped at different pitches, as if they'd assembled a band of sorts. It was alluring listening to the sounds of the trees swaying in the soft breeze. When she couldn't bear to keep walking, she came to a stop, still noticing everything around.

"Connor, this is so amazing. Do you come out here often?"

"I used to." He glanced away and wouldn't meet her eyes. Suddenly, something seemed to catch his attention. "Look at that." He pointed toward a congregation of dragonflies as they fluttered across the water, wings circulating in the magical space between the lake and air.

"Oh, my. That is a sight. I don't think I've ever seen dragonflies do that before." They appeared to do some kind of dance that was mesmerizing.

Connor's eyes were following their direction. "I can't say I have either. I think it might be a mating ritual, but I can't be sure."

"Whatever it is, it's lovely." They both sat down and watched the performance in a comfortable silence, until the dragonflies took off toward the heavens.

"I wonder where they are going?" Starla said.

"I wish I knew." He stood and held out his hand once more. "We best get going."

After another thirty minutes of hiking, Starla's throat was parched. Thank goodness Connor had remembered to bring the bottled water. She'd brought some in a thermos but forgot paper cups or glasses. It had been a long time since she'd been on a hike or picnic, so remembering everything was a challenge.

"So," Connor said. "Tell me about yourself while we walk."

"My life is pretty boring. Why don't you tell me about yours instead?" She stepped closer and studied his face from the side.

"I asked you first." He lifted an arched brow. "I thought it would be nice for us to get to know each other more."

"Okay, then." She smiled. "I own a catering business with my best friend. We started it seven years ago—at least, that's when we began saving for it. We both knew we would work well together."

"Is your best friend married, and is her husband okay with it?" Connor asked.

"Yes, *his wife* is excited to learn about the business. They just got married." She chuckled.

"Ah, your best friend is a guy. That doesn't happen often, but one of my good friends is a woman. I am her son's godfather," he explained. "You saw her the other day, actually, when she asked me to fix her washer."

"Yes, I remember. That's so nice that you are a godfather. Are you friends with her husband?"

"No, I was, but he passed away five years ago. It was sudden and unexpected."

"That's awful. I'm sorry for your loss." She knew how it felt to lose people you love. She missed her parents every day.

"Yeah, it was awful. He'd gone to buy some tile to finish the entryway, and when he got home and started the work, he had a heart attack." They both glanced up and watched a big eagle flying overhead.

"Sometimes people are born with heart problems and it goes undetected for years." Starla reached out and touched his arm. "I'm really sorry."

"We all knew he had an arrhythmia, but it was mild. He worked out—we met at the gym at least four days a week." He shook his head. "We never thought he'd die because of it."

"That's terrible. Maybe the doctors missed something," Starla said.

"Maybe." He nodded.

After a little break they continued walking again, the only sounds were the melody of birds chirping and the soft whispers of crickets and frogs. Starla inhaled a mysterious fragrance that drifted through the air. Flowers were blooming and covered the hillsides and pathways, and the colors were vibrant.

About an hour later, a sound called her attention, and Starla came to a stop after they'd rounded the corner.

"Oh my." She gasped as the magnificent waterfall came into view. The downpour flowed with bubbles of spray that changed colors. Tears filled her eyes. "I've never seen anything like this." It was almost as though it glowed a bright blue. She could have sworn that some of the rocks were shimmering with lights. It was hard to tell from her vantage point. Then, she saw an eagle soaring high above the waterfall.

"Lord, have mercy." She inhaled and took in the sight. "That might be the same eagle we saw earlier. I feel he's following us. "Do you think we are near his or her nest?"

CONNOR WATCHED STARLA FIGHT TO MAINTAIN CONTROL OVER HER emotions, then answered her. "We might be, you just never know out here." He stepped in front of her, leaned down and added, "It's God's country around these parts."

She nodded, glancing between him and the Grand Falls. "I can see and feel that." After a few minutes, she gave him a slight smile, but her eyes brimmed with tears.

"I'm sorry if bringing you here has made you sad." He felt as if his heart was being squeezed.

Something was going on with her, but he had no clue what it was. Maybe she'd recently had her heart broken. There seemed to be heartbreak in her eyes—he'd noticed it yesterday on the road. There had to be a reason she'd taken off from her home with only an overnight bag and taken a road she'd never been on.

After a deep breath, she glanced around. "I just realized... I've been so busy working and trying to keep everything perfect..." She took a deep breath. "I've forgotten to notice all the loveliness in the world." Her eyes met his. "I've never seen anything so beautiful—so —these are happy tears. Thank you so much for bringing me here." She stepped closer and wrapped her arms around him.

Connor couldn't think straight with her so close. God in heaven, her scent was flowery, like roses and gardenias on a spring day. Her fragrance wrapped around him as he hugged her in a warm embrace. "You're welcome," he said.

She released him and stepped back. "I'm sorry." She used her delicate fingers to wipe away her tears. "This place is so breathtaking. It made me think of heaven and brought up silly emotions, but I'm okay. I want to get a closer view."

Connor nodded and reached for her hand. There was no doubt he was more than a little attracted to this lady. He hadn't felt this way toward anyone in so long. Not like this anyway, not since Holly, and that scared the dickens out of him.

Once they got closer, the roar from the waterfall woke his senses. It was a force of nature, both dazzling and strong. Tranquility surrounded him, and yet pain still punched him in the heart, reminding him he still loved Holly. He glanced over at Starla and saw her still-wide eyes.

"Some of the old folks," he upped his voice a notch to be heard over the rushing water, "and natives call this Heaven's Hideaway. They say there is magic all around."

"I've never seen anything like it. Even the colors seem more vibrant. I want to touch the water."

Connor nodded. "Let's put our stuff over by the trees. It's quiet over there, or at least the sounds are muffled, and we can talk without shouting. The trees help to quell the noise."

After they got everything all set up, Starla laid out the blankets and put down plates and napkins. Connor took a minute to assemble the little tent and his one-man burner, which he hadn't used in a long time.

His backpack was filled with things he'd forgotten about, including coffee, his coffee pot, and some stainless-steel cups they could use. However, the old Jerky had expired, so he put it back inside his bag. The last thing he wanted was for either of them to get food poisoning.

"Where are the hot springs?" Starla turned and glanced around for any sight of them.

"Let me show you." He pointed. "You can see the steam if you look hard. They are a little hidden in the ground. Do you want to change before we head that way?" he asked.

"I have my swimsuit on under my clothes, and Ria loaned me a pair of flip flops. Did you bring something to wear?"

"No swimsuit." He arched a brow. "I normally don't wear anything."

"Oh." She blushed and fidgeted with her hands. It seemed she did that when she was nervous. He laughed inside.

"You can turn your head." He chuckled. "Once I'm in the water, you won't be able to see anything. The bubbles and color will keep your eyes safe, but I would like one of those towels over there," he said as he motioned toward the stack, "if you don't mind."

"Sure." She tripped rushing to get them.

Connor had to hide laughing again. She seemed a little shy, but very cute about it. However, the minute she slipped off her pants and shirt, the word 'cute' melted right out of his mind. He gulped air and his heart skipped a few beats. She wore a one piece, but the way it showed off her bottom and hugged every inch of her, made him realize he needed to focus on something else. If he didn't, there would be no hiding his attraction, so he turned and stared out toward the waterfall, trying to shake things off and get a distraction.

Thank God, when she handed him a towel, one was wrapped around her waist. "Whew," he said out loud.

"What is it?" she asked.

"Oh, I'm just glad you brought some towels. I forgot mine," he partly fibbed.

"I forgot a lot of stuff, too." She grinned. "When I left home, I forgot to pack shoes." She shook her head and wrinkled her cute little nose. "I don't know how I did that."

"Were you in a hurry?" he asked.

"I was." She chewed her bottom lip. "Let's go. I want to crawl into that water. My muscles are sore after that hike."

He nodded and got the hint. She didn't want to talk about why she'd left home in such a hurry.

CLIMBING INTO THE HOT SPRINGS WARMED HER SOUL AND REMINDED her of stepping into a warm jetted tub on a chilly day.

"Oh, Connor, this is wonderful." She sank into the water. "I don't know if I'll ever leave." As she chuckled, she noticed he was unbuttoning his shirt, so she laid her head back to give him privacy.

A few seconds later, she heard him climb into the water. "You can look now; I'm covered. This feels so doggone good." He sighed.

"How can it be so quiet here when we are actually closer to the falls?" She couldn't figure it out.

"There has never been an answer for that. One of the magical things about this area, I guess. Maybe all these rocks protect us from the noise or maybe it's the trees. Or maybe it's a secret of the water."

"I can still hear it, but the roar is softer." The water was making her skin tingle, and the soft breeze caressed her face. Everything lulled her as she gazed up at the massive sky. "I might not ever want to go home again," she softly said.

Here in this spot, she wasn't the Starla who was sick. Right now, she could push everything out of her mind and be normal like everyone else. So, she made up her mind—nobody in this town needed to know. And that was her final decision.

The passage of time drifted by in a relaxed silence and didn't seem to matter. A few hours later, while they ate lunch and enjoyed their surroundings, they watched as birds sailed through the sky taking turns skimming across the water. It was a beautiful sight.

Once they had eaten, they climbed back into the hot springs, and when she glanced over and noticed he was staring at the sky, it almost looked as though he had tears in his eyes.

"Connor," she said softly.

His eyes met hers. "Yes?"

"Are you okay?"

He didn't answer, and for a moment, she thought he wasn't going to.

"This place brings up a lot of memories. I'm okay, though," he replied, his voice husky and sad.

"Do you want to talk about it?" Starla waited.

"I don't know if I can. But thank you for asking."

"Okay, I understand. If you change your mind, I'm here."

"Thanks, Starla. So, tell me about your life. Do you have a boyfriend back home? Are you running away from a relationship?"

"No, no relationship issues. Actually, the last time I had a boyfriend was in high school." She chuckled, but knew it was fake.

Connor sat up straighter. "Since high school? Why?"

"Well, honestly, he broke my heart into a bazillion pieces. I haven't much trusted guys since."

"Do you mind me asking what he did?" Connor's eyes were gentle. "It's no fun to have your heart busted to pieces."

"He was my prince charming—or so I thought. We'd been neighbors and had hung out together since I was six. I was fifteen and he was sixteen. He'd treated me with total respect and told me over and over again how much he loved me. He was my first, well, you know." She felt her face flush. "We fell head over heels in love—at least, I did—but as it turned out, he was in love with a lot of girls."

"I'm sorry. How did you find out?" Connor asked.

"It was awful." Starla chewed her bottom lip again. "Even now, I hurt for my younger self." She sat up and adjusted her legs. "I wanted to surprise him and came home early from a weekend outing with my girlfriends. His parents were gone, but his car was in the driveway. I let myself in the house, and I climbed the stairs to his room…" She paused. "I heard the shower and knew it was him. He was an only child and home alone. So, I stripped off my clothes and snuck into the bathroom, only to find him with Vera Thompson, who also happened to be the girl I hated most."

"What happened next?"

"Oh, Vera laughed, and Jason just stared at me with this blank look. I left his school ring on the living room table and ran home—and that was that."

"I bet he felt like an ass." Connor shook his head. "Did he beg you to take him back?"

"No, sir. He gave the ring to Vera the next day from what I heard. They ended up going off to college together. But years later, I heard they'd broken up and that she'd married some guy who runs a rodeo and travels all over the place with him. As for Jason," she paused for a moment and chuckled. "From what I hear, he got fat and bald and is married to his third wife."

They stared at each other and laughed.

"Sounds like he got what he deserved, and you were saved from marrying him. I've never understood men who cheat. If you want to play around, stay single."

"You've never cheated?"

"Never," he said quietly. "I'm not that kind of man."

"So, there was someone special in your life?"

"Yes, she was my childhood sweetheart and we married young."

"I'm sorry, so you divorced?"

"No," he shook his head. "Widower."

"Oh my gosh, I'm sorry, Connor."

He nodded and went silent. There was no way she was going to ask questions. He could talk when it was right for him.

After a few minutes of staring out at scenery, his breathing told her he'd drifted off. Watching him rest gave her the idea to lean backward, too, so she closed her eyes and let her mind drift.

"Starla… Starla." She heard a familiar voice and opened her eyes. "We have to get going; the sun is going down."

"Heavens," she said as she looked at Connor. "What time is it? How long did we sleep?"

"A long time, and it's late," he answered. "We won't make it back before dark, but I have a great flashlight that will help guide our way."

The day had vanished so fast. She turned her head as he climbed out of the hot springs. The last thing she wanted to do was become attracted to a man who had just lost his wife.

Once he said he was dressed, she stepped out, wrapped up in a towel, and quickly got her clothes on. Connor took down the tent and gathered up most of the stuff. A few minutes later, they were packed up and on their way.

"We have about an hour of daylight left." He glanced up at the sky. "It's going to get really dark, which might slow us down."

"Is it safe to be out here after dark?" Her voice quivered.

"It should be, but we should find a good long stick just in case. I'm sorry I fell asleep for so long."

"We both did. I guess we were tired from all the exploring we did. Do you think we should pitch the tent and just sleep out here?" she asked.

"No, it's not that far. Unless, you're really afraid to keep going."

"I'm okay." She swallowed hard and prayed nothing would try to eat them.

It didn't take long for the evening air to grow crisp but not cold. After they had been walking for over an hour, the sounds of nighttime surrounded them. Nearby, the hoot from an owl made Starla jump.

"Guess he's saying hello." Connor took her hand in his and they both chuckled.

Starla held his strong hand and noticed that the reflection of the stars sparkled across the water, while the moon left an enchanting glow. Now, she wasn't nervous at all. In fact, she couldn't remember a time when she was less afraid of the dark. Somehow, the warmth of his hand with his strong yet gentle touch, made her feel as though everything would be all right.

"So," Connor started, breaking the silence, "did you enjoy yourself today?"

"Yes, I loved it. Everything was—" She stumbled, then landed with a hard thump on the ground.

"Starla," Connor said as he bent down on his knees, "are you okay?"

"As good as I can be after falling flat on my face." She felt like a klutz.

He moved the flashlight over her. "You look okay." He smiled. "Just a bit ruffled." He reached out his hand and pulled her up.

"Ouch." When she started to walk, she felt a pain in her foot. "What in tarnation have I done to myself?" She sat back down. "It's my foot."

"Let me take a look." He slipped off her shoe and shone the light on it. "Well, it looks like we *will* be spending the night out here. Your foot is either broken or sprained badly. It's already swelling."

"It can't be broken. I have to help Ria on Monday." Her voice quivered. "I promised."

"Now, don't you go worrying yourself over that. Ria will understand. The most important thing we can do is get you to a doctor as soon as possible—hopefully tomorrow. But tonight, you need to stay off it. You sit down, and I'll set things up." He patted her arm and stood.

"Connor, you must hate me. This is the second time you've had to rescue me. I normally don't cause this much trouble. I am a strong woman." She was beginning to feel like a pansy.

"I have no doubt that's true. You have not caused me any trouble. I'm the one who asked you to come on this hike. You asked me out to dinner."

"True. So, I guess I *can* blame you." They both cracked up as Connor moved to make camp for the night.

❦ 6 ❦

ONCE HE'D SET THE TENT UP AND HAD A SMALL FIRE GOING, THEY SAT around and watched the luminous lake. The moon was up high and cast a glow, lighting up the darkened water and giving the lake a mystifying glimmer. All around the trees Starla could see, fireflies twinkling like little magical lanterns. It was as though they were blinking a secret code.

"Connor, this is delightful. Listen to the frogs and crickets chanting as though they are in a church choir."

He laughed. "Or they are rocking and rolling." He strummed an invisible guitar.

She had to giggle. "Or maybe they are trying to sing some country-and-western song."

"Could be. Now look up at the sky." He pointed. "See those stars there?"

She tried to see where he was pointing. "Not sure."

He moved closer to her. "Right there—they look like they make the shape of a handle."

"Yes, I do see that. I've never noticed that pattern before."

"That, darlin, is the Big Dipper."

She gazed up into the heavens and her breath caught. "I honestly have never seen so many stars. My parents tried to show me once." She swallowed. "But I didn't care. I was a kid and it didn't interest me."

"I was the same way with my parents. Look." He pointed up again. "If you look just below the Big Dipper at that group of stars—that's Virgo. My wife taught me that." His voice went hoarse and he cleared his throat.

She looked into his eyes. "What was her name?"

"Holly." And that was all he said.

She knew that was enough from him, so she drifted into silence and nothing more was said again. Together, they gazed at the stars, not speaking out loud, but it was as if they were saying things to one another with their silence. When she took his hand, she could feel the tension fall away as he held on. This was a new sensation, the touch of his hand sent tingles through her entire body. She loved how warm and strong his fingers were. They talked until midnight, about their experiences as children, it was one of the most special times Starla had ever had with a man. When Connor helped her up, he paused and brushed a strand of hair out of her face. That simple gesture made her feel something toward him, she couldn't explain.

THE NEXT MORNING, CONNOR WOKE TO THE SOUND OF WATER RIPPLING and birds chirping. He'd slept like a rock and was sure as heck glad he'd brought two sleeping bags. The minute his vision adjusted to the morning light, his gaze swept over Starla, but stopped at her cherry-red lips. God in heaven, she was gorgeous, sexy and... rocked his boat, he'd like to... He rebuked the thoughts from his mind the minute she opened her droopy eyes.

"Hi," she whispered and brushed the hair out of her face.

"Good morning, sleepy head." Connor smiled. "I'd like to get up, but..." he nodded downward, "I don't have anything on. I don't mind, but I don't want to embarrass you." He lifted an arched brow.

Her smile reached her eyes and she turned over, facing the tent. "Okay, let me know when I can turn around. But I'll need you to leave so I can get dressed, too."

"Will do, little lady." He slipped on his clothes, folded his sleeping bag, and stood. "I'll go make some of that year-old coffee and hope we don't get sick from it. I'll take a drink first to make sure it's okay."

"So, in other words, you're willing to poison yourself for me." She giggled.

"Just call me Mr. Hero." He chuckled. "You'll be okay getting dressed by yourself? It might be a bit difficult with a hurt foot and all. I wouldn't mind helping."

"My arms work just fine, but thank you for the heroic offer," she said with humor in her voice.

"Understood." He left the tent and wished like hell she would have said yes. Knowing she may have been sleeping in the nude, did things to him.

Connor got the fire started and made the coffee. He was glad they had a little leftover food for breakfast, and he placed the remaining sandwiches and slices of pie on two plates and waited for Starla to finish dressing. What in the world was taking her so long? He moved closer to the tent to check on her.

"Starla, you okay in there?"

"Yes, just trying to figure out how to fold up this sleeping bag."

"Can I come in?"

"Yes," she said, sounding frustrated.

What he saw next caused him to choke back a big laugh. She was sprawled out on her stomach, trying to fold the darn thing. Her hair was all over her face, and when she looked up at him and blew her hair off her forehead, he doubled over, no longer able to control his laughter.

"What the hell are you doing?" he asked, still laughing. "Have you ever been camping or slept in a sleeping bag?"

"My parents always did this for me! And this thing is broken, anyway."

"Broken? And how, exactly, would a sleeping bag get broken?"

"I tried to do it just like you did yours, but it wouldn't go in that circle."

"Let me show you." He helped her up, and she limped off toward the opening of the tent. "Here, just like this." He zipped it up. "See, you have to close it back up first." Then he rolled it in a circle. "That's all it takes." He tightened it up and smiled.

"Oh," is all she said.

He helped her out of the tent and found a log for her to sit on. "Now, have some of this coffee—it's really not bad. I found some sugar but no cream."

"Thank you," she said, adding, "how far do we have to go?" She took a small bite of the sandwich on her plate and heard birds singing and squawking.

"Well, we didn't get far last night, so we still have a ways to go. How is your foot feeling?

"It's still really sore, but I can hobble. I may have to stop off and on, though."

"Can I see your foot?" he asked.

"Sure." She took off her shoe. "It's more black and blue than it was, but it's not as swollen."

He lifted her foot into his lap and examined it carefully. "Starla, there is no way you can walk on this."

"Well, I could try and crawl." She touched her foot. "*Ouch.*"

"I'm going to have to carry you," he said and meant it.

Just then, a sound made them both look up. "Oh Connor. run. Just give me a stick, and I'll try to scare him off."

Connor laughed. "Starla, seriously? You haven't spent much time in the wilderness, have you?"

"No," she shook her head. "Not since I was little with my parents."

"Well, would you look at that. What a beautiful wolf," he said. "He's very curious about us."

"I hope he doesn't want to eat us," she said nervously, twisting her hands,

"Nah, I think he belongs to the Indian woman, whose name is Hialeah. I was telling you about her and I remember hearing that he keeps his distance."

"Shadow!" A woman's voice called out from across the lake. "Come to me."

Connor stood, and Starla tried to stand but lost her balance. Luckily, he turned just in time to see her falling and caught her before she hit the ground.

"You need to stay off your foot. I've tried using my cell phone twice, but there's no reception out here," Connor explained.

Before Starla could answer, the wolf came tearing across some rocks and flew in their direction. Starla screamed, and Connor stepped in front of her with his stick. The wolf had never done this before, as far as he knew. This is a small town and he would have heard if someone got malled by a wolf.

"Shadow!" the older lady yelled again. "Stop." She was making her way across the water.

But Shadow didn't seem to listen. Shit, Connor hated to hit him, but would if he had to.

7

STARLA CLOSED HER EYES, KNOWING THIS WAS NOT GOOD. CONNOR would try to protect her, but maybe the wolf wanted to take her out because she was weak. He must sense it.

"Starla, stay very still," Connor said in a husky, but steady voice.

She opened one eye and stared deep into the creature's eyes. It was as though the wolf was gazing into her soul. She could feel him.

"Connor, put down the stick."

"What? No way," he snapped.

"Please, put it down." She reached up and grabbed it from his hand. "He's not a threat." She did not understand how she knew this, but she did.

The wolf sniffed the air and took a few more steps toward them. Connor tensed.

"It's okay," Starla said lightly to him. "Hi, Shadow."

He moved closer, looking between her and Connor.

"Good boy." There was something so powerful in his eyes that Starla felt a connection. Then, slowly as she moved down to the ground, he inched his way to her face.

"Starla, not too close," Connor cautioned.

"Don't worry," she said.

Before she could say another word, the beautiful Shadow licked her face. For whatever reason, his warmth brought up a flurry of emotions inside her, and tears trailed down her cheeks.

"Hi, Shadow." She wanted to hold him forever.

The older lady with white hair approached. "I'm so sorry." She sounded winded. "He's never done this before."

"Does he normally attack or is he friendly?" Connor asked.

"He has never attacked anyone and usually keeps his distance from strangers. He's *certainly* never done this. What are you doing out here, Connor?"

"Visiting the waterfalls," he explained. "You might say we got stranded."

Starla finally got her wits about her. She'd never paid much attention to dogs, but it's never too late to start, even if it's not really a dog.

"Hi." She looked up and smiled at the older woman. "He's very friendly."

Connor leaned down and moved Starla's foot out of the way. "Did he step on your foot?'

"No," she said. "He's been careful with it—almost like he knows I'm hurt."

"What happened?" Hialeah kneeled down and examined Starla's foot.

"I tripped last night in the dark. I'm so clumsy."

"Oh dear, is that why you were stranded?" She sighed and continued to study Starla's foot. "It's black and blue and you have some major swelling going on. You shouldn't be walking on it at all."

Connor nodded. "That's what I said."

"By the way," she glanced between Connor and Starla and continued, "my name is Hialeah, and I can help you with your foot if you like. I'm a good fifteen minutes away, but I have a truck that could take you back into town."

"Nice to meet you, Hialeah. My name is Starla."

"Nice to meet you." She smiled. "I've known Connor and his family since he was a teen." She winked at Connor. "I have some herbs that would help with the healing and the pain. It won't take away any bruising, but it can help speed up your recovery."

"I think I could walk that far if I had a stick to lean on." Starla glanced around, looking for a stick.

"There is no way you're walking. I will carry you."

"No, Connor. We have all this stuff." She waved around.

"I can take some and so can Shadow. He's good with carrying things, and I might be sixty-two, but I built my own cabin. I think I can handle this." Hialeah appeared serious.

The thing that surprised Starla most, was after Connor got everything ready, Shadow took the picnic basket in his mouth and waited for Hialeah to take the backpack. She picked it up as if it were nothing.

"There," she said as she adjusted the straps. "We are all set."

Connor walked over and nodded to Starla. "Ready, little lady?"

"I hope I don't break your back." Starla was worried.

"I work in construction and carry things all day that weigh more than you. I don't think that's going to be an issue." He swept her up in his arms. "Let's do this."

Sure enough, he carried her as though she was weightless. The hardest part was crossing over the lake on the rocks and not slipping, yet somehow, they all stayed upright. It was clear what had taken Hialeah so long to get across the water.

After about twenty minutes, they arrived at Hialeah's log cabin. The place sat in an open meadow with flowers of every color and mountains serving as the backdrop. Several trees stood close by and shaded the front yard. The aroma of burning wood fanned its way around them and the smell was divine.

"Well, I'll be." Connor said. "This sure as heck wasn't what I was expecting."

"It's lovely." Starla studied the cabin. "How in the world did you build this by yourself?"

"I used my two hands." Hialeah held them up. "It took me over two years, but I did it. I had some help from family, then hired a few things done, like the wood-burning stove, plumbing and electrical, but I did everything else by myself."

"Where did you live while you built this home?" Connor asked. "Being that I own a construction business and my family didn't mention you doing this, I find this down right mind blowing."

"In my camper." She pointed toward the cabin. "It's in the back. I used to keep it in the barn, but I needed more room for all my horses and other animals. Let me tell you, that barn was a mess when I first bought this land, but it was a good shelter, especially after I repaired things and put in some insulation. It kept us warm and safe."

"Us?" Connor repeated.

"Shadow was a pup back then. I found his mama dead, so, I took him with me. He was all alone and very frightened." She reached down and stroked his head. "I became his mama."

Starla inhaled deeply. "Bless your heart for taking such good care of him. Do you take care of all the farm animals by yourself?"

"I sure do." She smiled. "Let's get inside so Connor can give his arms a rest and I can tend to your foot." Hialeah led the way.

As they climbed the front steps, Starla noticed a pile of already-chopped wood with an ax sitting next to it. Chairs lined the front porch, and beautiful flowers and clay pots were all around.

"My word, did you chop that yourself?" Starla asked.

"Of course." She laughed. "I haven't been able to teach Shadow how to chop wood or carry water yet."

"I read that book." Starla smiled. "*Chop Wood, Carry Water* by Rick Fields. I was in college when I read it. Wonderful book."

"It sure is," Hialeah agreed.

They entered the house, and Starla was immediately enchanted. The aroma wafting inside was different, but nice.

"It smells wonderful in here," Starla said as she sniffed the air.

Connor nodded in agreement. "What is that? It's woodsy, but with something else too," he asked.

"Oh, it's sage and sweetgrass. I burn it every day." She pointed toward the sofa. "You can put her down there and I'll make us a pot of tea. Then, I need to see about your foot." She smiled at Starla.

"How do you get your water?" Starla had never heard of anyone living out in the middle of nowhere with no power lines or hookups.

Connor set her down, and she hadn't realized how warm his arms were until they were no longer there.

"Thank you," she whispered while she waited for Hialeah to answer. Their eyes met for a moment, and something in his eyes sparked, but she wasn't sure what it was.

"I'm on well and septic. The electrical, as you may have noticed, is solar. I'm off the grid." She headed toward the kitchen. "There are times it's rough, mainly during winter, but I manage to make it work. The cows get milked and the chickens lay delicious eggs."

"Looks like you did a fine job with this building and all you've done here." Connor ran his hand over the walls. "I'm impressed."

"Thank you," she said from the kitchen, and then turned on the water.

Connor glanced over at Starla. "I was supposed to pick up my godson today. He was going to help me work on my yard and was excited about it."

"Oh no, and you're missing it all because of me. I'm sorry." Shadow climbed up on the couch next to Starla and laid his head in her lap.

"Don't worry about it. I'll just need to contact him somehow."

Hialeah called out from the kitchen. "When my cousin came to visit, he found one spot that works. He marked it with a little flag down near the lake. He said texting works better."

"I'll go look, Hialeah. You okay, Starla?"

"I'm fine. I would like to let Ria know I'm okay, though, so she doesn't worry, and I don't just stand her up."

"I have her cell number. I'll text her too, if I can get anything sent out."

"Wonderful," Starla said and went back to smooching on Shadow.

Connor walked to the door, then paused. "He's a lucky dog." His voice was husky and the smile that lit up his intense blue eyes sent a shiver down Starla's spine.

When he left, she let out a long breath and fanned her face. Suddenly, the wood stove made her feel like she was burning up, she settled on one side of the sofa and leaned on the armrest.

Hialeah came into the room, carrying a wooden bamboo tray.

"I bet you're hungry, so let's drink some tea and eat some of these wonderful organic cookies. Everything is made from real ginger and fresh carrots. Just about everything I have, I make using ingredients from my garden and farm animals."

She handed Starla a cup of steaming tea with a smile. "Now drink that up, and we'll have a look at your foot." She motioned for Shadow to move. "He doesn't seem to want to leave your side."

"He's wonderful." Starla gazed down at him. "I know this sounds crazy, but I feel like I know him."

"I see. Tell me, what is familiar about him?"

"His eyes. When I first looked into them—I know this will make me sound like I should be shipped off to the loony bin—they reminded me of my father's."

"Your father passed away?"

"Yes, he did."

"I'm sorry to hear that." She took Starla's hand in hers. "Losing a parent is never easy."

"I lost both of mine close together." Starla felt tears stinging her eyes. "It's been a while, but, you know, I still miss them."

"How long have you had cancer? If you don't mind me asking."

"What?" The room spun. "How… did?" She pulled her hand from Hialeah's. "Please don't say anything, but how did you know?"

Hialeah patted her hand. "I won't say a word. I'm what they call a medicine woman, and Shadow gave me the sign. He gives me a signal when someone has cancer. Dogs can smell it."

Before they could finish their conversation, the door opened. "I got off a text to everyone," Connor announced. "Ria offered to come and pick us up. She knows where this place is and said there is an old road off Pinewood Lane she can take to get here."

"Oh, yes. That's how I get into town, its remote, but a good road. Ria and I have had many cups of tea together. I also helped her when she was suffering with the flu. Now, let's see what I can do to help you feel better."

Starla pulled off her shoe and held her foot out. "Ah," Hialeah, said and continued touching all around. "What you have is called a stone bruise. Let me get something." She stood and walked down the hallway.

Connor glanced down at her foot. "I'm sorry that you're hurt. How does it feel?"

"Not as bad as last night, but not good."

"Okay." Hialeah was carrying something in her hand. "Let me wrap your foot in this, and the pain should hopefully be gone by tomorrow."

"What is it?" Starla was skeptical when Hialeah wrapped a wet, muddy cloth around her foot.

"Now, you need to keep that on when you sleep tonight," She instructed. "And continue to stay off your foot."

"*What is that?*" Starla scrunched up her nose. "It smells… odd."

"You'll get used to it. It's a remedy for pain and healing—just natural herbs and things I use for broken bones. However, your foot is not broken."

Connor leaned over and studied the wrap. "What kind of natural things?

"Oh, a little comfry, cobwebs, and a few flowers."

"Cobwebs?" Starla's voice cracked. "What's that do?"

"It can help mend broken bones, heal wounds, and stop bleeding. Overall, it's a healing agent."

"Okay," she said as she glanced up at Connor, and he gave her a half shrug.

"If you like," Hialeah continued to wrap her foot, "I can come check on you tomorrow." She finished and wiped her hands on a towel.

Right away, the pain eased, and a cooling sensation ran through her foot. "For heaven's sake," Starla glanced between the two, "it's not hurting anymore."

"It will take away the pain but stay off your foot until I see you tomorrow."

"Okay, I will." Starla couldn't believe how fast the pain had stopped. "Can I walk on it at all?"

"No." She looked up at Connor. "Can you stay with her tonight and help her?"

"Yes, I can work it out. I have to run and feed my cat, but I can stay with her."

"I have to help out Ria on Monday." Starla couldn't just break her promise. "And Connor, I don't want to put you out any more than I already have."

"You're not putting me out. I wouldn't help if I didn't want to." His eyes sparkled with what appeared to be honesty. "I've enjoyed our time together."

"I'll come by tomorrow afternoon, and I'll bring Shadow because he hasn't taken his eyes off you and will not be happy when you leave."

Connor laughed. "Guess he's in love."

"Those two have a connection," Hialeah explained. "He was more than likely waiting for Starla to come. He's been watching for a long time. Animals know things we don't understand." She smiled and rubbed his head. "It's important that we pay attention to them."

Starla couldn't explain what she felt toward Shadow, but she knew it was something deep.

"I love him already." She reached down and stroked behind his ears. "And I do feel connected to him, but I have no idea how or why."

Hialeah stood. "We don't have to always understand everything. Sometimes life just surprises us in good ways. Usually, we accept them and don't question why. It's the hurtful things we get angry about and lose our faith over, letting emotions blister our insides."

Starla saw pain flash in Connor's eyes. She wanted to give him a big hug. Even though she didn't know what had happened to his wife, she knew whatever it was had sure hurt him. That much she could see.

A knock at the door made Connor turn. "That must be Ria." Shadow stood up straight and stared at the door.

Connor crossed the room and answered it and motioned for her to enter. "Well, I'm glad to see y'all are safe and warm. I was worried sick when Starla didn't show up for breakfast, until I saw your Harley parked out front. I thought maybe y'all were *busy*." She chuckled.

Hialeah moved across the room. "Ria, it's so good to see you. It's been too long, child."

They embraced, and Starla could sense the strong friendship between them.

"I know. It's been crazy, but I've thought about you often and wondered if you were still selling those wonderful eggs?" Ria let go and turned to Starla.

"Not to you," Hialeah said. "I have plenty extra for you to have. At least six dozen."

"I'm going to load up this stuff in your car, Ria. Is that okay?" Connor said.

She nodded and turned back. "Oh, Hialeah, that's so generous. Thank you. So, what's the verdict with your foot?" Ria asked as she moved next to Starla. "Is it broken?"

Starla shook her head. "No, thank goodness. I've been more worried about keeping my word to help you, than I have been about my foot."

"Miss Holloway, don't you dare worry about that. I can work something out."

"Your name is Holloway?" Hialeah asked, her voice going up a notch.

"Is something the matter?" Starla asked.

"What were your parents' names?"

"My mama's name was Ama Yona, and my father's was James Russel Hollaway. So, of course, my mama became Ama Yona Hollaway."

Hialeah stood, held up her finger, then headed down the hallway without a word in reply.

"I wonder what's going on?" Starla said as she glanced up at Ria.

Ria shrugged. "I have no clue."

After a few minutes, Connor marched back inside. "I went ahead and got everything loaded." He surveyed the room, seeming a little confused. More than likely, he could feel the tension in the air. "Anything wrong?"

"We don't know. Hialeah seemed a little shaken by my last name and the name of my parents." Starla frowned and wondered why.

"Really?" he said. "Where is she?"

"Well," Starla looked in the direction Hialeah had left. "I think she went to get something."

Connor moved by the couch, shifting from one foot to another. There was no missing his concern.

After a few uncomfortable minutes, Hialeah came back carrying an old wooden box that appeared to be handmade. She set it on the table and stared into Starla's eyes, unshed tears glistening in the old woman's eyes.

"What is it, Hialeah? Did I say something to upset you?" Starla felt horrible and did not understand what she'd done.

Hialeah opened the box and took out some pictures before speaking. "Ama Yona was my daughter." She handed some photos to Starla. "I should have seen the resemblance, but it never dawned on me to look so closely."

Starla lifted the pictures and felt her heart pounding. "That's my mama." She glanced up at the woman, she had just met—her Grandmother. "But how? She told me her mama had died. The only grandma, I ever knew was my daddy's mama, and she has dementia. She doesn't even know me anymore."

When Starla looked up at Connor and Ria, they both were obviously uncomfortable. "I know Ria needs to get back, but... I feel like I need to stay here and talk. Would that be okay if I stayed here with you?"

"Yes, of course." Hialeah nodded. "I would love that."

"No problem here." Connor said. "I'll go back with Ria and get some of your stuff. I can come back and bring it to you in a couple of hours. It should all fit in my bike's saddlebags, but if there's an issue, I can pick up my truck. I just need to run home to feed my cat and chickens, and then I'll head back here to check on things."

"Maybe you and Connor could stay the night. I have two spare rooms." Hialeah's eyes pleaded.

"Okay. Will that work for you, Ria? I hate to take up that room if I'm not there. Connor, I know you have a business to run."

"I don't have to be back to work until Monday. I'm the boss, remember?"

Ria walked over and touched Starla's shoulder. "Nobody has booked that room right now anyway. It's not a problem if you stay there or not. I'll see you two later." She embraced Hialeah. "What a blessing and a miracle that you two found each other."

Hialeah wiped away a tear. "I never dreamed anything like this could happen," she said just barely above a whisper.

Connor gave them both a soft look. "I'll see you in a bit."

The minute they walked out, Shadow got up and went to the door.

"You need to go out?" Hialeah crossed the room and opened what looked to be a doggie door.

Once Hialeah came back over and sat down, she took Starla's hand. "We can get a DNA test to be sure, but I have no doubt. You look just like your *aa-chee*." She smiled. "That's how we say *mother* in our native language."

"Is that why Shadow knew? Because we are blood relatives?"

"Yes, he knew my blood runs through your veins—just like he knows you have cancer. A dog's nose is a most powerful thing."

"Did you know my mama died?" Starla tried to swallow back the tears.

"No. I did not know where she was." Tears reflected in her eyes. "I did look for a short time, but not until her *aa-doh-dah*, her father, passed away. She called him *doh dah* when she was young. His name was Adahy, and they were as close as any two people could be. They fished, hiked, and played together." She picked up her tea and took a sip as a tear trailed down her cheek.

"What happened? Why did she tell me you were dead?"

"Because, in some ways, I was." She opened her mouth but shut it again. "Adahy forbid her to see your father. He was a white man, and her daddy wanted her to be with her own kind." Her face was stamped with pain.

"How did you feel?"

"I was okay with it. I tried talking to him, but I was raised to believe that the man is the head of the household, and that you must not go against what he says." Hialeah picked up another picture and handed it to her.

"That was your grandfather. He was a kind man, but more stubborn than five bulls."

"He was handsome and so... *big*." Starla said softly.

Hialeah nodded. "Yes, he was. When your parents came to us and told us they wanted to get married, Adahy became angry. He told her that if she did, he would never speak to her again—that she would no longer be his daughter and could never come back home." Hialeah covered her mouth, then took a long deep breath and started again. "I begged and pleaded for him to take back his words, but he never did."

Starla reached over and held Hialeah's hand. "They never saw each other again?"

"No, she came home while we were gone and left us a small note saying goodbye. She said that she'd always love us. As Adahy died, he cried out her name many times before he passed away. I didn't know why." Her breath caught. "Now, I know he was seeing her—she was there to guide him into the next world."

Starla chewed on her lip and tried to push down her emotions. "I miss my mama and daddy, but I resented him so much after she died. All he did was drink and hide out in his room. He was never the same. I felt as though he hated me for looking like her."

"I'm sorry you went through that with your father." She shook her head and continued. "I'm so glad we found each other." Hialeah squeezed her hand. "I've always wondered if she had children. I have two grandchildren by my son, but they live so far away that I rarely get to see them."

"I have more family?" Starla couldn't help but feel excited and wondered what they were like. "My mom never mentioned siblings?"

"I was pregnant when, Ama Yona left. We hadn't told her yet," Hialeah, said. "You have two first cousins and some second and third. Also, there is my sister, who is younger than I am, and lives in Colorado. She is going to want to meet you. She and Ama Yona were close."

"I didn't think I had any family left."

"We are not great in numbers, but we are your family. Now, let's talk about your health," she stated, just as Shadow walked in and put his head in Hialeah's lap.

"I have breast cancer for the third time. They want to remove my breast." Tears welled up in her eyes, but she blinked them away.

"How many opinions did you get?" Hialeah asked.

"Opinions?"

"Yes," Hialeah said without hesitation. "Did you see more than one doctor?"

"No, I've only seen the same doctor who has treated me from the beginning." She sighed. "I don't want anyone else to know."

"You mean your male friend, Connor?"

"Yes, well, no," she said, fidgeting with her hands. "Actually, I don't want anyone to know except for Oliver, who is my best friend. I have to tell him because he's also my business partner."

"What kind of business do you run?"

"We own a catering business." Starla couldn't help but notice the sparkle in her grandmother's eyes.

"That's wonderful." She patted Starla's hand. "Speaking of food, I want to talk to you about what we can do to kill that cancer and about getting a second opinion." Her grandmother stood, and in a shocking display, lifted her top. "See, I've had mine removed, but I refused chemo or radiation. That was over twenty years ago. I know now that I didn't have to get rid of my body parts." She let her top fall back down. "But I didn't get a second opinion, until it was too late. What I did isn't right for everyone, but it was right for me and it could be right for you."

"You only had cancer once?" Starla reached once again for her grandmother's hand. "I'm so afraid."

"Only once." She nodded and sat back down next to Starla. "There is a doctor I know, Dr. Norman Hatcher, who offers medicinal and herbal treatments, along with traditional medicine. He's fantastic, and although I knew a lot about natural remedies before, I've learned so much more from him."

"Where is he?" Starla guessed it couldn't hurt to get another opinion.

"Right here in Secret River Valley."

"Okay, we can go when my car is fixed. If you give me his number, I'll call when I get back to my cottage."

"Starla, how would you feel about staying out here with me? I'd like to treat you with some remedies that can help your immune system. I believe that's where it starts. Eating healthy and doing the right things helps to boost it and make it stronger. That way it can fight off cancer cells. Also, I believe in doing away with almost all sugar, especially when you have cancer in your body. It's important to have a good medical doctor though, but remember you are in charge of your treatments. Just make sure your doctor supports what you want also."

"Really? I read something about eating healthy, but my oncologist told me I could eat whatever I wanted. He said it didn't matter."

"Yes, I've been to those who say that as well, but since you've already tried it his way two other times, maybe you might want to try it another way this time."

Starla agreed. "I do. They've been wrong about everything so far. They told me that if I went five years cancer free, more than likely it wouldn't come back. Yet, here it is for the third time." Starla inhaled a shaky breath. "I want to fight it off for good."

"You can do that. Together we will beat the tar out of it." They both laughed, and Hialeah rose from the sofa. "I'm going to start dinner for you and Connor. What I'm going to make will feed your immune system, and it tastes amazingly good, he won't know what I'm doing." She left the room.

Shadow came to her and she could've sworn she saw a smile in his eyes. What was it about this wolf that made her feel like he was an old friend? "You're a good boy and I love you." She bent over and embraced him. "I think you've captured my heart, Shadow." She laughed and heard Connor's bike.

A few minutes later, Connor came walking in with her overnight bag. "I forgot to ask you what you wanted me to bring." He glanced between her and Shadow. "So, I just grabbed your bag and took everything I could find." He held it up. "Where should I put it?"

Hialeah called out from the kitchen. "Put it in the last bedroom on the right side. You can't miss the purple bedspread."

Connor walked away, but he paused and stuck his nose in the air. "Something smells doggone good." Starla's mouth went dry. The way Connor moved down the hallway made her almost swallow her tongue. How could he look so enticing after the heartfelt conversation she'd just had with Hialeah? If she had even a smidgen of decency, she'd stop ogling his behind and control her mind in her grandmother's home.

It only took him seconds to find the room and place her bag inside, and then he walked toward her. "I need to grab my own overnight bag and I'll be right back." He walked to the door, and, once again, her eyes were glued to his jeans and chaps, not to mention his wide shoulders that filled up his shirt and accentuated his narrow waist.

Suddenly, he turned back around to face Starla. "After I get my stuff, do you want to go sit on the front porch? It's a beautiful afternoon."

She pulled her eyes away from his and stared at his strong jaw. Although, she was sure he'd busted her, or was reading her mind, when he gave her a slow grin.

"Sure, that sounds good." She swallowed hard and saw his eyes flicker with what appeared to be laughter.

"Starla." The way he said her name was sexy as hell. "Anything else you need, darlin?" He stared into her eyes and wouldn't release them. She felt as though he was pulling her deeper into the depths of temptation.

"Ah, no. I'm fine." She tripped over her words and watched as he opened the door.

She hadn't realized she was holding her breath until she exhaled and mumbled, "Lord, have mercy."

"What in tarnation? Starla, you have to see what's out here." His voice sounded excited. "I've never seen anything like this." He backed up slowly. "Hialeah, you have to come and see what's out on your front porch."

For a minute, Starla's heart stopped beating. As he was backing up slowly, she couldn't help but wonder if he might need to shut and lock that darn door.

"Connor, you're scaring me." Starla felt her voice crack.

"No, it's beautiful." He put his finger to his lips. "Shhh!" He whispered, just as Hialeah walked in the room.

"What did you say?" Hialeah asked, holding a small bowl, and still mixing it. "Is something wrong?" Her attention went past Starla to Connor.

"Look at this," he quietly said. "I've never seen anything like this in my life."

Hialeah walked with ease to the door and sighed. "Oh, that's Blaze."

"Blaze?" Connor tilted his head and a confused expression slid across his rugged and handsome face.

"Yes." She turned around and called to Shadow. "It's Blaze." He hopped up and practically ran out the door.

"That's Shadow's best pal." She smiled as she mixed again and stepped closer to the door. "*Osiyo,* Blaze." Hialeah chuckled. "*Dohitsu.*"

Starla couldn't understand what her grandmother was saying, so she went to stand, but a sharp pain went through her foot. "Oh, darn it."

Connor turned. "Let me carry you out to the porch." He strolled over to her, and she caught her grandmother's smile just before she headed back to the kitchen.

"I am not going to let you break your back." She held up her hand. "I just need a walking stick."

He muttered something under his breath and, ignoring her, lifted her in his arms. "Now, take a look at this," he said as he walked over to the front door and gestured with his chin.

"Heavens to Betsy. I would have never…"

Right in front of her, a bald eagle sat next to Shadow. Seeing the two side by side was out of this world.

"I can't believe this," Starla exclaimed.

Connor walked across the porch and sat her down on a chair. "I know," he said, while they watched the two wild creatures move around the front yard. "In all my days, I've never seen anything like this. I wish I had a camera."

"I have one. It's in the bag you brought. Do you want to get it?" Starla asked.

"You bet." He winked.

8

CONNOR TOOK OFF DOWN THE HALLWAY AND HOPED HIS TRUE FEELINGS weren't showing. Having Starla in his arms had caused his heart to race and every part of his body to respond. There was something special about her—something he hadn't felt since... Holly. Guilt washed over him. How could he dare to have feelings for anyone again? He was a louse—a no-good low-down snake.

Starla's bag was exactly where he'd left it, so he unzipped it in search of the camera. "Holy crap," he said under his breath. Jesus almighty, her clothes were folded in a neat array of perfection. Never could he remember seeing anyone's suitcase or overnight bag packed with such care and precision. As he continued to stare at the bag's perfectly packed contents, his eyes caught sight of a journal titled The Big C. He knew he shouldn't read it, but he couldn't help himself. Well, he could, but didn't. What the heck was The Big C? When curiosity got the best of him, he opened the notebook to the first page. Written across the middle was, "Having cancer" but the entry was dated five years ago. He took a deep breath to steady himself. Why did she carry an old journal with her? Closing the book, he saw the camera and pulled it out, making sure everything was put back in order. Okay, shake it off and walk out there smiling. There was no way he could let her know he'd seen her journal.

A few minutes later, he arrived back on the porch. "Here you go, Miss perfection, I've never seen a suitcase packed like that."

Starla flushed. "I know, I'm a neat freak. Do you want to take the picture? You are able to move around better than me, after all." She gave him a tender smile that made him feel as if his insides had melted.

"Sure." He had just snapped pictures when Hialeah stepped outside to join them.

"Dinner is on and cooking in the oven," she announced.

"It sure smells good." Connor responded. "My stomach has been yelling at me."

"Won't be long—about thirty minutes or so." She moved down the steps. "I want to get Starla something from my barn. I'll be right back." She crossed the yard, stopping to stroke the eagle's head and leaned down to kiss Shadow. What a sight. Even as Connor captured the moment with pictures, he still couldn't believe his eyes.

The minute Connor glanced up, he caught Starla staring at him. From the look on her face, he was sure she had been checking him out again. His gaze met her chocolate-brown eyes and her cheeks turned pink, confirming his suspicions. The way their eyes connected caused his heart to flip. He needed a distraction.

"Smells like Hialeah is cooking something pretty doggone tasty." He rubbed his stomach.

"Maybe I got my cooking skills from her," Starla said. "I've loved working with food since I can remember. I would help my mama in the kitchen."

"So…" He glanced around to be sure Hialeah couldn't hear him. "You think she is really your grandma?"

Starla nodded with tears in her eyes. "She showed me pictures of my mama. I always wondered why she didn't talk about her mother—

my grandmother. All she told me was that she had died. Whenever, I would ask to know more about her, she'd say she couldn't talk about it." Starla wrung her hands. "My daddy told me to stop bringing it up because it hurt Mama too bad. Suddenly, she placed her hand across her forehead. "I caught her crying many times when she was alone. Now I know why."

Connor moved his chair closer when he saw tears roll down her cheeks. He took her hands in his, trying to soothe her.

"I'm sorry you're sad."

She nodded and swiped away the tears. "I'm happy more than sad, it's just all so emotional."

Hialeah came up the stairs. "Here you go." She handed Starla a beautiful hand-carved walking stick. "This might help you to walk without hurting yourself." She stared at Starla's face and her eyes turned tender.

"Goodness. That sure is beautiful." Starla stood and clutched the gorgeous stick, which looked very much like a cane. "This is perfect. I love it."

"Good, now try it out. See if you can go down the steps."

Connor stood, wanting to make sure she was okay as she moved down two steps and did so with ease. "Wow, that seems to work great." Connor grinned.

"I would like you and Connor to go down to Solitude lake." Hialeah pointed. "That's a special part of the water. I'll send Shadow to fetch you when dinner is ready. That water has healing powers, so be sure to stay there for a while." She stuck her hand in her apron. "Snack on some of these until dinner." She handed Connor a bag full of string peas that looked baked. He wasn't much into anything like healing waters or magic, but for Starla, he might try.

Connor swooped Starla up before she protested.

"Connor, what in the dickens do you think you're doing?" She noticed his grin spread during her protest.

"Well, darlin, I can tell you that I'm not doing brain surgery." He handed her the cane.

"Really, and here I thought you were fixin' to cut my head open." She chuckled.

When they got down to the lake, Connor placed her on the ground and handed her the walking stick. Even though the pain was still intense, the support it offered, helped immensely. There was no way she wanted Connor to know she was still hurting, so she smiled and focused on her surroundings.

The little lake sparkled as the sun shone across the ripples of water. Little dandelions floated all around while the sounds of birds chirping echoed through the air. Starla had never seen a lake shaped like a diamond or looked so silver.

"This is different—but breathtaking." Starla moved closer and looked around. The lake was lined with trees and the scent of something different wafted toward them on a breeze.

Connor slipped off his chaps. "Let's get in the water. Hialeah said it has healing properties, so let's find out if it can heal your foot," he said as he rolled his eyes. "I've heard the stories, but I have to warn you. I don't hold faith in them."

"What stories?" Starla asked while bending over to pull off her shoes, but before she could finish the task, Connor leaned down and did it for her.

"Oh, just how some of the lakes out here hold magic and can heal emotional and physical pain. Some of the elders in town believe it even can heal illnesses." As he rolled up his pants and took off his shoes, then shirt, she tried to focus on the sun. It was going down behind the mountain, and traces of orange, yellow, and red filled the sky. It was like a perfect painting of the horizon.

By the time she pulled her eyes away from the beautiful sunset and glanced over toward him, he had stepped even closer.

"Ready? Can I carry you into the water?" he said, his voice low and husky.

"Actually, that sounds good." She was nervous about stepping in the lake on her sore foot and she loved being close to him.

With that, he swung her up into his massive arms and walked toward the body of water. His skin was warm, and, Lord have mercy, chills traveled down all of her.

After a few steps, he eased her down into the lake. She dipped her warm hands into the cool water, making ripples.

"How is that?" he asked, holding her steady. "I don't want you to fall."

"I'm fine." A splash made them both turn.

"Look at that." Connor pointed. "Talk about a big fish."

"It was." Starla watched as another fish jumped into the air. "Holy wow."

Connor cracked up. "That would make a good meal."

A few seconds later, a sweet scent encircled them again. "Connor, do you smell that?" A honey-like fragrance hung in the air. "That's about the sweetest aroma I've ever inhaled."

"I think I smelled something even better just before I sat you down."

"You did? I guess I missed that. What did it smell like?"

He moved closer. "Like you."

"Me?" she gulped for air.

"Yes, you." He arched a brow and bent down, brushing the hair from her face. "Starla, you smell sweeter than my mama's apple pie with brown sugar sprinkled on top. And, I promise, you look more delicious than any treat she's ever made." He gave her a slow, easy grin.

Starla couldn't seem to catch her breath. His eyes drew her in with a subtle magnetism, causing her legs to turn into mush. Before she could say anything in response, he traced his tongue across her bottom lip and mumbled, "You taste sweeter than pie, too." A moan came from his throat. Or was it her throat? Hell, she didn't know.

Oh, lord have mercy, A tingle ran up her back all the way to her neck. He tasted like maple and mint. She felt as if electricity was pulsing through her. At first, she thought maybe it was from the water—maybe she was reacting to its magic, but the truth was simple. It was Connor. He was making her feel things she'd never experienced.

He caressed her face with his large but gentle hands and pulled her closer. She had no choice but to gaze into his ocean-blue eyes. "Connor," she whispered.

Suddenly, they heard more splashing, and before Connor could move them out of the way, they were both knocked into the water.

"Damn," Connor said, laughing as Shadow continued jumping around. He rubbed his face and playfully scolded the dog. "Your timing sucks." He stood and reached out to Starla.

Shadow licked her face. "I guess we'll need to change now." She hugged the wolf, then took Connor's hand.

"I think so," Connor agreed. "I don't think Hialeah would like us dripping all over her furniture." He pulled her up. "Are you okay? I can carry you..."

"No, actually the water did help my foot feel better. At least it's not hurting right now." He continued to hold her hand and helped her to shore.

Once they got closer to the cabin, they saw Hialeah out on the front porch. When she realized they were drenched, Starla noticed amusement in her eyes.

"So, what in the world happened?" She held up her hand to Shadow and looked down at him. "You have to dry off first. I have a feeling you caused them to be drenched."

As if he understood, he shook his fur and his eyes showed guilt. He found a warm place in the sun and lay down.

"Let me get you kids a towel." She took off into the house.

They both sat down and Starla tilted her head back and let the sun warm her face.

"Did that stick help you to keep the pressure off your foot?" Connor asked.

"Yes, as a matter of fact what little I used it, I noticed it helped. I don't feel any pain right now." She looked at him and saw what she could only guess was doubt in his eyes. "I know, I know, but it's true. The pain is gone."

He looked down at her foot. "Well, the most important thing is that it's not hurting right now."

Hialeah walked out and handed them both a towel. "When you both dry off and change, come on in the kitchen. Dinner will be waiting for you."

They took the towels and dried off the best they could, then they sat in the sun for about ten minutes. The warm breeze helped them to dry off.

After Starla cleaned up in the small bathroom, she walked into the bedroom and opened her suitcase. Everything was in its place except her camera, which she'd left in the living room. She picked out a pair of slacks and her blue shirt. This would just have to do until she could get into town. These were not the kind of clothes she should wear out here. As she sat down on the bed, she lifted her foot. How could it not hurt anymore? Even the swelling had gone down, which made her think about her cancer.

Her mind drifted back to the day in the oncologist's office when he came in holding her chart, which held the news of the results.

The door opened, and she gulped for air. The look on his face was not good. His frown lines increased as he ran his fingers through his salt-and-pepper hair.

Dr. Langley sat down and met her gaze, then put on that fake smile she knew all too well. His almond-shaped, nut-brown eyes flashed with pity. She tried to prepare herself, but her heart sank down into the pit of her stomach.

"Miss Holloway, I'm sorry," he drawled. "It's returned, but this time we can't take any chances. We suspect it may have spread to other areas." He cleared his throat. "We will need to remove your breast and possibly some lymph nodes." His voice was so low it was almost inaudible. "We should begin treatment right away."

"You want to remove my breast?" Her throat closed with emotion. There was no way to control the tremor in her voice. "I'm only thirty-three. How can this be happening again?"

The room spun, and the floor shook beneath her as his words echoed in her mind. They had to take her breast and it might be in her lymph nodes? She'd lose her hair and get those awful sores inside her mouth. What about her business? Things weren't the same as they had been five years ago. Now they were booked solid, and Oliver couldn't do it all on his own.

Was she going to die? She needed to breathe before she passed out.

"Starla." She heard her grandmother's voice in the hall. "Do you want to come and eat?"

"Yes." She pulled her mind back from the heartache and opened the door. "I'm starving." She smiled her best smile and laced her arm through Hialeah's.

In the kitchen, she watched Connor as he scanned her from top to bottom. His gaze made her hotter than a two-dollar pistol.

"Well, now, you look all gussied up. I feel underdressed." He winked.

"Sadly, these are the only clothes I brought—except my jeans, which need to be washed." Starla sighed.

Hialeah smiled. "I have some clothes that might fit you. After dinner, we can go check them out." Her grandmother pointed to a chair at one end of the table and she sat at the other. "Now sit a spell, relax, and chow down."

"I don't know what you cooked, but it sure smells great." Connor lifted his nose in the air and rubbed his stomach.

Starla couldn't believe the way the casserole melted in her mouth.

It was loaded full of vegetables, and she was positive the spices were tamarack, ginger, and garlic with fresh basil and quinoa.

"This is wonderful." Starla glanced at her grandmother. "Now I know where I got my ability to cook."

"You come from a long line of folks who might as well be chefs, because they can cook up a storm."

"Really?" Starla tilted her head and waited for her grandmother to explain.

Hialeah swallowed a bite of her food and took a drink of water. "Your great grandma owned a bakery and was the talk of the town, where we grew up. People would line up to get a loaf of her fry bread. It was the best. Grandmother learned it from a Navajo woman and as time went by, she perfected it."

After her grandmother finished her stories, things went silent and Starla couldn't help but feel excitement to meet a family she never knew she had.

There wasn't much more chatter during dinner except the occasional groan of approval. Once they finished up, Connor and Hialeah started cleaning the dishes. Starla wanted to help, but they wouldn't hear of it, so she walked with her new cane out into the living room.

The sounds of crickets and bullfrogs floated in through the windows. It was as if they were calling her name to come out to the front porch, so she hobbled her way out the door and plopped down into the rocking chair. The moon hung in the sky and the heavens were filled with millions of twinkling stars. Everything about the night enchanted her. While she took in the beauty around her, Shadow came and sat by her side.

"Hi, boy." She scratched his head as they both looked out at the view.

"How's your foot?" Connor asked again as he stepped outside and peered over at her.

"Honestly, it's much better. I'm still being careful, but the pain is essentially gone."

"Can I see it?" Connor asked and moved closer.

"Yes, the swelling has gone down." She pulled off her shoe and raised her foot. "See."

He sat in the chair in front of her and examined it. "Actually, the swelling hasn't gone down that much." Their eyes connected.

"What do you mean?"

"Just what I said. There is still swelling, but it's wonderful that you're not in pain."

Starla nodded. "You're right about that."

Hialeah joined them with some tea in hand. "Here, drink this." She handed Starla a cup. "He's right about what?"

"Look." She held up her foot. "The swelling has gone down some and it's not hurting."

Her grandmother nodded. "I told you that the water in Solitude Lake is healing."

Starla's thoughts drifted to her cancer. "What kinds of things does it heal?"

"It can heal everything from emotional issues to serious disease. Although, severe ailments take more than just the healing water. You have to soothe your insides with positive thinking and good, healthy food."

"Okay, I'll give that some thought," Starla said.

Before Hialeah could respond, they heard a car coming down the unpaved road. It was late, but they could see the dirt flying all around due to how fast the car was going.

"Who in the world?" Hialeah stepped forward. "Nobody ever comes out to these parts, especially at night. Unless, they are lost."

Connor stood. "That's Ivy. How did she know how to find me?" He trotted out to the driveway to meet her.

Shadow stood and growled. "Uh oh. He must not like strangers at night." Starla noticed that the fur on his back was standing on end.

"He doesn't normally act like this. I need to put him in my room." Hialeah snapped her fingers and pointed toward the house. Reluctantly, Shadow did as he was told and walked slowly inside.

Starla stood, wondering if there was a problem. She looked on as Ivy stepped out of her car and spoke to Connor, seeming distraught. After a few minutes of conversation, Connor wrapped his arms around her. Something was wrong. Starla went back into the house to give them privacy just as Hialeah came back out to the living room.

"So, Ivy is the young woman who lost her husband about a year after Connor lost Holly, right?"

"I think so. I'm not really sure about the timing, but he did mention that he was her son's godfather." Starla twisted her hands. "I hope everything is okay. I just met her for a minute the other day when I broke down."

Right then, Connor walked inside. "I'm sorry, but I need to go. Ivy is having a hard time with Austin. They can't find his cat. I guess Tommy, one of my employees told her I was out here, when she stopped by my house, he was dropping off some supplies."

"Okay, I'm sorry to hear about his kitty," Starla said, and she meant it. The poor kid.

"I'm going to go help them look." Connor ran his hand through his hair. "It shouldn't take too long. I'd like to come back if that's okay?"

"I'd like that." Starla glanced over at her grandmother.

"Here, take this." Hialeah handed him a key off the wall. "Just in case we are already sleeping."

"Thanks a million. I should be back soon." He smiled and took off toward Ivy's car.

"So, you met her?" Hialeah said again.

"Yes, for just a second. I don't think she liked me, though."

"What makes you say that?" Hialeah sat down and examined Starla's face.

"Just the way she looked at me. It was like she was shooting daggers at me with her eyes."

"Maybe she was jealous." Hialeah stood. "I need to let Shadow out, and maybe you should talk to Connor—tell him about your suspicions." She headed down the hallway.

"No. They seem awfully close."

Starla wondered about Connor's friendship with Ivy. Was that all it was? She knew how things must look to others—people had wondered if there was more between her and Oliver. But, from the moment they'd met, their friendship was strong. When Oliver dated Thea, it was obvious they were a match. She'd loved Thea from the start and pushed for them to recognize that they belonged together. Looking back, she knew she would have never given Thea a dirty look or been jealous of her and Oliver's relationship. All she'd ever wanted was for her best friend in the world to be happy.

Interrupting her thoughts, Shadow came bounding into the living room with Hialeah not far behind him. His fur was still up as he ran over to the front door.

"What's wrong with him?" Starla asked. "He looks angry."

"That's a very good question. Maybe the rumors I've heard about Ivy are true."

"Rumors?" Starla tilted her head.

"Some say she's not a very nice person. Come back here, Shadow!"

Shadow looked up at Hialeah. "Sit," she commanded. "What's gotten into you?"

9

IVY PULLED INTO HER DRIVEWAY, AND AUSTIN RAN UP WITH TEARS sliding down his cheeks. "What if he never comes back home? I can't find him anywhere. I've gone knocking on doors, Mama, just like you said I should do."

Connor's heart broke. Austin loved that cat. However, Connor was concerned over Ivy leaving him home alone at night.

"Don't worry, bud. We'll find him." He touched Austin on the shoulder as he got out of the car.

"Toby's never run away before." Austin's bottom lip trembled.

Ivy walked around the car and faced Austin. "How about you and Connor go search for Toby together, and I'll go get that cat food and open it. If I walk around with it, maybe it will entice him to come home."

"Okay, Mama." Austin took Connor's hand.

"Here, take this." She leaned into the car and handed them a flashlight.

"Good idea." Connor said as they took off in search of the family pet.

After spending nearly twenty minutes looking for Toby, Connor felt like a big old pile of dog poop. There was no sign of Austin's beloved kitty anywhere.

"Connor! Austin! I found Toby."

The look on Austin's face was brighter than the moon. "Mama found him." They both trotted back toward the house.

"Where was he, Mama?" Austin asked, winded from running back to the house.

Ivy smiled. "I don't rightly know. He just came up to me after I tapped the can for the hundredth time. He's inside eating now."

Connor released the air from his lungs. The last thing his godson needed was to lose anything else. The poor kid had been through enough.

They all turned to head inside, and Austin took off at full speed.

Once in the kitchen, Ivy stopped and touched Connor's arm. "I'm sorry I interrupted your night. I shouldn't always depend on you." She cast her eyes downward.

Dang it, he wished she didn't look so sad. "It's okay, sweetie. I'll always be around for you and Austin." He took her hand and squeezed it.

"But you were on a date."

"No problem, she's very understanding." He glanced around. "I should be getting back, though. They're waiting on me."

"You don't want a slice of my famous apple pie?" She waved toward the counter.

"Oh, boy. I have been eating healthy all day, that does sound good, but I would like to use your restroom first."

"Go ahead. I'll get the pie ready for us." Connor nodded and took off around the corner.

When he entered the bathroom, he couldn't believe his eyes. The place was trashed. What in tarnation does she do all day? She had time to pick up—even just a little bit. The towels were strewn across the floor, there was makeup all over the counter, and the mirrors were filthy. Garbage overflowed out of the trash bin and shoes, toys, and clothing were everywhere. Given the state of everything else, there was no way he would look in that tub—no telling how dirty it was.

Connor washed his hands and dried them on his jeans. Did he want a piece of that pie? Maybe he'd just pass and get back to Starla.

A few seconds later, he walked by the mudroom and noticed that Austin was lying on the floor with his cat. "Look, Uncle Connor. He's fine."

Connor bent down and rubbed the little fur ball. "He is. Now, come on out to the kitchen. Your mama is cutting some pie. Maybe she'll give you an extra big piece since I have to take off."

As they arrived in the kitchen, Ivy was pulling out the pie. He was glad it had taken her so long because he changed his mind about staying. "Look Ivy, I'm taking off, so I'll have a piece of that pie tomorrow. I need to go pick up my truck."

"Oh, all right." She smiled. "We will save you a piece. Don't you want me to give you a ride?" She gave him a questioning look.

"I don't want you driving this late." Connor shook his head. "I'll see you both tomorrow. It's a nice evening for a walk to my house, anyhow."

"Bye, Uncle Connor." Austin hugged him around the waist.

Connor squeezed him back. "See you in the morning, slugger."

On his way through the living room, he couldn't help but notice the mess. What the hell? He just couldn't understand how she could do this.

Trying to ignore how she lived, he stepped out on the front porch. His mind instantly drifted to Starla. There was no missing his heart going into overdrive as he thought about getting back to her. Even the fact that he'd only known her for a few days, didn't stop him from wanting to get to know her more.

"Wait, Connor." Ivy stepped out on the porch. "It's only a little after nine," she said as her face dropped. "Please let me give you a ride."

"Are you sure? What about Austin?"

"He's getting his jacket and yes, I'm sure. I picked you up and your Harley is there. I want to do this." She handed him the keys. "You can drive out there, and I'll drive home."

"Okay." He agreed. "Sounds good." Austin stepped out on the front porch and they all headed to the car.

He slid inside and stuck the keys in the ignition. Kachunk. Again, he tried to start it. Kachunk.

Ivy shook her head. "Is this night haunted or what?"

"It could be the battery." He got out of the car and opened the hood and saw Ivy climb out. "I can't tell in the dark." He handed her his tiny flashlight. "Shine that right here." He pointed at the area around the battery.

After twisting the cables and trying to see the problem, he stood up straight and sighed. "Well, I guess I could call my brother. What time is it now?"

"It's not that late. I could wait and call Fred tomorrow. I'm just so broke…" Ivy looked down at the ground.

"No, you don't have to do that. I'm sure I can fix it in the morning."

"Oh, Connor." She gave him a big hug. "I'm so sorry. Why don't you just sleep on the couch? That way you'll already be here to take a look at it tomorrow morning."

"I don't know. I really need to get back out there." He glanced around. "I guess I could have a piece of that pie and give it some thought."

After they had pie, Austin climbed into bed with Toby. The little guy looked up at Connor with droopy eyes as he tucked Austin in. "Good night, Uncle Connor." He almost sounded sad. Connor couldn't pinpoint why, but something was bothering his godson.

"Good night, buddy. I'll see you tomorrow." He leaned down and kissed his head. "Love you."

"Uncle Connor?" Austin glanced up and his lip quivered. "I'll see you tomorrow for sure, right?"

"Of course. You okay, buddy?"

He nodded, but he could sense that Austin was still upset.

Connor made his way out to the living room and plunked his ass down on the couch. Man, it sucked that he was missing out on the evening he had planned. And he had no idea how he could sleep in this mess. There were soda cans all over the coffee table with dirty dishes, socks, shoes, and even a damn bra. Jesus almighty.

"Here are some blankets for later." Ivy walked in and handed them to him. "Do you want to watch a movie with me? I could make some popcorn and get cherry soda."

"Not really." He tried to smile, but he couldn't take his mind off Starla. He needed to either get home or back to the cabin. Jesus, she walked out of the room like she hadn't heard what he said. What the hell?

"Ivy." She stepped back in the living room. "I'm fixin' to go to my house." He headed toward the front door. "I'll come back in the morning and check on your car. I just don't feel right leaving Starla and Hialeah waiting for me." He opened the door and gave her a wave. Then, he took off before she could pitch a fit and try to stop him.

He walked toward his house, the breeze nipping at his cheeks, and the quietness of the evening left nothing to do but let his brain ponder. He had this gnawing feeling about Austin. Maybe he missed having a dad. Or maybe he was just tired.

What in blue blazes was wrong with him? He'd never run out on Ivy and Austin before. Why had he'd done it this time? Ivy was like his sister and Austin his godson. Shame on him.

By the time he arrived at his house, it was ten thirty. He checked on his cat, grabbed his truck keys and rushed out the door. Finally, on his way back to the cabin, he passed through some nearby neighborhoods and noticed all the little white lights that shone in the windows of some of the homes. Many folks in town were married with children, and the fact was, he'd never have what they did. Not now, not ever. Holly was gone, and there wasn't anything or anyone who could ever fill the void she and their unborn baby had left behind. Not even the beautiful, alluring, Starla, whom he'd almost kissed.

Is that what he was hoping for? Someone to take Holly's place? Like the sun going down behind a mountain and never coming back, a sense of loss enveloped him.

Overwhelmed by the sudden onset of loneliness, he slowed down, pulled over to the edge of the road, and mentally slapped himself. Maybe he should just turn around and go home. Leaving Ivy and Austin reminded him of how he'd let Holly be on her own that night. He'd failed Holly and should have been with her.

"Shit." He released a tremulous breath and made his decision. A few minutes later, he whipped the truck around and headed back toward home. What he really needed to do was to stop by to see Ivy and apologize, but it was late, so he'd do that tomorrow morning.

There was no reason he should be walking into something with another woman. He wasn't deserving of anything good ever again— not in the way of love. The best thing he could do was to stay away from Starla Holloway, but he had to go get his Harley. That was easy. He'd ask Ivy to give him a ride tomorrow morning after he fixed her car.

STARLA OPENED HER EYES TO SEE THE FIRST RAY OF SUNSHINE PEEKING through the window. The night had dragged on while she waited for Connor. It was well after one in the morning when the sound of the lake hitting against the banks lulled her to sleep. The wind had blown just enough to make the ripples soothing.

The morning sound of a woodpeckers tap-tap-tapping filled the room. The world was waking up and life was starting all over again.

She was in fear of falling in love with everything about this place, even though she had only been there for such a short time.

"Life," she whispered as a pain etched its way into her heart. Would she have a full life, or would the cancer steal it away? So many things she wanted to do and see. Even more so now, she had family to meet and get to know. She shook off the fear and instead allowed her thoughts to return to Connor. Did he come back last night? Did she sleep through it?

Maybe he had been quiet. She rose and slipped on her robe, but the minute she stepped into the hallway, she knew he hadn't come back. The door to the guest room they had made up for him was wide open and she could see the bed was made.

They must not have found the kitty, or Connor had gone on home instead of returning to the cabin. Coffee called, so she went into the kitchen and pulled down everything she'd need. Once she filled the craft with water and ground the coffee beans, aroma filled the air. Was there any smell as alluring as caffeine first thing in the morning? Heck no.

Minutes later, her cup was filled to the brim. With ease, she tiptoed out on the front porch and realized her foot wasn't hurting at all. The morning breeze fanned its way across her shoulders, making her shiver. Off in the distance, she could see birds taking flight and small animals scurrying around on the ground. She caught sight of Connor's bike, and imagined him sitting on it, while thinking about their almost kiss. Chills went through her and goose bumps crossed over her.

"Good morning, sweetie. I guess Connor didn't come back last night." Hialeah stepped onto the porch and eased down on the chair with a cup in her hand. "Thank you for making the coffee."

"You're welcome and no he didn't come back." Starla glanced at Hialeah's cup. "Are you drinking the coffee I made?"

"Oh, it smelled wonderful, but no." She chuckled. "But, it was still nice for you to do that. We need to wean you off coffee as well."

Starla frowned. "Why?" She held her cup a little tighter. "I love coffee."

"Because it's acidic, and we want to keep your pH in good balance. Coffee complicates that."

"I guess I love acidic things." Starla shook her head, "I can't give up my coffee."

"Moderation, my dear, moderation. We need to go into town today and get you an appointment with Dr. Hatcher. He was the one I was telling you about."

"Sounds good." Shadow came strutting out onto the front porch. He gave a part howl and part bark.

They both laughed. "I guess he's putting in his two cents," said Starla.

"He wants to be fed." She stood and waved him inside after her.

Just then, Starla heard a vehicle approaching and knew it must be Connor. Sure enough, he pulled up in Ivy's car—with Ivy.

Starla put her coffee mug down before she headed out to greet him and watched as they both climbed out of the car.

"Starla," he said as he approached. "I'd like to introduce you to Ivy, since I didn't do that the other day. Ivy, this is Starla."

"Well, how do you do?" Ivy stuck out her hand, but it didn't feel like a friendly gesture and her voice sounded sharp.

"Good, and nice to meet you." Starla smiled and shook Ivy's cold hand.

"Likewise, I'm sure."

Starla's teeth hurt from the false sweetness that dripped off Ivy's tone.

"I had to come and get my bike. It was late when we got done last night and I started to come out, but I didn't want to wake you, so I went on home."

"Did y'all find the kitty?" Starla asked.

"Yeah, we found him pretty quickly." Ivy smiled. "Only took a few minutes."

Connor cleared his throat and Starla noticed he appeared nervous. "I need to head on back to my house. I have a ton of work to do today. I let some of my clients move into my office because we fell behind on their house, so I need to make sure they get settled." He walked toward his bike. "I'll see you later. Ivy, thanks for the ride."

"All right," Ivy said, "But I need my keys." It took no rocket scientist to see she didn't like leaving him.

"Here they are." He handed them to her and nodded.

She turned and almost threw herself into her car. Connor seemed oblivious to her body language, although, when she took off, stirring up dust from her speed, he paused and took a long glance in that direction.

Connor turned and met Starla's eyes. "Sorry I didn't make it back here. I really did almost make it out here last night, but I turned around."

"Why?" Starla was perplexed.

"I need some time to think about the why of it," he mumbled.

"I see." Starla's face heated and she wrung her hands. He needed time to think about the why of it? What the hell kind of answer was that?

"Well, I better let you go." She knew her voice was short. "I'm getting ready to go into town with Hialeah."

He nodded, got on his bike, and drove out of her life. Just like that. Maybe it was for the best. Not even a goodbye or thank you for the lovely day, or it was nice almost kissing you.

She stormed inside the cottage. "To hell with him," she said without thinking, as usual.

"What's the problem?" Hialeah asked. "You look upset."

"I guess I am. Connor came by to get his bike with his friend and barely said goodbye." She glanced down at Shadow. "He almost kissed me yesterday—probably would have had we not got knocked into the water." She squatted down in front of her new friend. "Maybe you knew it wasn't a good idea." She hugged him.

As though he knew she was upset, he kissed her face. "Ah, you are such a good guy. Even if your kisses are full of slobber." She laughed. "I'll be okay. I've been through worse."

"You know that boy has been through hell and back, too."

"I know he lost his wife. That must have been awful."

"Yes, but it's the way he lost her." She frowned. "Let's eat breakfast and talk. I heated the leftover quinoa from last night and cut up some fresh fruit." They sat down at the kitchen table while Shadow finished his food. He stopped and stared, then took off to the living room.

"He doesn't beg," Starla mentioned.

"No, he doesn't like what we are eating. If he did, he might stare at me for a few minutes longer before running off."

"What were you going to tell me?" Starla asked.

"Well, you know Connor lost his wife, but do you know how?"

"No, but I'd like to know."

But, before Hialeah could continue, they heard the screen door slam and a blood-curdling scream. "What in the world?" Hialeah jumped up from the table when she heard Shadow's fierce barking. He was angry.

Starla trailed behind her and saw it was Connor's friend Ivy, with fear in her eyes staring at Shadow, who obviously didn't like her.

"Shadow. Get over here," Hialeah demanded. "Now." She gave a pointed look to Ivy. "He doesn't like uninvited guest."

Shadow's fur was once again standing on edge. Hialeah pointed inside and left with him.

"Connor is already gone," said Starla.

"I know. I was wondering if I could have a word with you." She smoothed down her hair and plastered on a smile. Her eyes wide still watching the direction that Shadow went.

"Okay. Would you like a cup of tea or breakfast? We have some quinoa and fruit."

"No, thank you. This will only take a minute and I don't want to go near that beast."

"Okay." Starla stood, waiting and trying not to be offended by her calling Shadow a beast and wondering how she got back here so fast. She must have driven way over the speed limit, if she lives in town or she just turned around and came back.

"I want you to stay away from Connor. He's been through a lot, and he's not ready for anything serious." She crossed her arms over her chest, and any pretense of friendliness vanished.

"I just met Connor. We're barely friends."

"Good. Keep it that way. Stay away from him—far away."

Starla felt her neck flush and the heat turned to flames. "I think that Connor is old enough to make his own choices. Even though we don't have any future plans, I don't recall him mentioning he had a date planner or body guard in the short time we have spent together."

Ivy stepped closer. "Look, you've been warned." A growl came from her voice. "It's in your best interest if you stay clear."

"Is that some kind of threat?" Starla held her ground. "Because, I've had worse threats than you."

"Well, aren't you dramatic? Just consider it a friendly request." She turned and walked toward her car. "By the way, you're not his type. He's always been attracted to women with a fuller figure, if you know what I mean." She grinned. "See you later."

Starla stood there in disbelief. How dare this woman tell her to stay clear of Connor? She wasn't planning on chasing him down—he had just taken off without so much as a goodbye or I'll see you later. However, she didn't like some blonde telling her what to do. She wondered if Connor knew Ivy was interfering in his personal life. It was pretty dang clear that Ivy wanted to control Connor's life, maybe more, than he even knew.

As she strolled back toward the cabin, she realized how blindsided she felt. She stepped inside and glanced at her anxious grandmother, trying like heck to pull it together.

"What in the world was that all about?" Hialeah asked.

"She wants me to stay away from Connor. No biggie. As I mentioned, I've been through worse. I just wasn't expecting to get a warning about a guy I just met. I wonder if Connor knows how territorial Ivy is."

Her grandmother arched a brow. "I was wondering the same thing."

Starla moved into the kitchen and sank down onto the wooden chair. "He said they were just friends and she was his best friend's wife. Speaking of his wife, you were going to tell me more about her before we were interrupted."

"Not right now. I need to get ready, so we can go into town. I was hoping they could see you at the clinic today. We'll talk later, it would take too long, and I want to get you an appointment." Hialeah turned and left the room.

Starla picked up her spoon and tasted the quinoa. Surprisingly, it was still warm and had a wonderful nutty taste to it. With every bite, she wondered if she should tell Connor about Ivy's little visit. But how could she approach him? She didn't know where he lived nor did she have a clue if she'd ever see him again.

AFTER A CRAZY MORNING, CONNOR ARRIVED BACK AT HIS HOUSE. First thing when the sun rose, he had gone to fix Ivy's car, which ended up just being a loose connection to the battery, but he left it charging anyway. Then, he made sure the Owens were doing okay and settling into their temporary home at his office. He had every single guy working to get their house finished. Hopefully it would be done in two weeks, if not sooner. But even with the delays, the family seemed happy to stay at his office. At least now, the kids had a place to stretch out and watch TV.

He went down the hall and entered his home office. Everything was quiet; the only sound was the chickens and the old clock on the wall ticking away. Plopping down in his desk chair, he turned on the computer and waited for it to load. Loneliness suddenly wrapped itself around him so tightly he almost couldn't breathe. God, how he missed the sounds of laughter and his wife singing off key, reverberating through these walls. The ache in his chest made him think of Starla. He felt terrible when he saw the look on her face as he left, but he didn't want attachments. No way. He'd been there and done that.

Taking a trip to his favorite bar might be a good idea. Usually he went out of town when he needed to blow off steam, but right now, he needed a quicker solution. Being around Starla had brought up desires he didn't want to think about, and he didn't want to act on them. She wasn't the kind of girl that he could do a one-night stand with.

Starla was special. He knew that the minute he found her stranded on the side of the road. But he'd been out with a lot of beautiful women and had long nights filled with hot sex. It would wash away the pain of losing Holly, but only temporarily. "Shit." Someone was ringing the doorbell which pulled him away from his gloomy thoughts. He stood and moved down the hallway to his living room.

He swung it open and found Ivy standing on his doorstep. "Hi, what's up? Everything okay?"

"Yes, have you eaten?" She moved past him without so much as a hello and walked inside.

"No, I can't rightly say I have. Not since last night at supper." His stomach growled right on cue.

"Well, I'm here to save the day." She glanced around. "Are you alone?"

"Yes. I'm working from home until the Owens house is ready, remember?"

"Oh, right. Well, would you like to grab a bite to eat?"

"Sure." He didn't want to, but since he had to eat and go shopping for groceries, he could take his truck and get both done in one outing.

"You might want to take your car since I am going grocery shopping afterward."

"That would be great. I need to pick up some things, too." She grinned with a spark of something he couldn't quite decipher in her eyes.

He nodded and guessed she might be lonely. Like him, sometimes it was so overwhelming that it made it hard to breathe. Her situation would get better if she'd start dating someone. Which begged the question, had she dated at all? Maybe he'd bring that up at breakfast. He grabbed his hat and they took off.

The minute they entered Logan's Diner, they saw the place was filled with the usual sounds of chatter and clanking plates. Breathing in the rich fragrance of coffee almost caused him to salivate, plus the aroma of fried eggs and bacon, made his stomach growl like an old bear.

Ivy stifled a laugh. "Well, I guess you are hungry."

"I guess so." He rubbed his stomach. "I sometimes let myself run on empty."

"Now, Connor. That's not good for a growing boy." She laced her arm through his and they found a booth facing the lake. Outside, the morning was gorgeous, filled with the hustle and bustle of people on bikes and pedestrians walking from place to place. The one thing Connor always loved about this town is how you can see the water from every business. Today it was extra amazing the way the lake sparkled and cast a golden glow throughout Secret Lake Park.

"Hey, mister. What are you thinking about?" Ivy studied his face.

"I was just thinking about you," he lied. "I was wondering if you were dating anyone." He saw her eyes darken.

"Now, I don't ask you about your time on your so-called retreats." She narrowed her eyes.

"Yes, but you know what that's about."

Connie walked up to the table. She was such a sweet girl and had been working there for about a year now. She was fresh out of high school and working her way through college. He respected her for that. Everyone in town did. The way she cared for her grandma and handled so much for a young kid.

"I didn't see y'all come in. I just saw you when I delivered food to one of my tables." She set down two waters in front of them. "Either of you want coffee?"

"Yes," they both said in unison.

"I'll grab the menus, too." She turned and left.

"So, are you going to answer my question? Are you dating anyone?"

Just then, Connie handed them the menus and set their coffees down. "I'll be back in a few minutes to take your order."

"Thank you." Connor smiled and watched her cheeks turn pink.

"Well," Ivy shot a look towards Connie, "if you must know." She picked up her napkin and placed it on her lap. "I'm not."

"Why not, Ivy? You're beautiful, and I know a few guys who would trip over themselves to date you."

"I'm not ready." Her eyes filled with unshed tears. "I don't want to talk about it. Can we just have a nice breakfast together?"

"I just worry about you, that's all." He reached across the table and touched her hand.

"Please don't. I'm just fine and dandy." She smiled, but something was off, and he knew it.

They both studied the menus for a few minutes. "I'm ordering the Bounty platter this morning. How about you?" He looked at Ivy.

"I'd like the light start." She smiled.

Right on cue, Connie approached the table with the tablet and pencil in her hand. "So, have you both decided what you want?" She glanced between the two of them.

"Yes," Connor looked at her, then down at the menu and read their orders.

After a long wait and uncomfortable silence, the waitress came and set down their food.

"Here you go. Be careful. The plates are hot."

Ivy slumped back in her seat. "Did you have to go gather the eggs and slaughter a pig?"

"I'm sorry about the delay. We are so backed up." Connie's cheeks turned pink again, but this time she was obviously embarrassed because Ivy was rude.

"Don't you be worrying your pretty little head over it." Connor glared at Ivy. "This looks great, doesn't it?"

"Yes." Ivy said nothing more.

Dang, had she always been so doggone rude? He winked at Connie, and she gave him a tiny smile and strolled away.

"What in the world has gotten into you, Ivy? It wasn't nice to talk to her like that."

"I'm just tired, that's all. It's been a hard week." She picked up her fork and took a bite of her Vegetable-and-cheese omelet. "Oh, this is really good."

"You might want to tell Connie that." He jabbed at his sausage, still frustrated with her behavior, especially toward someone as sweet as Connie.

"I'll be sure to tell her how wonderful it is when she comes back."

"If she comes back," Connor mumbled as he took another big bite.

The place got busier and sure enough the Mayor strolled in, alone this time. A pin could have been dropped and heard, as he walked up to the counter and took a seat. Even the cooking and dish clanking, got quieter. He was in the dog house with the entire town. Nobody approved of what he had done to his wife. Connor had to admit, it was a shock to find out he had taken up with a woman young enough to be his daughter. Hell, she was young enough to be his granddaughter.

STARLA AND HIALEAH WALKED OUT OF THE SECRET VALLEY CLINIC and had two hours to kill before their appointment with Dr. Norman

Hatcher. If only she could stop being nervous. One would think she would be used to doctors by now. Since she first got cancer, Dr. Langley had been her one and only physician.

The carefree laughter of children pushed away her thoughts and brought a smile to her face. Across the street, children were running and playing at the park. It seemed like they were there on a school outing.

Hialeah chuckled. "The teachers at Valley Lake Elementary School teach their students at the park once a week." She pointed. "They must be on recess."

"How neat. I would have loved that as a child." Starla continued to glance around, taking in how wonderful the town was. The way all the stores faced the lake was something you didn't see often. Had she ever seen anything like that? Not that she recalled.

She was excited to visit some of the little shops and maybe even pick up some clothes and shoes. As they headed down the street, a slight breeze tickled her cheeks, making her forget any worries she had. Wind chimes hung on the streetlamps and it was as though they played in harmony.

The morning was gorgeous, the blue sky stretching out as far as you could see toward the horizon. Only a few small clouds dotted the sky. People were chatting away with each other as they walked in all directions. A lady with long dark hair and pale skin who seemed to know Hialeah waved at them. The few cars that drove down Chestnut Lane slowed down and would nod or smile as they passed. The town might be small, but everything about it was charming.

"This is wonderful," Starla said to Hialeah.

"I've always loved it here." Her grandmother's eyes lit up. "It's home in many magical ways." They continued walking.

"I've never been to a town where people were so friendly." Starla glanced around once again.

"It is delightful, but it's not without drama and some well-kept secrets."

"I guess you'll have to fill me in." They passed by a little place called Hamburger Delight. "Oh, my stars! Something smells good in there." Starla stuck her nose in the air and slowed down.

"It has some of the best hamburgers you'll ever find. Pure, one-hundred percent grass-fed." Her grandmother smiled. "I stop in once a month and treat myself to one."

"Aren't all cows grass fed?" Starla was perplexed.

"Yes, but most are also fed grains. Cows are meant to graze out in pastures, not fed grains and corn." She furrowed her eyebrows. "They do that to fatten them up for slaughter, and it's against nature."

"Oh, that's good to know." Starla hadn't had a clue but was glad to find out now. She couldn't help but wonder how much nutrition had to do with health. The old saying was you are what you eat.

The next store they stopped in front of was The Sweet Shop. Starla stepped closer and peered through the window. "I better stay out of there. I have a weakness for chocolate."

"In moderation, dark chocolate is good for you." She waved Starla back over toward her and pointed down the side of the street. "Let's go this way. The natural foods and herbs are down here. You could also check on your car. Blue Sky Auto Repair is right around the corner."

"That's great, and I see more stores down that way."

"Yes." She nodded. "The Sunny Side shoe store is just past the herb shop. I could meet you there when I'm done."

"Sounds wonderful," Starla agreed.

After Hialeah left to go shopping, Starla checked on her car and learned that the owner was waiting on the new parts. He explained that the radiator's cooling fan had burned out. Heck, she hadn't even known radiators had fans in them. The part he needed would arrive on Thursday, and she'd at least have her car back.

As soon as the shoe store came into view, she made a beeline straight to the front. Once she stepped inside, the smell of leather drifted all around. Shoes lined the walls, and in the center of the store were comfortable-looking chairs. They even had purses and scarves displayed along one wall.

A short, dark-haired woman approached.

"Hi, how can I help you?" The bell on the front door rang, and a lady with two kids walked in and waved.

The short lady waved back. "Hi Trudy, I'll be with you shortly."

"No hurry, Janet. We're shopping for tennis shoes. You know how long my children take to decide on anything, so no rush." She guided her teen girl and younger boy toward the sneakers that lined the wall.

"Sorry about that." Janet's smile was warm as she rubbed her hand through her short, curly hair. "Are you looking for something in particular?"

"Yes. I left home without any shoes." Starla chuckled. "I have sneakers, but I'd like something casual and nice."

"My name is Janet as you heard. I'm the owner." She stuck out her hand. "Are you new in town?"

"Yes. Well, I got stranded here after my car broke down, but I've decided to stay for a few weeks." Starla didn't want to go into all the details about her grandma, but she figured the town would find out sooner or later. "And, I connected with my grandmother who lives here. My name is Starla Holloway." They shook hands, and both smiled.

"Well, bless your heart, Starla. I heard you found your Grandmother." They released hands. "Welcome to our town. We are small but friendly. Now, let me show you some shoes, and you can tell me who your grandma is. I probably know her." She led Starla down the far aisle that had every shoe you could think of in every color imaginable.

Right away, Starla saw a pair she liked. "Oh, these are cute." She held them up to look at the price tag and almost swallowed her tongue. "Whoa, a little out of my budget." Her face heated as she set them back down.

"Those are the Tabitha Simmons loopsy slingback sandals. Aren't they cute? They're on sale for almost half off."

Starla laughed. "That's still out of my budget. I try not to spend over a hundred dollars for a pair of shoes."

"Well, then let's look on this side." She pointed to another area. "Most of these are less than a hundred—some are way less."

Starla spotted a pair of Fenta shoes in white and gold. "These are adorable. Just what I was looking for, and at this price, I can buy a few pairs in different colors."

"What size do you wear?" Janet asked.

"Big feet—size seven." She lifted her foot and chuckled.

"Smaller than mine and honestly that's not big." Janet found a box with size seven shoes below the display pair and handed them to her.

"I'd like some for walking, too, but I don't want sneakers. I already have those," Starla explained again.

"How about some women's walking cradles? Great for walking and they are so cute." She held up a peach pair for Starla's approval.

"Oh, wow. I love those, and I love the red ones, too. Let me try them on, and, if they fit, I'll take both."

Starla tried on both pairs and they fit like a glove. Just as Janet was bending to gather them up, the lady with the two kids peeked around the corner holding shoes stacked up to her chin. "We are ready when you are, but no hurry. We could go eat and come back."

Starla waved her hand. "Go ahead, Janet. I want to look around some more."

"Okay, if you're sure."

"I am." She really did want to look at everything.

Janet took off for the front to ring up the shoes for Trudy and the kids.

Starla loved all the scarves and purses. She picked up a multicolored scarf with peach and blue butterflies with a purse to match. This was wonderful. When was the last time she splurged on herself and bought new things? Too long ago to remember.

She did not understand where she would wear the accessories. Maybe she'd take Hialeah out to dinner this week. That would be a treat, and they needed to spend time getting to know each other better, anyway. Her mind drifted to Connor and wondered if she saw him again, would he notice her new shoes. More than likely not. Did guys even notice those things? Which led her to wonder if she'd ever see him again. She looked at her watch and realized there was more time to shop.

When she finally made her way toward the counter, Janet was running a credit card from Trudy. The teen girl smiled and looked Starla up and down. She was sure pretty with long blonde hair and blue eyes. As a matter of fact, her eyes were the spitting image of Connor's, which made her think of him again.

Trudy turned and grinned at Starla. "Did I hear you say you broke down outside of town?"

"Yes," Starla answered, wondering why she was asking.

"Oh, you must be the lady my brother-in-law helped. I'm Trudy Whelan. I'm married to Connor's brother, Duncan. It's nice to meet you." Her green eyes sparkled with friendliness.

"Nice to meet you, too. I'm Starla."

The young girl's face lit up. "Starla. I love that name. I'm Megan."

"Thank you. Megan is a pretty name as well." Starla noticed the boy, who was no more than twelve, staring at her, so she grinned and asked, "What's your name?"

"I'm Tucker. Nice to meet you, ma'am," he said, like a good southern boy. His eyes were green like his mother's and he had brown curly hair just like her too. He was a handsome kid.

"Nice to meet you, too," Starla said and watched his cheeks turn crimson.

Before Starla could say anything else, her grandmother walked in and waved. "I'm finally done." She sighed.

Janet stared at Hialeah. "Well, I'll be. I heard you found each other and you sure look alike."

Trudy glanced at her watch. "It was so nice meeting you, Starla." She turned toward Starla's grandmother. "Good seeing you, Hialeah. I wish I didn't have to run. I'd love to hear more about how you two found each other. Connor never gives all the details. I have a meeting in fifteen minutes and I'm afraid I'm already running late." She turned and gathered her credit card from Janet. "I hope to see you around town, Starla. Maybe we could have lunch or tea one day."

"Sure, that would be great. Connor knows how to reach me," Starla explained.

"Wonderful." She turned to leave but stopped and gave Hialeah a hug before she did. "I hope to see you again sometime soon as well. It's been a while."

"It's been too long." Hialeah hugged her back.

Trudy released Hialeah and rushed toward the door. "We have to hurry, kids." Like a bolt of lightning, they all flew out of the shoe store loaded down with bags.

Janet laughed out loud. "That woman sure has her plate full, but she's always happy. I think it might have to do with being married to one of the Whelan brothers. Every woman in town would like to snag one of those boys." She lifted an arched brow. "Nothing but pure sexy."

Starla glanced toward the door. "I would imagine so if they look anywhere near as good as Connor."

Hialeah laughed and said, "Oh, they do. Even an old woman like me notices a good-looking man when she sees one."

All three of them cracked up as Starla paid the bill and took the bags. "Thank you for all your help, Janet."

"And thank you for coming in. I hope to see you again soon." She handed Starla the receipt.

After one last goodbye, they stepped back outside and into the beautiful day. It had warmed up and the breeze was still there, but it was much lighter. The clouds were all but gone, and out by the lake, kids were still running and laughing. The town was amazing. Even though Starla had only been there for a short time, she was feeling a real connection to the area.

Hialeah tapped Starla's fingers. "Would you look at who's coming our way?" She pointed with her chin.

"Oh, no," she said lightly. "I don't think he wants to see me anymore. He's with Ivy, and she hates me."

"Well, now, avoiding him is going to be next-to-impossible in this town. And Ivy is not a nice person. Believe me," Hialeah huffed out.

As they headed toward each other, Starla couldn't get the memory of the almost kiss out of her head. What in the heck had made him run away?

Before she could blink, they were standing in front of each other.

"Hello, Starla and Hialeah." Connor gave them a nod. "Hope y'all are having a beautiful day."

Ivy glared and barely said hello.

"We are," Hialeah said. "I hope you both are enjoying yours as well."

"Oh, it's been precious," Ivy said with sarcasm. "We just had breakfast, and now we are going grocery shopping, but we had to stop by the bakery first and grab some goodies." She put on her fake smile and threaded her arm through Connor's.

"Well, we'd better let you go." Starla said and tried to act friendly but knew she failed. "We have an appointment. See you two later." Making sure she didn't even look his way, she took her grandmother's hand.

❧ 10 ❧

CONNOR STOOD WATCHING STARLA WALK AWAY FEELING LIKE A jackass. What in Sam Hill was wrong with him?

"Come on. Let's go grocery shopping. I have to pick up Austin soon." Ivy tugged on his arm and led him down the street to the store. Connor was more than a little distracted, thinking about Starla. He watched as a guy carried a crate of fresh vegetables into the store, managing to balance everything.

Ivy almost yelled. "Connor, are you coming or you going to stand out here all day?

A few minutes later, they walked through the door and grabbed grocery carts. However, Connor remained standing at the front of the store watching Ivy move to the produce section. He reflected on his behavior. How could he treat Starla like that? He was being ridiculous, and he knew it. After all, he damned near kissed her, spent the night camping with her, and then left without even making plans to talk to her or see her again. Jackass was a good word to describe him.

Coming to his senses, he looked over and saw Ivy by the apple bin so he walked up to her. "Here are the keys to my truck. Go ahead and take it back to your house when you're done here. I'll be there to pick it up later."

"Why? Where are you going?" He placed the keys in her hand.

"I'm going to right something, I did wrong."

On his way out the door, he turned back and saw Ivy still staring at him. He probably should have given her little more to go on, but she didn't need to know what he was doing.

On foot, Connor combed the streets searching for Starla. After he walked by Blue Sky Auto, passing the fire department and Fred's towing, he turned down Secret Valley Road. Maybe they went home. "Damn it." He headed toward the grocery store, passing the gym, bakery, and coffee house.

After about thirty minutes, he stopped and gathered his thoughts while he stood in front of the clinic. Damn, they must have left. Just as he was about to turn around and head back, he saw Starla and Hialeah sitting in the waiting room through the window. Both were thumbing through magazines until a nurse came out. They set down the magazines and followed her through the door, which he knew led to the examination rooms. His stomach took a dive. Was something going on with her? Starla's journal came to mind, and he remembered what she had written.

Was she ill again, or was the appointment for Hialeah? Now he felt like crap. He stood, looking into the clinic waiting room for a good five minutes, before he headed back to the store and found Ivy.

"Change of plans again. Let me get my shopping done, and I'll give you a ride home."

Confusion washed across her face. "Okay," was all she said.

Thankfully, she didn't ask many questions, and he hurried and bought what he needed. His cart was almost filled when he stepped up to the checkout counter. Ivy was at a different register paying for her items, but he could see an odd look on her face. She wasn't a happy camper, that much was clear. Sometimes he felt she was too involved in his life. Sure, she was a good friend, but she was pushy, even if she had the best intentions. They'd both been though horrible losses, so maybe he should cut her some slack. They had spent so much time together after she lost Larry. There had been times he had been in fear she'd take her own life. For some reason, he felt she was unstable. Years had gone by and it seemed they were just too damn dependent on each other. Maybe what they needed was to take some distance.

Speaking of his own life, all he could do was hope Starla was at the cabin soon. He would go out to see her, after he put his groceries away. Maybe bringing them lunch would help compensate for his bad behavior. And, maybe she'd share what was going on with her. He shouldn't expect her to tell him anything personal, since they'd only known each other a short time, but he could hope.

A few hours later, Connor arrived at Hialeah's house, but nobody was there except Shadow, who gave him a friendly welcome. He put the bag of food on the table under the tree and plopped down in the chair beside it. Fifteen minutes went by with no sign of Starla or her grandmother. He got up and made his way down to the lake and put the food in the ice chest in the back of his truck. Shadow was trailing along beside him.

Standing there in the soft sunlight, feeling the gentle breeze, and hearing the sounds of nature all around him brought up memories from the past.

The night had been beautiful with stars twinkling in the sky and the moon was big and luminous. He'd heard a splash in the water and knew Holly had jumped in. He had paused wondering why she would swim at night, after he asked her many times not to do that. Then, he thought he heard her talking, but he figured it was only to herself. He slipped off his pants and was unbuttoning his shirt when he heard a bloodcurdling scream.

"Holly!" He listened for her voice and heard nothing. He couldn't even hear her swimming. Maybe she had climbed out and something scared her.

"Holly," he yelled again, but the sounds of the frogs and crickets were the only noises echoing in the night.

He took off at full speed and reached the bank where her shoes and towel lay untouched. "Holly." He jumped in, thinking he saw movement out in the water, but it was too far away and at first, he thought it was her. He swam with all his strength, then he saw her floating. It wasn't until he reached out and grabbed her arm, he noticed her body was lifeless. "Lord, no!" he cried as he swam back to the shore, carrying her as best he could. Nothing—no breathing, no sound, no heartbeat.

"Help!" He cried out repeatedly. "Please, someone!" He didn't know the first thing to do and had never learned CPR, but he turned her onto her back, supported her neck, and blew air into her lungs. He had seen others do that before. Finally, some people came from the other cabins and offered help.

"What happened?" an older man asked as he took over and seemed to know what he was doing.

"I don't know. I heard screaming and got to her as soon as I could. I've often told her not to swim at night, at least not alone." He felt tears burning his cheeks. She had to be okay.

"I have a pulse—it's weak, but it's there." The man continued working on her.

After a few minutes, an ambulance arrived with sirens blasting. The rest of the night was a blur. He recalled that Ria had been by his side and kept telling him everything would be okay. But somehow, deep in his heart, he knew it wouldn't be.

The ride to the hospital was fast, and the events that followed were almost dreamlike as the paramedics ran Holly into the emergency room and he followed. Doctors and nurses rushed to her side and worked on her for what seemed like forever.

One nurse walked up to him. "I'm sorry. You're going to need to leave."

"I'm her husband." He refused to budge. "I need to be here for her."

"You need to get out of our way." She pointed to the corner. "Stand over there."

As soon as he stepped to the side, every alarm around her went off. Unlike similar scenarios on TV, there was no yelling or rushing around in a panic. Just doctors putting a tube down her throat, taking the paddles, and laying them on her chest. Nobody came in to save the day. Only two doctors and two nurses continued to work until they paused, looking up at the clock and called the time of death.

His heart slammed against his chest. She was gone, and she wasn't coming back. She simply lay still and pale. There was no last-minute effort to save her.

The nurse walked up and touched his arm. "Is there someone we can call for you?"

"Call? How about God? Where is he?" That was all he said.

By the time he walked out into the waiting room, his family and Holly's parents were standing in a huddle, waiting there for him. Ria must have called them. That was the moment he found out just how weak he was. Thank God for his dad, who caught him as his legs gave out.

Tears filled his eyes and the sobs coming from him were foreign. In the fading background, he remembered hearing cries from her mom and dad, even today that still haunted him. Why had she died? They tried to introduce suicide but dropped that idea. A large size bump was found on the back of her head. Where did it come from and how did she get it? There were no rocks. She wasn't near the dock. They'd even questioned him, but eyewitnesses saw him looking at the stars just before they heard her scream. There was no doubt she had been depressed, but lord have mercy, she was pregnant—and she was happy about it. Why would she take both their lives? The police agreed and dropped it to accidental death. He had told none of the family about the baby. Why break their hearts even more, when everyone was already torn apart?

"What are you doing?" Starla surprised him. "Are you okay?" With a tilt of her head, she studied him.

Connor stared into her hot chocolate eyes. "I'm fine. Are you okay?"

"I'm good. Went downtown and bought some new shoes and clothing," she said, glancing down at Shadow and scratched his head.

"Starla." He cleared his throat. "I would like to get to know you better, but I want to be one-hundred percent honest about something." He moved closer. "I'm scared."

"You're scared of me?" Confusion etched her eyes.

"Yes and no." He took her hand. "I told you that I lost my wife. What I didn't tell you is, it damn near killed me, and...well—are you sick?" Damn it. Now that he'd blurted that out, he couldn't stop the rest from tumbling out of his mouth. "I saw you at the clinic today, and why did you run away from home?"

With a look of sadness, she let go of his hand. "I am. I have cancer and it's my third time. Given what you've just told me, I don't think you'd want to chance being with me."

STARLA WATCHED HIS FACE TURN AS PALE AS THE PUFFY WHITE clouds. "I should have told you after you almost kissed me." What had she been thinking? It wasn't a secret that his first wife had died, and here she was holding back something that might make him afraid to date her.

"What did the doctors say today?" Connor asked.

"He felt it would not be necessary to remove my breast, so that's some possible good news. They are going to start running more tests next week, so I'll be here for a while. My other doctor didn't seem to agree when he called him today. He's worried that it's worse than that."

Connor took her hand again. "I still want to know you, take you out on a date, if you want to. I like you a lot, Starla."

"How did your wife die?" Starla softly asked as she watched the leaves flutter across the lawn.

There was no missing him wince. "They really don't know. I'll never know how she died, nor what happened."

"Can we go sit down? My foot is a tiny bit sore after all the walking." She waved toward the picnic table under the tree.

After they sat down and exchanged looks, Hialeah brought out two glasses of tea. "I'm going to be inside working with some herbal recipes. Are either of you hungry?"

Starla shook her head. "Not yet."

"I brought some food over. It's out in my truck." Connor pointed. "I have it chilling for when everyone is hungry."

"Sounds good." Hialeah rubbed her stomach. "I'll eat when y'all are hungry." She turned and headed toward the cabin.

"I'm so sorry about your wife." Starla swallowed her tears. "How do you think she died?"

"I'm going to tell you something." He paused. "But I don't want her family to find out. I haven't even told my family."

"Okay." She studied the serious look in his eyes.

"Holly." He swallowed hard. "Was pregnant. Only two months, but we were expecting a child." Tears misted his lashes. "She'd already had one miscarriage and that drove her into a deep depression. We hadn't told the families yet because we wanted to be sure it would take. The miscarriage depressed her, put her down to her knees, but she was so happy to be pregnant again. There is no way she killed herself. Which is what they thought initially."

Taking a deep breath, she asked, "But depression is why they thought she killed herself?"

"Yes," he whispered. "But she didn't. She had a knot on the back of her head. They just figured she bumped her head earlier in the day or something. The police officers didn't know for sure how it got there, so it was all speculation, and nobody was in that water with her. I would have been a suspect, but there were witnesses that saw me standing outside looking up at the stars and getting ready to go in the water, when she screamed."

"Oh no." Starla took his hand. "Connor, that is just the most dreadful thing I've ever heard."

"I know. I've never wanted her family to find out about the baby. It was bad enough losing their daughter, but to find out they lost a grandchild too? I just couldn't do it. I should have been clearer about her swimming alone. I don't know why she did that. I had told her many times it wasn't safe to swim alone, even more so at night. But because the resort was full that weekend. She must have thought it was safe. It was almost pitch black and I had no idea she'd go in by herself."

"Oh, Connor. I hope you don't blame yourself."

"Of course, I do." He stiffened. "It's my fault. I should have been there with her."

"You didn't know any of that would happen." She gently squeezed his hand.

Connor glanced down at their fingers entwined. "What I do know is I'll never find out how she died. How did her head get a gash on it? She had no enemies. Everyone loved her."

"It does sound strange. Were there any boats in the water or anchors or anything that she may have hit?"

"No, they searched and tried to find what had caused it. They couldn't find anything. So, they ruled it an accidental death. The whole thing has never made any sense." He dropped her hand, stood and paced.

"Did the police know she was pregnant?"

"Yes. I begged them not to put it in their report or tell her family. The baby was left inside her." Tears filled his eyes.

Starla lost her breath. "Oh, Connor." Silence hung between them. She got up and moved next to him. Without thinking, she wrapped him in her arms and held on tight. "I can't even imagine."

He sucked his breath in. She knew he was holding back from crying, so she held him tighter.

"I'm sorry," he apologized. "I didn't want to do this in front of you." He inhaled deeply. "I've never done this before."

Starla released him and stared into his sad eyes. "I'm glad you did. I want to be here to help you."

"I feel like I've known you forever." He ran his hand through his hair. "I should be letting you share your feelings. After all, you're going through a lot..." He paused. "Tell me everything the doctor said today."

It was obvious he wanted to change the conversation. "He is going to remove the lump and check me every thirty days at first. I'm going to do what Hialeah did and see how it goes. If the tests show anything coming back, we will go from there and make a new plan."

"How do you feel about that?" he questioned.

"Good. Really good. But you know what?" She smiled.

He looked at her and tilted his head. "What?"

"Right now, I'm starving."

They relaxed at the same moment and headed off to get the food.

IVY HAD GONE OVER AND KNOCKED ON CONNOR'S DOOR, HOPING HE was back from seeing that skinny chick. But he wasn't and that just down right pissed her off. What was he thinking spending time with someone he barely knew? Damn it to shit, she had to stop him from seeing her. Now she was in a sour mood.

"Austin, get in here and pick up your toys!"

Things were a mess again. After Connor's last visit and the

disapproval in his eyes, she didn't want him to see it that way again. It wasn't her fault it was a wreck. Austin was a messy child.

"Austin, get in here and clean this mess up." This was getting on her last nerve. She heard him plowing through the house.

"What, Mama?" he asked, sounding winded as he came to a halt.

"Look at this. I want it cleaned. Until you have everything done, you can't watch TV or go outside. Do you understand me?"

"Yes, Mama." He started picking up his toys and appeared to be nervous.

She walked toward him and put her hand up, but he backed into the corner. "I'm sorry, Mama." He hid behind his hands, acting like a little coward.

"Well, just get it done and you won't get punished." She sneered. "You better keep your mouth shut when you talk to Uncle Connor. Do you hear me?"

"Yes, Mama." He gathered up his toys.

"He doesn't need to know all our business. If you don't stop telling him stuff about how messy our house is, we are going to move far away, and you'll never see him again. And don't you dare tell him anything else if you want to stay in this house and around your friends."

"I won't, Mama," he cried. "I promise."

"Just shut up and get this cleaned up. Stop acting like a big bawl baby or I'll make you regret it."

"Yes, ma'am." His tears dried up as he continued cleaning up the living room. "I watched Uncle Connor clean and I can make it look real nice, Mama."

"Okay, I'm going to take a long bubble bath. I expect everything to be spotless when I come out. I don't want to have to hurt you again and make up another story to tell your school."

He swallowed hard. "Okay."

"Damn boy," she mumbled. She'd never wanted kids to begin with. Living in a small town was a pain because those nosey teachers had been asking why he keeps getting hurt. It was her dead ass husband who wanted kids in the first place. Now she was stuck acting all domestic and shit. Connor didn't make it easy, he was so protective of Austin. And to boot, he'd told her to find a man. Why the hell would she do that? She was the grieving widow. She'd stay that way until she got what she wanted.

In the bathroom, she turned on the water and poured bubble bath inside. This whole damn thing with him hanging out with Starla was beyond anything she understood. What the hell did he see in her? There wasn't much to her. Her breasts were as flat as pancakes, and she had just plain old brown eyes. And what about that ass? It wasn't very big. What the hell would a man hang on to? Holly wasn't skinny like that. She at least had a figure.

Holly had been Ivy's best friend since childhood, and they'd done everything together. Sometimes, Ivy did miss her. It was sad that she had to die. But she didn't deserve Connor either. Holly had lost his one and only child, and, well, sometimes you just have to be punished. Had Holly quit her job like Connor wanted, maybe she wouldn't have lost the baby. Then, Holly went into a horrible depression and made Connor look sad all the time. That just about did Ivy in. Seeing him hurt like that, she knew she had to make it all better.

Sure, she knew it would be worse for a while, but she'd be there to help him and console him. Just thinking about him made her throb in ways that drove her insane. She turned on the radio and cranked up the sound and took out her toy from behind the towels. Fantasizing, she imagined his face and his oh-so-big hands. The images in her head made her body jerk as she came apart. Her last thought was, she would do what she had to do to win Connor.

ONCE THEY WERE DONE WITH LUNCH, STARLA WATCHED THE BIRDS AS they flew in circles, gliding on the breeze. Her mind drifted once again to how much she'd grown to love the area. The landscape offered miles of meadows and trees. There were silver cobwebs lacing through the stems of some of the plants, and the blooming roses were the most stunning she'd ever seen. The sun had cast a lovely glow across the lake and spread colors hard to describe. How could a person not fall in love with such a beautiful display?

"What are you smiling about?" Connor caught her eye.

She stood and held out her hand in reply. When Connor entwined his fingers with hers, she led him over to the roses she had been admiring.

"All my life, I have loved roses." She reached for the yellow blooms and touched the velvety petal. "I saw a singer perform in southern California once when I was a child, and I remember her last name was Rose. She was amazing and had long, red hair. There was just something about her. So, now, every time I see a rose, I remember her. But tonight, I'm not happy just because of that, it's everything about this place."

Connor reached out and touched her other hand as she caressed the petal. "A redhead, huh?" He arched a brow. "I bet she wasn't as gorgeous as you."

A knot formed in her stomach when she glanced up at him and they held each other's gaze. As she stared at his strong features, her heart slammed in double-time.

"Okay, what are you thinking now?" He angled his head. "Suddenly, you look so serious."

"I just got lost in my thoughts." She paused, feeling her face heat once again. "You are the one who is beautiful. I'm just a plain Jane compared to you."

A grin spread across his face. "Well, thank you ma'am. But I have to disagree. There is *nothing* plain about you, Starla Moon."

At a complete loss for words, she changed the subject. "You know, I really do need to call Oliver."

"Ah, he's your business partner, right? Did all this talk about how handsome I am, make you think of calling him?"

"Yes, in a way. I've missed him and his wife a lot. They are both stunning and my best friends."

Connor moved even closer to her side, and her legs buckled. Jesus, he was the sexiest man she'd ever met. "Will you go out to dinner with me tonight?" With a soft touch, he lifted her chin and it was as if his gaze hypnotized her. Her head nodded yes, and she couldn't have stopped it if she wanted to.

"Is that a yes?" His smile grew wider.

"Uh huh," she said and swallowed what felt like a hair ball stuck in her throat. Somewhat easing the growing tension between them, they moved over to the folding lawn chairs and sat down. They shared a relaxing silence, but there was no way she could stop thinking about what Ivy had said. How could she? It's not every day you get such a blatant warning to stay away from someone. Even though Starla would not let it stop her from going on a date with him, she knew a storm was brewing. She could feel it in her gut.

"Connor." She looked over at him. "Can I ask you a personal question? You don't have to answer if you don't want."

"Sure, ask away. I've already told you more about myself than I've told anyone else." He reached over and brushed a pine needle off her leg. "I'd say you know more about me than anyone in this town."

"Are you..." she inhaled deeply, "involved with Ivy?"

"Absolutely not." He shook his head to punctuate his quick response. "She was Holly's childhood best friend. If anything, she's like a sister to me."

"Oh, okay." She fumbled with a couple fallen leaves that had landed in her lap. "Could that be why she is so protective of you? In my encounters with her, her tone didn't reflect sisterly-type concern."

"What do you mean?" He tilted his head.

"I don't know if I should say anything more, and please don't tell her I've brought this to you. Can you promise not to say anything?"

"Sure." He gave her a half shrug. "What is it?"

"She came over to see me and told me to stay away from you. I guess she was worried I would somehow hurt you, but it felt like a warning—a big warning. She was pretty upset."

"Are you kidding me?" There was no hiding his shock.

"No, afraid not." She watched his jaw clench.

"It came off like she wanted you for herself or that maybe you two had dated and had kept it a secret. I just don't want to hurt anyone."

"Never, not once." He stood and looked out at the lake. "Almost a year after Holly passed, Larry died of a heart attack. He was one of my best friends. So, Ivy and I clung to each other, but we were never close in that way. Plus, Larry and Ivy made me and Holly Austin's godparents."

"Wow. How old was her husband?"

"My age. We went to high school together. None of us saw it coming. Not even his doctors. He had a small arrhythmia, but it was minor—nothing serious—or at least that's what they said."

"That is awful. He was so young."

"It was hard on everyone. Ivy fell apart, and I think she became very dependent on me—too dependent. But she doesn't control my life or choose who I see. I'm surprised she came to you. It's not as if I've been celibate since Holly's death. In fact..." He stopped talking and winced. "Never mind."

Starla laughed. "I get what you're saying."

"I guess I went a little crazy about a year later, and I didn't hide it very well. But I calmed down later on. I realized I was trying to push away the pain."

Starla reached over and took his hand. "I understand."

"You do? Why, did you go through a wild phase, too?" He arched a brow.

"Oh, heaven's no." She chuckled. "I've dated maybe three guys since I graduated from high school. And back in those days, I had that one boyfriend, I told you about. Since then, I've dated two guys, but only once in a while. So, dating three guys since age sixteen, is a little less than wild."

"As beautiful as you are, that's hard to imagine." He winked. "I bet you had to say no a lot."

"Not really." Her gaze clung to his. "I'm so busy that I don't have time to meet anyone. Our date will be the first I've had in a long time."

"Not sure you'd call what I was doing before *dating*," Connor stared into her eyes. "This will be my first real date since Holly passed away."

Starla nodded. "I'm just worried because Ivy made it perfectly clear she didn't want me dating you. I hope this doesn't mess with your friendship."

Connor pulled her up and wrapped his arms around her waist. Just being close to him made the cool afternoon turn warm. "I want to go out with you. Like I said, Ivy does not get to tell me who I can spend time with."

"Okay." She smiled as she ran her fingers over the neck of his shirt. He shivered under her touch.

"Starla."

"Yes?" She looked up at him.

"You are sexy as hell." He leaned down, his lips close to the base of her neck, and inhaled.

Heat swarmed her face. "Thank you," she said in a quiet tone. "I've never thought of myself that way."

"Oh, Miss Moon, you should." He kissed the top of her head and lingered there. "You always smell so good." He leaned back and grinned. "As much as I hate to say this, I need to get going. I have a lot of work to do. Want to meet me at my house around five or would you rather I pick you up?"

"Well, Mr. Wyland, I'd love to meet you at your house, but I need to know where you live." She chuckled.

11

CONNOR WAS DOWNRIGHT PISSED OFF AS HE DROVE HOME THINKING about Ivy. Maybe she was trying to protect him, but from what? Why would she behave like that? He had a mind to go over there and tell her to butt out. Hadn't she told him to stay out of her life when he suggested that she date? But Starla had asked him not to mention anything to Ivy. He had no choice but to keep his trap shut. So, he took a deep breath, focused on his date with the very lovely Starla Moon, and planned on having a good time.

An hour later, after stopping by the construction site again, he pulled up to his place to find Ivy and Austin waiting outside. Since he wasn't expecting them, maybe they were checking on him or perhaps something was wrong.

Connor opened his door and slid out of his truck. Taking another deep breath, he walked to where they were at the side of the house. Austin was sitting on the fence, wearing a cowboy hat and boots. Damn, seeing how much Austin looked like his dad made Connor miss his friend. Larry would never get a chance to see his son grow up.

Ivy glanced over and brushed some hay off her pants. "Hi, Connor. We stopped by to ask if you would like to come over for dinner."

"That's nice, thank you. But I have a date tonight." He waited to see her reaction.

"Oh, okay. So, you're making one of your trips out of town then," she said with no tone or angry look.

"No." He walked over to Austin and tousled his hair. "I have a date with Starla. I'm taking her out to dinner."

"Can I go?" Austin asked. "I like dates, and Starla is a *really* pretty name."

Connor cracked up. "I don't think so, cowboy. This is an adult date." He picked Austin up off the fence and playfully tossed him into the air and caught him.

"Uncle Connor, put me on your shoulders!" He laughed. "I want to be taller than you and Mama."

Connor placed Austin on his shoulders and walked around the yard. Ivy followed them, but there was no missing the scowl on her face. What the hell was the matter with her?

After playing a few more minutes, Connor set Austin down. "I need to have a word with your Mama. Maybe you could run inside and play with Spanky—he could use some loving." The back door is open, and there are some fresh cookies on the counter if you want one. Mrs. Owens baked some delicious peanut butter ones."

"Yes!" he said as he pumped his fist and ran off.

Once Austin was out of earshot, Connor turned to face Ivy. "Is there something about Starla you don't like? I noticed you didn't look very happy when I said I was taking her out."

Her face softened. "Of course not. I don't even know her. As far as I know, she's just someone who got stranded in town and she's going back home soon. But I've seen the way you look at her, and I don't want you to get hurt. So, I do worry."

"And how's that?" Connor hoped she'd fess up about her visit to see Starla.

"It's almost the same way you looked at Holly. She's not Holly, Connor."

"I don't need you to tell me *anything* about Holly," he snapped. "I sure as hell know she's not my wife."

Ivy's lips trembled. "Okay, that's fair. I just worry about you. That's all." She mumbled so softly he almost didn't hear her as a tear trailed down her cheek.

"Shit, I'm sorry, Ivy. I shouldn't talk to you like that." He pulled her into a warm hug. "You and Austin mean the world to me, and I love you both. But I'm ready to start dating again, and I really like Starla."

"Okay." Her expression soured, and she pulled away. "I need to get going to start dinner anyway or go out and get something."

"I'll go fetch Austin for you."

When he brought Austin out to meet her, she was already in her car and the look on her face sent a chill down his spine. The minute Austin climbed into the backseat, she put the car in gear and tore out of the driveway. No smile, no wave, nothing. Despite her mood, guilt tore through him. She'd always been good to him. However, she shouldn't have approached Starla and said those things. Maybe a little time apart from Ivy would be a good thing. He could still pick up Austin without going inside.

As he continued to stand there, lost in thought, he remembered something Larry had said.

"Ivy's a good woman, but don't ever get on her bad side."

At the time, Connor had thought Larry was kidding and he'd had a good laugh over it. But as he remembered the look on Larry's face, he thought about that conversation. *"She has a bigger temper than I ever knew. Sometimes, I get out of the house when's she's angry."*

Larry told Connor about his bird and how one day, after having it for years, the bird had bitten Ivy. Two days later, he found it dead. His little neck had been twisted. Larry was torn up. He thought Ivy had done it, but she swore she hadn't gone near that bird. She had even cooked his favorite supper to show him how bad she felt. But Larry always harbored resentment toward her for his suspicions, and Connor had tried his best to help Larry get over it.

Now, seeing that scowl on her face before she left, made him wonder about Ivy. Maybe her temper *was* worse than anyone knew. After a few more minutes of pondering, Connor remembered he had things to do. He was still covered in dust from the construction site, but he'd clean up once he was done with his chores. So, he gathered up his tools and went to work in the back yard.

STARLA STOOD IN THE BEDROOM AT HER GRANDMOTHER'S CABIN thinking about the good news again. Dr. Hatcher had told her there was no reason to remove her entire breast. He explained that the cancer was very tiny and said it was barely stage one. As she thought about the rest of her appointment, she stuck her hand where the lump had been and couldn't feel it. Had it shrunk? Dr. Langley had said it was more advanced and suspected it might have spread to her lymph nodes. However, her new doctor didn't agree. His office was sending the new findings to her old doctor and see if he'd change his mind after they showed him the results. She prayed the results were conclusive and that Dr. Langley would agree with the same course of action. It was her body and she was the CEO of her own health.

Pulling her attention away from her medical issues, she focused on her new cream-colored dress. Although it was simple, it was beautiful. It hung just above her knees, and when she turned side to side, she loved how it looked when it flowed. The spaghetti straps were adorable, and the embroidered neckline was perfect. She bent down and slipped on her new white-and-gold sandals. "Perfect," she said. "I love them." As she admired the complete outfit, there was a knock on her bedroom door. When Starla opened it, Hialeah greeted her with a smile and a glass of lemon juice.

"Well, my word. Don't you look gorgeous?" She handed Starla the glass. "Drink this before you go, and please, no alcohol. Not even wine."

"Why no wine?"

"The short of it is because wine contains mycotoxins. I won't explain further right now because that would make you late for your date." Her face softened. "Connor sure is a stud. If you don't come home tonight, I won't worry." She smiled.

"I'll be home." Starla lifted an arched brow. "I don't usually go on many dates, much less have sex on the first one."

"Well, my dear, have you ever dated a man like Connor?" She grinned.

"Ah, let me think…" She put her finger to her chin and glanced up. "Maybe a few." She laughed. "In my dreams, anyway. By the way, are you sure you're okay without a vehicle?"

"Yes. Now get going." Hialeah pointed toward the door.

After they had hugged and said goodbye, Starla climbed into the old truck. "Well," she patted the dash, "don't you break down on me." With that, she started the engine and left.

As she drove through the heart of town, people waved and smiled, and she did the same even though she didn't recognize any of them. They were friendly, small-town people, that much was clear. As she passed the downtown park, she noticed it had quieted down compared to earlier that day. There were only a few people walking around, some holding hands. A couple with two small boys were buying hot dogs from the stand near the swings. It was becoming apparent that Secret Valley River was a place anyone could call home, and she couldn't wait to explore more.

Following the simple directions Connor had given her, she pulled up to what appeared to be his house. It had to be since his Harley and truck were both in the driveway.

"Oh, wow," she said lightly. The place was lovely, not at all what she expected.

She beheld a white Victorian-style home that looked like it could have been plucked from a Thomas Kinkade painting. The light-yellow shutters and the little white picket fence left her speechless. As she opened the truck door and stepped out into the cool afternoon, she noticed a cat lying on a rocking chair clearly uninterested.

Just as she opened the gate, Connor came from around the house and slowly lifted his hand to wave. As he approached the truck, he pulled a pocket watch from his pants, and there was no missing the guilty look on his face.

The chill in the air did nothing to cool the temperature that had just climbed to at least a hundred. She swallowed, trying to rid herself of what felt like a major lump lodged in her throat. Connor stood shirtless with dust peppering every single inch of his body.

"Hello, Starla. I'm sorry; I lost track of time." He tried to brush off the dust coating his sweaty, bare skin.

She couldn't stop scanning all of him and gave no hoot about the dust. *Lord have mercy.* Never had she seen a man so hot in her life. It wasn't like she hadn't seen him partly shirtless at the waterfall. He was covered with water for the most part though.

"Wow." Her voice was barely more than a whisper.

"Excuse me?" he said.

Once she pulled her eyes away from his biceps, she found her full voice. "Oh, nothing. I was just talking to myself." She gulped as his dark blue eyes landed on her, his gaze taking her hostage.

"What?" Starla asked nonchalantly, trying like heck to act normal.

"You're just so damn…" He paused and slowly looked her up and down. "*Fine.*" His voice was low and sexy as it vibrated through her.

"Thank you." Her heart warmed. "Remember, I bought some new clothes and shoes downtown. It was a fun trip."

When he stepped closer, she imagined her fingers running down his chest.

"It won't take me long to shower and get dressed." He took her hand. "We can still make our reservations, if you don't mind waiting for me to get ready." He leaned in, gave her a slow, soft, kiss on the corner of her mouth, and then paused. His breath hitched, and he didn't move.

His musky, outdoor fragrance caused her belly to tighten and her heart pounded like a drum.

"Starla." He moved closer. "Can I..." he whispered, his lips so close she could feel his breath, "kiss you? I know you have your new dress on and I'm a little dirty and sweaty."

"It's okay, yes. Please do."

At first, his kiss was slow and easy, but once she parted her lips to allow him more access, the tip of his tongue brushed her bottom lip. The heat from his kiss made her head spin. Then, he glided deeper, probing, exploring, and making her shiver.

His groan pulled her in deeper, and she became aware of every sound around her. She could hear the thump of his cat jumping off the chair onto the porch. There was no way to explain how she knew what each sound was, she just did. The rustle of the leaves blowing across the yard, the sound of Connor breathing, and the echo of her own heartbeat played in her head. And his taste, oh sweet heaven, was like pure honey with a dab of something she was too drunk with passion to recognize.

"Starla," he whispered and pulled her closer, pressing all that was hard against her. His big hands tugged her to him, leaving no question whether he wanted her.

And never had she wanted anyone like she wanted him.

"Can we go inside?" His breath felt warm against her ear.

She wondered if he could feel her trembling. "Yes, that might be a good idea." There was this feeling deep in her gut, they were being watched. More than likely by a neighbor. She glanced around and saw nobody, but still...

Once they climbed the porch steps and walked inside, he shut the door and locked it. Then, with a look that lit her on fire, he moved her so her back was against the door. Not one word was spoken as he traced his fingers down her neck, arms, and hands. His unshaven jaw tightened, and his eyes were smoky.

With ease, he moved his hand just under the hem of her dress, his eyes fixed on her. Connor had a commanding presence and she was thrilled by it. There was no doubt her legs would buckle soon. If only he'd carry her to the couch… sweet Jesus, his touch inched further up her thighs. A noise came from her throat, one she'd never heard. She was ready to give herself to him, totally and completely.

Then, with no warning, he stopped his upward trail and moved his hand to her waist with a look that could have bored into her soul, then stepped away. What was he doing?

To hell with food. To hell with him cleaning up. She'd take him now, dirt and all.

"Starla." He cleared his throat. "I'm going to get in the shower and take you to dinner." He kissed her softly and then backed away. As his gaze glided from her head to her toes, he moved across the room and sauntered down the hallway. "Make yourself at home," he called over his shoulder.

Starla braced herself against the door and slid down to the floor. What in the world had just happened? She'd almost had her first orgasm right there in the man's living room. That wasn't a way to show off her manners, now was it? Speaking of manners, what kind did he have, leaving her breathless and…and in this *condition*. There was no way he could have known she'd never had an orgasm. That's not something you go around telling everyone. She'd thought maybe the cancer had something to do with it. Yet even back in high school, her boyfriend had never accomplished that feat. She'd always faked it.

While she attempted to quiet her heart and catch her breath, she glanced around the room. The first thing that grabbed her attention was the wooden mantel lined with photos. After a few more seconds, she regained her composure and got up and crossed the room to look.

She picked up a picture of Connor that was obviously taken on his wedding day. Oh, my lord, his wife was stunning. They both looked incredibly happy. Tears wet her eyelashes. Connor looked so playful and handsome, and his bride's long black hair flowed down around her shoulders, her amazing emerald-green eyes shining bright. Other pictures revealed the connection between the two, their love clear by the way they gazed at each other. Starla swallowed hard, wondering how it would feel to have that with someone. Never in her entire life had she experienced such a great love, and, deep inside, she knew she never would.

Setting the first picture back down, she picked up another one. There was no mistaking Connor, even though he was much younger, in a large group that was obviously his family. His father was handsome. All the guys pictured were exceptionally good looking. His mother was gorgeous, and the only other female was tiny with long blonde hair like her mother's. She was so pretty. One girl with six brothers. That had to be insane.

She then noticed a picture of an older man and woman she assumed were his grandparents. They looked happy as they stood on the front porch of a large cabin and it appeared as if there was a lake behind them. Was that taken around here?

There was also a snapshot of his wife and Ivy. The pair couldn't look more different from each other if they tried.

Starla jumped when she heard a knock, then keys jiggling at the front door. She watched as it opened.

"Oh, hi." A tall, attractive man, looking to be in his thirties, smiled and took off his cowboy hat. "Sorry for just walking in, ma'am. I didn't know Connor had a guest." He had a playful smile, much like Connor's.

"He's in the shower right now." Starla didn't know what else to say.

As if he sensed her discomfort, the stranger crossed the room and held out his hand. "I'm Duncan, Connor's older brother. And you must be, Starla. I heard about your car breaking down outside of town and that you found your grandma here."

"Yes, it's been a real adventure. Oh, I believe I met your wife at the shoe store." She shook his hand and realized just how small this town was. "Nice to meet you. I was just looking at the pictures on the mantle."

"Nice to meet you, too. You'll soon learn that those pictures don't tell all. We are a large bunch of crazies." He chuckled. "I didn't mean to startle you."

"You didn't," she lied. "Connor was running late when I got here, but he should almost be done."

"Well now, that sure ain't good manners. Maybe I better have a long talk with my little brother," he replied. "He should know better than to keep a beautiful woman waiting."

Before she could answer, the bathroom door opened and shuffling that had to be Connor, echoed into the room.

Duncan called out, "Hey, brother. Sometime tomorrow you need to get your ass over to the house, so I can have a talk with you." He winced. "Sorry ma'am. Looks like I've lost my manners, too."

Connor stepped out into the living room with a towel slung over his bare shoulders and his hair still damp. Starla swallowed hard and tried to reel in her attraction.

"What is it?" Connor took the towel from around his shoulders and finished drying his hair. "I don't have too long to talk now. We have dinner reservations."

"So, I heard. But we have ourselves a little problem."

"What problem?"

"The problem you created when you told Megan you'd talk to me about letting her go to that damn prom. Now, she and her mama are on me like a hound dog hunting for a fox. I can't hide from either one of them."

"Should I step outside?" Starla asked.

"No," they both said in unison.

Connor put the towel back around his shoulders. "Well, why don't you let her go? Whether you like it or not, she's a big girl now."

"Only when hell freezes over will my daughter go out on a date with a boy. In case you forgot, she's only fifteen."

"Jesus, Duncan. We're talking about the prom, not accepting a proposal of marriage. You can't stop her forever."

"Fine, I have the perfect plan, then. Since you think she should go, you are going to chaperone her and her date." With that, Duncan turned and headed toward the door.

"Like hell I am." Connor's jaw twitched.

"Like hell you *aren't*." Duncan scowled as he put his hat back on. "You brought this on yourself. Get yourself ready to be at our house on Friday in three weeks at six, and wear something nice. If you don't show, she ain't going. Nice meeting you, Starla." He tipped his hat. "Sorry, our introduction was under these circumstances." He left the same way he had come in.

"Jesus Christ." Connor stared at Starla. "I knew I should have stayed out of this."

Starla tried not to laugh, but she couldn't help it.

"What is so doggone funny?" Connor asked.

"I can just see all those young high school girls swooning over you." She laughed harder.

"Is that so? I wouldn't laugh if I were you. You're coming with me and all those high school boys will have their eyeballs popping out when they see you."

Starla closed her mouth and shook her head. "No way. I've never been to a dance—high school prom or otherwise."

"Well." He stepped closer. "Now you're going to one with me."

"I am, huh?'

"Would saying please be appropriate right now?" He stepped even closer and hooked a finger under her chin to tilt her head up toward him.

"It might help convince me." Darn it, she couldn't think clearly when he was so close.

"Would you please accompany me to the school prom?" He grinned.

She nodded. "Yes."

"Thank you." He moved back, giving her a long look with his blue-suede eyes that sent heat searing through her. After holding her gaze few seconds more, he walked back down the hallway.

Holy shit, this man was driving her insane.

❧ 12 ❧

IVY WALKED THROUGH THE DOOR AND SLAMMED IT. "AUSTIN, WHERE are you?"

"Right here, Mama." He came running toward her, wearing that same pathetic look his father always wore.

"Did you do everything I told you to do?" She glanced around the living room, and things looked pretty good.

"Yes, I did everything. Can we go get pizza tonight?"

"I suppose so, now that we don't have company coming over."

"Where did you go, Mama?"

"Just for a walk to think about things," she snapped. "Now, let's get going. We're going to pick it up, so we can bring it home to eat it here."

"But I wanted to play the games there," he whined.

Grabbing him by his hair, she shook his head. "What have I told you about being a big baby and arguing with me when I tell you something?"

"Sorry, Mama." He held his hands up, trying to shield his face, but she popped him on the cheek anyway.

"Get your ass in your room and change those ugly pants right now." She pointed. "And don't you *ever call* that bitch, Starla pretty, or say her name is pretty again, understand?"

"Okay." Austin turned and ran to his room, but not before she picked up a shoe and hit him in the back. She watched the sissy bend over and act like it had hurt him, but after a few seconds, he shook it off and continued to his room. As much as she hated to admit it, she had to give him credit for not crying this time, like he had when she socked him in the shoulder. There's nothing worse than a big old bawl baby.

Ivy went to her room and punched the wall. That chick was trying to make Connor hers, but there was no way Ivy would let her do that. Not after how hard she'd worked to get him for herself. Her entire adult life should have been spent with Connor. Adding fuel to her raging thoughts, she pulled down a box from the shelf, and she couldn't help but smile as she opened it and pulled out Holly's hair clip. She kept the trinket hidden so well that no one would find it, especially considering it might still have dried blood on it. But on the off chance someone came across it, she had a story to explain why she had it. She'd practiced what she would say repeatedly.

"I found it in the water, officer. It was the next day." *Sniff, sniff.* "I was so distraught over the sudden nature of her death that I kept it." She placed her hand over her heart. "Yes, I saw the blood, but it was my best friend's blood. I just couldn't let this one last piece of her go." She used her charm and cried her fake, crocodile tears. "Damn, I'm good. I should win an award." She laughed, then caught Austin standing in the doorway, his eyes wide with shock.

"What are you looking at?" She slipped the clip back in the box and glared down at him.

"I didn't know you had Aunt Holly's hair clip."

"You better not tell anyone. Don't make me do something that I might regret. I kept it after she died. I have it because she was my best friend."

The little shit nodded as he continued to stare at her. "I said, *what are you looking at?*"

"Nothing, Mama, I'm just hungry."

"Get your ass in the car *right now, unless you want another broken bone or something worse.*" She inclined her head toward the door and watched him run just like his chicken ass daddy.

The minute she stepped outside, her anger reignited. What the hell was Connor thinking, kissing that whore in his front yard for everyone to see? This thing between him and that bitch was going to end. No matter what it took, she'd put a stop to that bullshit.

❧

CONNOR HELD THE TRUCK DOOR OPEN FOR STARLA AND WATCHED HER slide inside. Man alive, she was tilting his whole damn universe. He wanted her and wanted her bad—but every damn time he kissed her, he felt a rush of guilt. Holly was gone, and nothing could ever bring her back again. It wasn't as if he was cheating when he'd been with other women, and he'd never felt guilty before. But then again, he didn't give two shits about any of them. Starla was bringing up tidal waves of emotions that scared the hell out of him.

He had never cheated on Holly, even in college. Remembering Holly's age when they'd first been together, reminded him just how young Megan was. Maybe it was a good thing he was going to that dance after all. Just maybe—her daddy was a little smarter than he was.

"Are you okay?" Starla asked. "You've been awfully quiet."

"Yeah, sorry about that. I was just thinking about Megan going to the dance." He sighed. "Perhaps it's a good thing I'll be there. I remember being her age."

"Oh, I see." She chuckled.

Connor started the truck and pulled out of his driveway.

A few minutes later, Starla looked around as they pulled up to the restaurant. "This area looks wonderful. I thought you were taking me to the Dragonfly Inn because it's right down there." She pointed. "Which reminds me... I need to go see Ria soon."

Connor turned and faced her. "I thought about taking you there, but I wanted a bit more privacy tonight, so I chose Taste of Heaven."

"That's a very nice idea, Connor. This has a great view. Right near the water."

Connor placed his hand on the small of her back and opened the restaurant door for her. The freshness of the evening washed over him, chilling his warm face and calming his nerves. The second they walked inside, the aroma of onions, garlic, and ginger floated through the air and his stomach did a flip. "Hell, this place smells good." Looking around, he knew he'd made the right choice in bringing her here.

Macie, whom he'd known forever, glanced up at them. He liked her new hairstyle, white and spiked. Spunky just like her.

"Hi Connor. We have your table all ready for you." She grabbed two menus. "Just follow me." She gave Starla a small wink.

"Macie, this is Starla. She's new in town and staying out with her grandmother, Hialeah and her wolf, Shadow."

Macie met Starla's eyes. "Oh, I can see the family resemblance. In fact, I'd heard about the fated reunion not long ago. I've known Hialeah since she came to town, and I've known this juvenile delinquent since he was in diapers." Macie put down the menus, motioned for them to sit down, and waved to a young guy walking on the other side of the dining area.

"Thank you." Connor said. "And don't you be telling her any secrets about me and my diapers."

"Oh, before I forget, how's Austin's shoulder?" Macie asked, her concern apparent.

"His shoulder? I didn't know anything was wrong with it and I just saw him today."

The kid came and set the ice water down on the table and hurried off.

"Really?" Macie's eyes widened. "He had a nasty bruise and told his teacher he'd fallen down the stairs on the front porch at your house. We have all been worried about him. He seems to have bruises all the time. Belinda Rogers, who is the assistant teacher for his class, came in here for lunch and talked to me about it."

Connor was perplexed. "If that happened while I wasn't there, nobody told me about it." The very idea that Austin had been hurt was upsetting, and he was confused about why Austin would lie about where he got hurt, or did he just not say anything?

"We have all been praying for him. He needs to see a doctor," Macie whispered.

"I'll see that happens." How long had this been going on? What was wrong with Ivy? She couldn't just ignore something like that.

"I'm sorry, Connor. I thought you knew, since it's been happening so often. I didn't mean to spoil your evening."

"It's okay." He reached out and touched Macie's arm. "Thank you for your concern."

"I'll be back in a few minutes to take your order. Tonight's special is Chicken Marsala with baby potatoes and asparagus."

They both nodded as Marcie walked away.

"I can see that upset you." Starla touched his hand. "You really didn't know anything, did you?"

"No, but I'll deal with this later. Right now, I want to enjoy my evening with you." He laced his fingers through hers.

"I want to have a nice time with you, too, but I know you're worried about your godson. Why don't we take a rain check on dinner and maybe grab something quick to take back to the house? You could go see Austin while I set everything up for us."

"Are you sure?"

"I'm positive."

❧

THEY RESCHEDULED THEIR DINNER RESERVATIONS AND TEN MINUTES later walked into the pizza house. "Wow. It does smell good." Starla inhaled the aroma and realized how long it had been since she'd had a piece of pizza, just as her stomach growled like an old, hungry bear.

Connor laughed. "I guess someone's hungry." Suddenly, Starla noticed Connor squinting and staring farther into the restaurant.

Sure enough, Ivy and who she assumed was Austin, were standing at the counter. No sooner had she spotted them, when Connor took her hand and headed in their direction.

"Hello." Connor greeted the pair in a stern tone.

Ivy whipped around, a large grin plastered to her face. Never had Starla seen a smile so big shrink so fast.

"Hello, *Connor*." She nodded to Starla.

"Uncle Connor!" Austin threw his arms around Connor's waist and stared up at Starla. "Did you come to have pizza with us?"

"Not this time, kiddo. But I was coming to see your mom. This is, Miss Starla that I was telling you about.

He smiled. "Hi, Miss Starla." He reached out and gave her a warm hand shake.

I have something to discuss with your mom." He glanced at Starla. "How about you hang out with my date, for a minute while I go talk to your mama?"

Austin glanced over at Starla with a nervous look on his face.

"That would be fun, Austin. We can play those games." Starla pointed to the arcade sign which hung above some double doors. "I have some quarters we can use."

Austin's face lit up as he looked at his mom. "Can I go play with Starla?"

Ivy nodded. "Go ahead." Even though she agreed, she didn't look happy.

Starla took Austin's hand and noticed as he looked back at his mom twice. Why was he so nervous? Maybe his mother had made him afraid of Starla. The poor little guy seemed shaken to the core.

The second they got inside the arcade and the doors shut, he looked back over his shoulder one more time. Suddenly, he took her hand and pulled her hard around the corner.

"Help me, please," he whispered as tears gathered in his eyes. "Tell Uncle Connor to help me."

Oh lord, he was terrified. "Save you from what, honey?" Starla knelt to his level and brushed the hair out of his face.

"My mom's been hitting me more and more." He shivered. "She has Holly's hairpin and she's mad that I saw it. She told me if I didn't be good, I'd end up with something worse than a broken bone." He took a deep breath. "I'm afraid of her."

❧ 13 ❧

CONNOR STEPPED OUTSIDE WITH IVY AND STUDIED HER FACE. "WHAT the hell is going on with Austin?" Not wanting to be in the way of patrons walking in and out, he pulled Ivy off to the side to continue the conversation. "I just found out he's been getting hurt a lot lately. Can you explain that for me?"

"He's just been a bit clumsy this week," Ivy said, with a serious look on her face. "You know how rough little boys can be."

"According to what I heard, this has been going on for a few months now," Connor snapped.

"Like I said, he's a young boy. He's going to get in accidents from time to time."

"I want you and Austin to come to my house, and I want him to show me these injuries. We can all eat pizza there."

"I can't tonight, Connor. I have things to do."

"Well, come to my house when you're done then."

Ivy stared out at her car, her expression grim. For a minute, Connor feared she was going to run off.

"What if something's wrong with him?" Connor paused. "Since you're busy, I'll take him to my house."

"But you're on a date. I don't want to disturb that."

"It's fine." Connor's insides churned. "Go on and do whatever it is you need to do. I'm taking Austin."

"But—"

"No buts, Ivy. He's my godson, and I'm taking him."

"All right. Can I at least speak to him before I go?"

"No, I want to take him now." Connor meant it.

"Okay. Fine." She stormed away, and he watched as she got into her car.

When he walked back inside, he didn't see Starla or Austin, so he headed for the arcade, but he didn't spot them there either. Just as he turned around and looked in the pizza parlor again, he thought he heard Starla's voice. All the zipping and pinging sounds from the arcade games made it hard to hear anything else.

Heading toward the direction of the voice, he rounded the corner and saw Starla down on her knees hugging Austin. He was clearly distressed.

Connor walked closer and put his hand on Austin's shoulder. "What's up, bud?"

A pained look flashed across Starla's face, and she subtly shook her head.

Austin turned, tears glistening in his eyes, and looked up. "Can I come home with you, Uncle Connor?" He glanced around with fear etched in his eyes. "Where is my mama?"

"She went home. And, of course you can come home with me. Let's get that pizza and go to my house." He tousled Austin's hair.

It didn't take long to order a pizza and get on their way. When they pulled up to the house and climbed out of the truck, Connor didn't miss how upset Starla had become. Something was off, and he knew it. Maybe she was upset about their date night after all. Or it might be something else. She had asked him to give her a rain check, so that made no sense, it must be about Austin.

LATER THAT EVENING, CONNOR TUCKED AUSTIN IN BED WHILE STARLA stood at the door looking at him. How in God's name could his mother hurt him? She needed to tell Connor everything Austin had told her, but she wanted to wait until the boy was asleep.

Austin gazed up at her. "Could you read me a story?" His eyes pleaded, and there was no way she could refuse.

"Sure. Are there any books here?" She looked around the room but came up nil.

Then Connor reached under the bed, producing a stack of at least three books. "I have some of his favorites."

"Great. Which one would you like me to read?" Starla sat on the edge of the bed.

Connor handed her all three books and her heart melted like a toasted-cheese sandwich. She wanted to eat him up.

"I want, *The Knight and the Dragon.*" Austin interrupted her thoughts. "That is my most favorite." He pointed toward the book.

Connor made his way toward the door. "I need to go make some phone calls while you read. Is that okay?"

"Yes, of course." Starla opened the book to the first page, and Austin cuddled down in the bed with a happy glow on his face.

As she read, she couldn't help but notice that the pictures were wonderful and so well done. "Once upon a time, there was a knight in a castle who had never fought a dragon." Starla tried to use her best voices to make the characters and the story come alive.

Austin was fast asleep before she made it halfway through. With ease, she placed the book on the nightstand and studied the small boy as he slept. Once again, sadness filled her heart. Because of her bout with cancer, she'd never be able to have children. But if she could, there was no way she'd ever abuse her child. A few minutes later, she turned off the lights, partially closed his door, and headed down the hall, coming to a standstill when she heard Connor talking.

"I should be able to do something. I'm his godfather for Christ's sake." He was clearly upset. "I don't have a fucking clue what rights that gives me, but I'm taking them anyway." He took a deep breath and let it out. "Okay, so you'll have him call me tomorrow?" Starla quietly moved to the doorway. "No, I want to keep him here. I'll take him to work with me if I have to. I'm not sending him back into that house with Ivy. You should see all the bruises. He's covered." When he noticed that Starla had entered the room, he motioned for her to sit down. "I will. Thanks, Duncan. I'll drop him off tomorrow morning."

Connor hung up the phone and sat down next to Starla. "Some date I am." He gave her an apologetic smile and brushed a loose strand of hair from her face.

"It's okay. This is way more important than a dinner date. I feel so bad for Austin. I'm sad about those bruises. I saw how bad they were, when you changed his shirt." Starla touched Connor's arm.

"Me too and I'm damn well going to do something about it." He sighed. "You are so special, you know that? Thank you for reading to him." He leaned in and placed his lips on hers.

His lips tasted of basil and sweet tomato sauce. "I want to talk to you about what he told me," Starla mumbled against his mouth.

Connor moved back and looked into her eyes. "What did he tell you?"

Starla gathered her thoughts, scrambling for the right words. "He said he was afraid of his mom—she has some kind of hairpin that belonged to Holly." Starla watched Connor's face go pale. "Maybe he and his mom had an argument, and... God, I hate telling you this."

"No, you're doing the right thing. You mentioned a hairpin. Did he say what kind?"

"No, but he did say it had Holly's initials on it."

Without saying a word, Connor rose from the couch and paced the room. He finally stopped and stood by the window staring out.

"The night she died." He turned and faced her, then swallowed hard. "She was wearing a hairpin, and it had her initials on it. We never found it." His voice almost inaudible, his fists clenched at his sides. Starla could see the questions forming in his eyes. "I don't want to ask Austin about it. I can't imagine what he's already been through," Connor said. "But I have to find out."

"Do you think Ivy would do something like that?" Starla couldn't breathe just thinking about it.

"I don't know. I need time to think this over and figure out what to do from here." Her attention was dominated by the seriousness of his expression.

Starla touched his arm. "I should go home and let you sleep. If you want to bring Austin out to my grandmother's tomorrow, please do."

"I'm taking him over to my brother's house but thank you. Not sure I want you involved in all this. I don't want her paying you another visit, especially with the way things stand right now. Do you want me to wake Austin up, so I can give you a ride home?"

"No. It's not that late. I'll drive myself. I need to get Hialeah's truck back to her anyway." She stood and kissed his cheek. "I'll see you tomorrow."

Connor walked her to the door and tried to smile, but his face was pained with worry.

Once she pulled out of the driveway and headed down Evergreen road and past Secret Lake, she let herself take in all the beauty around her. The moon hung in the sky above the mountains, and for some silly reason, the sight made her think of the man in the moon. If he was there, she prayed he would watch over Austin and help ease Connor's pain.

As she passed by the little storefronts, her mind drifted to Oliver and their business. She needed to call him and make sure everything was okay. He'd be home by now from his honeymoon.

Turning onto Secret Lake Road the entire area got dark and made her tremble. There wasn't another soul on the road. She thought about how different traveling was where she lived; you were never alone on the road, not that she could recall. Then with no warning, someone pulled up behind her. The headlights were on high, and she wished whoever was driving the vehicle would turn the dang things down.

But the car got closer—so close she was afraid they would rear-end her grandmother's truck. She sped up to put distance between them, but they got even closer. What the heck? As a last resort, she slowed down and pulled over to the edge of the road, so they could pass, but they glided over as well.

"Breathe, Starla." She fought to keep her imagination from getting the best of her, but despite her efforts, Ivy came into her mind. Could that be her? Starla pulled back onto the road and the car behind her did the same. She tried her best to see who it was, but the lights were too bright. If nothing else, the good news was that she was in a truck, towering above the tiny car intent on trailing her.

Could Ivy have killed Connor's wife? Is Austin's life in danger? Maybe Connor should go to the police. The thought sent a shiver down her spine. "Stop it, Starla. It's nothing." She checked the rear-view mirror and saw the car was still there, but once again the lights were so bright she couldn't make out what kind of car it was, but it did look blue. When she arrived at the dirt road leading toward her grandmother's house, she made a right-hand turn. The car stayed behind her, not losing an inch.

She clutched the steering wheel, her grip so tight it was turning her knuckles white, while she hit bumps and bounced all around. Her heart pounded so loudly that she could hear nothing else. Just as sweat was dripping down her neck, the car behind her stopped and, thank God, started turning around. She inhaled deeply. They must have realized they'd taken a wrong turn and gone back to the main road. She exhaled the fear and laughed at herself. Why was she freaking out over a car behind her? That was just downright silly.

Once she pulled up to her grandmother's house and stepped out of the truck, the lake came into view, her breath calmed, but her body shivered. The pale light of the moon flickered across the water, leaving what looked like little sparkling stars behind. The night was cool, and the sounds of the frogs and crickets soothed her soul. This place was peaceful, she took another deep breath. "I love it here," she said to the stars.

Just as she got midway to the yard, a sound caught her attention. Shadow was running toward her, and then he stopped abruptly. His hair raised, standing on-end, and a low growl came from deep within his throat.

"What is it, Shadow?" Starla glanced around but saw nothing. Once again, a chill slid down her back and made her shiver. "Come on, boy. Let's go inside." He stood his ground and continued to growl.

Just then, the front door to the cabin opened, and her grandmother stepped out on the front porch. She looked so adorable wearing a native-pattern robe, her hair hanging down her back in a silver braid.

"Everything okay? I wasn't expecting you home so soon."

"It's a long story."

Her grandmother waved her inside. "Well then, come share with me. I just brewed some wonderful tea."

Once she reached the house, she realized how happy she was to be inside.

Her grandmother handed her the tea. "Now, did something bad happen? You have worry written all over your face and you're as jittery as a cat in water."

Starla's teacup rattled in her hands and she gripped it tighter. Shadow was right by her legs, and it seemed as though he was trying to calm her down, too.

"Someone was following me, and after I drove down this road a bit, they turned around. I thought everything was fine, but when I got out of the car, I heard a noise and Shadow started growling."

"Could have been a creature of some kind. We get a lot of wildlife out here. My guess about someone following you is, someone was lost. I've had a few people show up here not knowing where they were. There's a road about one mile down that leads to camping sites. Although this is an odd time of year for camping, but the weather has been nice. I've never had any trouble out here."

"Oh, whew!" Starla felt relieved. "I was letting my imagination run away with me." She took a sip of her tea. "This taste wonderful."

"Thank you. It's passion flower, and it's very relaxing. Now, why did you come home so early?"

"Oh, what a stressful night," Starla said and explained everything that had happened.

"This is very upsetting. I'm worried about you and Connor and especially that poor child." Hialeah shook her head. "I always had a feeling something was wrong with that girl."

"Really?" Starla examined her grandmother as she waited for her reply.

"Yes, and I hated feeling that way. I remember her being rude to a store clerk one time. Everybody in the store saw it, too. It was very unsettling."

"I'm not sure if Connor knows that side of her."

"I would bet he does," Hialeah interjected. "Most people in town have seen her act that way."

Starla's mind was reeling. She couldn't push away the sinking feeling she had every time she thought of Ivy.

"Well, considering what we know now, I do wonder if she's evil," Starla said, wondering if Connor would see that too. Thinking about poor Austin and what he had been through made her heart heavy.

❦ 14 ❦

STARLA AWOKE TO STRANGE NOISES THAT SOUNDED LIKE SOMEONE WAS running and a door slamming. Was she dreaming? She heard someone yelling for Shadow outside—her grandmother. What in heaven's name was going on? She jumped out of bed and took off down the hall.

"Grandmother," she called, noticing an orange glow shimmering along the walls of the living room. The minute she reached the front door, which was wide open, she saw flames engulfing the barn.

"Hialeah, Shadow!" There was no answer. She slipped on the shoes she'd left on the front porch and hurried toward the fire. When she got closer, she saw her grandmother running out of the barn, leading two cows. Starla gulped and ran faster.

"What can I do?" she yelled over the crackling noise.

"The animals—we have to get them out," Hialeah cried.

Starla rushed inside and gathered chickens, carrying some and shooing the rest toward the opening, but some ran back inside. The baby goats followed her and seemed like they knew what they needed to do. With every passing second, smoke filled the air, making it hard to breathe. She coughed and hacked.

"Oh, my god." Starla looked up to find that the ceiling was on fire. As her sense of urgency turned to panic, she grabbed a few more chickens and darted out as embers and planks of wood came crashing down behind her. "All the goats are out." Starla coughed again and turned to go back for more chickens.

"No!" Hialeah grabbed her arm. "We saved all the big animals. We can't save anymore. It's too dangerous." She had tears in her eyes. "We need to get these animals far away from the barn. It's going to fall. Let's lock them in the second pen. At least they will have a small shelter there." The chickens left inside the barn were clucking and screaming in panic. It was heartbreaking and Starla's legs became weak.

Having agreed upon their plan, they herded the animals out into the open pasture, so they wouldn't be hurt. Thankfully, she could no longer hear the sounds coming from the barn.

"Where is Shadow?" Starla asked while her grandmother stood next to her horse, trying to calm the mare.

"I don't know, and I can't find my cat." She glanced around. "Shadow wanted to sleep on the porch last night, so I haven't seen him since I ran out toward the barn. I thought I saw him take off in another direction, and I yelled for him, but he didn't come." She glanced around.

"Shadow!" Hialeah called out over and over repeatedly. But he still didn't come.

"Do you think the fire scared him?" Starla's heart was sinking as they both turned and watched flames consume the barn.

"No, but I do need to get the flashlights," Hialeah replied.

"I'll run and get them." She touched her grandmother's arm gently before she made a mad dash across the lawn and back into the house. Where were the damn flashlights? She looked in the kitchen, but then she remembered they were on the fireplace. After collecting them, she grabbed her jacket and ran as fast as she could back to her grandmother.

When Starla reached Hialeah in the open pasture, they continued to call for Shadow. After about ten minutes, they paused just as the barn fell to the ground in a loud, booming crash. Soon, the structure would be nothing more than ashes. Thank God it was on dirt and the lake was behind it.

"Do you think we should worry about anything else catching on fire?" Starla glanced around. "Do we have a hose or any water source?"

"No, not now. It was hooked up to the barn." Hialeah touched her brow. "I should have put in another one. All we can do is pray that the embers do not fly past the water source, or toward the field. If it does, you'll need to take the truck and go for help. We had good rain and snow this year, so it should be fine."

"Should I do that anyway?"

"No, we don't know how the fire started and I think someone will see the flames and come. Even if they don't, we need to find Shadow."

"You're right." A lump formed in her throat and tears filled her eyes.

"Did you hear that?" Hialeah's eyes darted toward the lake. "That was him howling." Hialeah made her way toward the sound, and Starla followed.

"Shadow," Hialeah called out again. The creature's sound was gut wrenching.

Once they arrived at the edge of the lake, they saw Shadow curled up on the ground.

Hialeah fell to her knees. "Shadow," she cried. "What happened to you?" He didn't move.

Starla took the flashlight and shone it on his body. There was blood, but Starla couldn't tell where it was coming from. Her heart was thumping hard in her chest. Tears flooded her eyes and ran down her cheeks, but she swiped them away with the arm of her jacket.

Hialeah pointed to his head. "Shine that light right here." Starla did, and the beam revealed a large gash. She sucked in a breath. "What in God's name happened?" She leaned down and touched his face.

"I need to take him into the lake, and then we need to carry him inside the house. Can you help me?"

"Of course," Starla agreed. "How do you think this happened?"

"I don't know." Hialeah shook her head. "Maybe an animal fight. Or maybe he tried to rescue the animals and was hit by the falling debris." They placed their hands under him.

"Okay," Hialeah said. "Let's lift him now." Going slowly, they made it to the edge of the lake.

They carried him into the water, holding him just enough so it rushed over his body and injured head. Starla was shivering, as was her grandmother. But seeing Shadow appear so lifeless broke Starla's heart. Would he survive this? Were they doing the right thing? Judging by the tears that slid down Hialeah's cheeks, it appeared she didn't know either. Every now and again, Shadow would lift his head, but he was so weak that he couldn't hold it up for long.

"Okay," Hialeah, said. "Let's take him inside and get him warmed up."

Somehow, they managed to carry him all the way back to the house without too much trouble. Once inside, they took him to the kitchen and lowered him to the floor.

"We need to clear off that table and put a sheet and blanket over it. I need to check his wounds, and I can't do that while he's down here."

"Where are the sheets and blankets?" Starla asked.

"I'll go get them. You can clear off the table." Hialeah exited the room.

Starla rushed around, pulling everything off the table and placing it on the kitchen counter. Only a few minutes had gone by before Hialeah came hurrying back and placed a sheet and blanket across the table.

"Let's do this gently." They lifted him again and placed him on the makeshift bed.

"Stay with him." Hialeah's face showed worry. "I need to prepare a poultice." She left the room only to return about five minutes later with bottles and bags full of indecipherable ingredients. Starla watched her as she mixed, adding pinches of this and that at the kitchen counter.

Once she was done, Hialeah walked over toward the table and leaned close. "This is going to burn for a second." She kissed his head.

"Would you mind coming close to his face to soothe him while I do this?" Hialeah asked. "He needs love and support right now."

"Okay," Starla said as she leaned down, stroking his forehead and his ears. "You're okay, boy."

Watching her grandmother clean his wounds, picking out particles of something from his wound, was fascinating. But what was even more intriguing was the poultice she used. After a few minutes of prodding, Shadow seemed to relax. Seeing his tension lessen, Hialeah returned to the sink and reached for a bowl in the cabinet. She mixed liquid together and filled up an eye dropper with the solution.

"Here, boy. You need to take this." Hialeah placed the dropper in his mouth and squeezed, letting him drink it.

After she bandaged his wounds, Hialeah gave him a small drink of water, then she took another blanket and covered him.

"He will sleep now, and the rest and medicine will allow him to heal." Her voice trembled as she gazed into Starla's eyes. "Someone bashed him in the head with a rock."

"Oh, my gosh." Starla felt as if she couldn't breathe. "Are you sure?"

In silent reply, Hialeah motioned toward the living room, dimmed the lights, and waved at her to sit. "I'm a hundred percent sure. I was pulling out smaller rocks that were lodged inside his wound. The impact had to be incredibly forceful and maybe even more than once to leave shards of the rock so deep in the gash. What I can't figure out is how they got that close to him. My thoughts are they did it while he was asleep."

"How would they get that close without him knowing?" Starla was perplexed.

"That's something I can't figure out." Hialeah shook her head.

Starla thought about the entire evening—the fire, the unknown person who had followed her back to the house—and Austin's words echoed in her brain.

"Are you okay?" Hialeah asked, concern evident in her voice.

"It was Ivy. I know it was. She hit Shadow. Maybe she attacked him while he was sleeping on the front porch, or maybe she lured him away or maybe he was drugged, wait where is his water dish?

Hialeah jumped up, unlocked the doors and headed outside. "It's on the front porch and I'm going to have it tested."

Ivy's the one who started that fire, and she didn't want Shadow to warn us," Starla said just above a whisper. "She's evil and dangerous."

"You could be right, but regardless, we need to notify the police." Hialeah went to the closet in the living room, then locked all the doors again and windows. She pulled down a long shotgun from over the shelf, took some bullets out of an ammunition box, and slid them in the gun. "In the meantime, however, we are going to protect ourselves." She also retrieved a handgun and handed it to Starla. "That is loaded, and you need to keep it with you at all times."

"I haven't used a gun before." She felt as if her insides were jumping all over the place.

"All you have to do is point and shoot—aim between the eyes if you have to. I'm going to stay out here on the couch, so I can check on Shadow. Everything is locked up, and these doors are strong. I know because I had to build them that way to keep the bears out. The animals are safe in the smaller areas." She moved toward the couch and pulled off the afghan that was thrown over the back. "Let's try to get a little rest. I'm going to change my damp clothes and so should you. You can go on to bed. Everything is going to be fine. I'll keep an eye out to make sure no more fires start up."

"Okay," Starla agreed. "Wake me if Shadow gets worse or you need me."

"I will." They embraced.

Starla entered the bathroom, peeled off her wet clothes, and put on some fresh sweats, a tee shirt, and a pair of warm socks. Being prepared was important if she needed to get up. Her bed called to her, and Lord, she was beyond exhausted. Even though she was uncomfortable with a gun, she placed it on the end table next to her head. It was well within her reach if she needed to use it.

Pulling the comforter around her, she shivered. The only sounds, other than her chattering teeth, was the slight breeze rustling the tree branches and the far-off sound of the cows mooing. More than likely, they were still traumatized over being uprooted from their home so abruptly. Should she shut the window and lock it? No, she was safe. There was a safety stick in the window, and nobody could climb through the little opening. But even though she felt safe, her mind wouldn't quiet down. Her grandmother needed to get a phone. Having only one spot where they could get cell phone reception wasn't enough. And the thought of being out there looking for a place the phone might work, sure as heck didn't feel safe. Not with Ivy roaming around.

She lay awake, listening to the night sounds, the ribbet of a frog, the sigh of the wind. If only everything had been a dream and the fire was not real. The events of the day played like a scary movie on repeat in her mind's eye. At some point, hours later, she finally dozed off, but nightmares plagued her. The sounds of the chickens squawking and Shadow's chilling howls echoed inside her head.

Her eyes popped open as she freed herself from the nightmare. Her chest tightened with anxiety just thinking about the day ahead. The police needed to be notified, and she needed to call Connor. Now, that it was daylight, she could find the area where the cell phone worked. It was by the lake heading east.

The house was quiet when she opened her bedroom door, so she tip-toed across the hall to the bathroom and turned on the water. The minute she stepped in the shower, she almost melted as warmth rushed over her. The entire night she had felt a chill, even bundled up in the warm blanket. Between the nightmares and the fear in her bones, there had been no hope for a restful night.

The hot water turned cool, so she shut it off, grabbed an oversized towel, and dried off. Suddenly, there were loud voices coming from the other room. She threw on her clothes, picked up her gun, and then skittered down the hall in her bare feet.

The minute she rounded the corner, she saw it was Connor and the sheriff. They stared at the gun in her hand, eyes wide, so she set it down on the lamp table.

Connor crossed the room toward her. "I'm thankful you're okay." He wrapped her in a hug. Being in his arms almost brought her to tears so she did her best to push them back.

She felt her stomach form a knot of nerves, and there was a brief silence between them before she spoke. "I'm so glad you're here. Where's Austin?" She glanced around, hoping to see him.

"He's with my sister-in-law. He's fine." He pushed the hair out of her face and kissed her brow.

"How did you find out about what happened?" she asked.

"I came out to see you and saw the damage. Hialeah was outside tending to the animals. When she told me you were still sleeping, I went to get the sheriff."

Starla gazed over at Hialeah. "How's Shadow?"

"Still weak, but he's better. He ate a tiny bit of food, so that's a start." She gave a small smile.

The sheriff cleared his throat. "I have to radio for the fire department to get out here to assess the damage. How much did you lose?"

Connor interjected. "Starla, this is Dan Brown. Dan, this is Starla."

He touched the brim of his hat. "Nice to meet you, ma'am. Sorry it's under these circumstances, though."

Starla nodded, and her grandmother handed him a piece of paper. "I went out to the fenced area and the old coop to take a headcount. I lost about ten chickens and my old cat." Tears misted in her eyes. "Smokey was nineteen." She sighed. "I was sure I saw her run out of the barn before it collapsed, but she's unaccounted for."

"I'm sorry," Starla said and moved to stand by her grandmother. "I forgot about the cat. I never see her around the house much."

"You know, I don't know where she came from," Hialeah explained. "She just showed up here one day and claimed the barn as her own. I put a bed out there. In the winter, she comes in the mudroom to sleep. But the rest of the time, she sleeps out there. She's an old cat and has been fixed."

"Maybe she's hiding and will show up later," Sheriff Dan said.

"I hope so." Hialeah handed him the paper.

The sheriff took it and continued taking notes. "Any other losses, besides these? Was there any equipment, hay, or saddles destroyed or damaged?" His eyebrows furrowed. "You will need to write all this information down again and place a claim with your insurance company. Take your time, though. It's hard to remember everything so soon after you've been through something as traumatic as this."

Hialeah nodded. "I do feel a little fuzzy on the details."

"Can we sit?" the sheriff asked. "I want you to tell me everything you remember about last night. I will file a report as soon as I get back to the station, so we can get to the bottom of this."

"Would anyone like coffee or tea?" Starla offered.

Connor headed toward the kitchen. "I'll make coffee. Y'all need to tell the sheriff everything." As he looked at Starla, a worried expression fell over his face. "Hialeah told me you were followed home last night. You need to tell Dan everything you can remember about the car."

❧ 15 ❧

STARLA AND HIALEAH TOLD THE SHERIFF EVERYTHING THEY KNEW, including the details about how someone was trailing behind Starla with their high beams on.

"So, you didn't get a look at the person driving the car?" the sheriff asked again.

"No." Starla shook her head. "Their bright lights were on, which made it hard to see. I was afraid I'd crash if I tried to look anywhere other than the road. Wait…" She paused. "I did notice that the color of the car was blue, when they first pulled up behind me."

Connor added. "Damn—Ivy's car is blue," he said while he set the coffee mugs down on a tray with cream and sugar. "Dan, in the last few days, some interesting information has been brought to light about Ivy's possible involvement with Holly's death.

Considering this new evidence and the strong case forming against her as the culprit for this crime as well, I think we need to reopen the investigation and consider Ivy as a suspect for what happened here last night too."

"That's not up to me." The sheriff's face turned a chalky white as he lifted the coffee to take a sip. "That's up to Alvin—he's the deputy sheriff, and he's the one who closed Holly's case. Right now, let me get this information in to him..." He paused. "Do you think these ladies might be in danger?" He glanced at Connor.

"You look awfully pale," Hialeah said to the sheriff. "Are you okay?"

"I guess. In truth and off the record, I never trusted that girl. She broke my wrist once when we were in junior high." He looked down at his coffee. "I was too afraid to tell anyone because she was a girl and she threatened to break both my little sister's arms if I did." He sighed. "Over the years, I pushed the memory out of my head. She seemed to outgrow her mean-spirited behavior. Even still, I was never friendly with her."

"Jesus Christ, Dan. That's awful. I'm going to stay out here, if it's okay with you. Duncan said he'd keep Austin at his house for the next week or so. I'd feel a whole lot safer with Austin there."

Hialeah smiled. "We would love your company, wouldn't we, Starla?" She looked over at her granddaughter and gave her a tiny grin. "I'd feel a whole lot safer too, with you here," Starla said and added. "Oh, Officer Dan, we have a sample of the water that was in Shadow's drinking dish. I think he was drugged."

"I'll need something to put it in, but we can get it tested." Officer Dan took more notes.

Starla swallowed hard. "Shadow would normally have alerted us."

Hialeah nodded. "He would have been all over someone doing that."

After last night, Starla was feeling a tad nervous over what might happen next. It was a lot to take in—especially after what Sheriff Dan had shared about Ivy. Being followed, the barn fire, and then for someone to have attacked Shadow was too much to happen in one night for it to be coincidence.

After the sheriff left, Connor and Starla headed out to check on the animals. Hialeah stayed behind to tend to Shadow.

As they strolled around the grounds in a comfortable silence, Connor threaded his fingers through hers.

"I do need to run into town and talk to an attorney about Austin. He's stopping by my parent's house at noon to discuss what legal action needs to be taken." He sighed. "But I don't like leaving you all alone out here."

"I was going to run into town, too. I need to call Oliver. I also think Hialeah wants to take Shadow to the vet and let him stay there until he's better. Maybe we should all go together. We could wait in the car while you see the attorney." She stared into his eyes.

"Don't be silly. My parents would love to meet you, and they already love Hialeah. I would feel better having you both come inside with me, so nobody is waiting out in the car alone."

Connor stopped walking and stood as if he were frozen when he saw the barn, which was only rubble and soot. The smell of burnt dust still lingered in the air.

"I can't believe this." Connor shook his head. "This is a total loss."

"I know, and the poor animals." She glanced out at the overcrowded area they now inhabited. "They really don't have the shelter they need."

"I'm going to fix that," Connor said. "I have enough spare supplies. With the help of a few friends, I can get something up while she waits on the insurance company. Until then, I'm going to get a tarp and make a cover. I have some two-by-fours in the back of my truck, and they are tall enough to serve as stakes for the tarp in the meantime. Then we can get some hay in town and bring it back. That will help keep the animals warm until we get them shelter. Unless, I can get some guys out here today. I'm going to try."

"Oh, Connor." Starla stepped in front of him and wrapped her arms around his neck. "You are the best." He circled his arms around her waist and pulled her closer.

"It's really no big deal." He paused. "I will keep you and Hialeah safe. You have my word."

"A lot has happened in such a short time," Starla said just above a whisper, but they both fell silent when they heard something.

"*Meow*." They turned toward to the partially burnt tree that stood by the barn.

"For heaven's sake," Starla almost cried. "That's Smokey." She moved quietly toward the cat. "Here, kitty, kitty." The cat moved away. "Smokey, please don't run." She got down on the ground and crossed her legs. "Here, girl. Here, kitty." It took a few minutes of convincing, but the cat finally moved close enough that she could scoop her up. "We need to get her inside. Some of her fur is singed." Starla held Smokey tight and kissed her head.

They set Smokey up in the mudroom with fresh water, food, and a soft bed. Hialeah cried as she soothed her old cat. Besides a small patch of fur scorched by the fire, she was the picture of good health.

"I'm so thankful you were able to get her." Hialeah stroked her head.

Starla reached over and gave her some love too and nodded.

It was a team effort to get Shadow into Connor's truck, but thankfully, there was a nice area in the full-size cab to make him a bed.

Ten minutes after they left and arrived at Pet Love Veterinarian office, Starla noticed it was right next door to the medical clinic, which made her think of her upcoming tests and biopsy—another mark on her already-scarred breast. But right now, she had to push away her anxiety and fear for her health, so she could focus on the more immediate tasks at hand.

Shadow didn't appear nervous and seemed to know Dr. Ross. Starla was surprised he would treat a wolf. But he was just a dog in disguise.

Dr. Ross, a tall man with graying hair and dark brown eyes, smiled at Hialeah. "I'm going to give him IV fluids and keep him here a couple days for observation. And, Hialeah, I want you to know that there will be no charge. I heard what happened on your farm last night.

You've been through enough." His eyes lit up when he looked at her grandmother.

"Are you sure? I can't take advantage of you like that," Hialeah said.

"You can take advantage of me whenever you like." He winked, and Starla watched as her grandmother's cheeks turned from pink to scarlet red.

"What do think about the gash in his head?" Hialeah changed the subject. "Do you think he needs stitches?"

"No. You stopped the bleeding, and it's already started to heal."

"Well, thank you, Dr. Ross," Hialeah said with a small smile.

"You're welcome, but call me Howard, please. I've told you that before."

Hialeah nodded, her cheeks even rosier. Both Hialeah and Starla kissed Shadow on the head before they turned to leave the room.

When they stepped out of the vet's office, Starla paused. "I need to call Oliver. He should be at work." She dialed his cell but couldn't get through. "This phone gets bad reception around here." She frowned. "I need to get in touch with him."

"You can use my cell." Connor reached into his shirt pocket. "I have unlimited calling, or you can use one of the landlines."

"I'll just wait and try again from your brother's house. If I can't get through, I'll use the landline as long as it won't be any trouble."

"It won't be any trouble." Connor gave her a soft smile.

Once they drove down Secret Lake Road, they turned onto Pinewood toward Evergreen Road. The area was spectacular, giving way to trees and flowers of every color. A little bridge crossed over the lake with swans swimming together in the crystal-clear water. Somehow, she already felt like she belonged. How was she going to leave in eight days? She knew she had to go because of her business, her best friend, and her other grandmother were all back in Louisville. Maybe she could extend her trip for another week. After all, she wanted to continue seeing the doctor here, and needed to get that biopsy, which was extremely important.

When she saw Connor's brother's house, she was speechless. The place was gigantic—a real Victorian-style structure. The wraparound porch was incredible.

"Goodness gracious." Starla placed her hand across her heart. "This house is something else."

"Thank you." Connor smiled as he turned off the truck. "We built it."

"Wait until you see the inside," Hialeah added. "I was here for their open house and the first Christmas party. You did a fine job, Connor."

"Thank you, ma'am. We aim to please." He opened his door. "Don't either one of you touch that handle. I'm coming to open it."

He walked around the truck and opened the door. It was sweet how he helped Hialeah down. He was such a gentleman with so much sex appeal, it left Starla breathless.

"Uncle Connor!" Austin came running out the front door and down the steps. "Are you here to pick me up and can I pick up my cat? Sometimes mama forgets to feed him."

"Hi, kiddo." Connor gave him a big hug. "You are going to stay here for a few days while we get things straightened out and we will pick up Toby. Now, I'd like you to meet Starla's grandma, Miss Hialeah."

She leaned down and looked into his eyes. "Well, it's nice to meet you, Austin."

"Nice to meet you, too. I've seen you before." He stepped closer to Starla. "You're Miss Starla's grandma?"

"I am." Hialeah smiled.

Before anyone else could speak, the lady Starla recognized as Trudy from the shoe store stepped out the screen door and onto the front porch.

"Why don't y'all come on in and have some cookies and coffee?"

She was adorable with her chocolate-brown curls going in every direction. Her smile reached her green eyes, making them shimmer. She was not heavyset, but she was definitely filled out.

Connor nodded toward the house. "Go on ahead. Starla, I'd like to show you around if you're up for it."

"I'd like to call Oliver first, if you don't mind."

"Sure thing." He nodded and lifted Austin onto his shoulders. Starla watched as they walked up the stairs into the grand home.

She pulled her phone from her pocketbook and dialed. It rang twice before someone picked up.

"Hello, vacation lady. I hope you're having a good time."

"It's been interesting, to say the least. I have so much to tell you that I don't even know where to start." Her voice broke, and she couldn't control the tears as they trailed down her cheeks.

"Starla, what the hell is going on? Are you okay?"

"So much has happened." She inhaled deeply as a giant lump of anxiety formed in her throat. "I guess I'll start from the beginning."

After spending a good fifteen minutes on the phone, she told him everything, not leaving out any details except one. The C-word.

"We're going to come out there tomorrow. I'll get Rachel to hold down the business. She can do it; she's really good."

"No, just wait and come on the weekend." She sighed. "We should know more by then."

"Starla," he said, sounding unsure. "Is the cancer back?"

"Yes and no." She knew that sounded confusing, but it was the best she could do by way of explanation. "The doctor here says I'm not even in stage one."

"What did Dr. Langley say?" he asked. "How long have you known?"

"Can we talk about this over the weekend? I need to get back inside. There is so much we need to do with insurance and attorneys today."

"I guess. But if you need me, you better call, and Thea and I will be right there. Is that clear?"

"I promise. I miss you. Tell Thea, I miss her, too."

"We love you, kiddo."

"I love you, too," she said with a sniffle. "I'll see you on Saturday?"

"We are coming Friday night. I'll call," he said, leaving no room for arguments.

Starla hung up the phone and collected herself. She wiped the dampness from her cheeks and started up the stairs. Just as she reached the porch, she heard tires squeal against the pavement. A loud thump followed. Ivy was headed her way.

"Where the fuck is my son?" she growled. "I have a mind to call the police and have you and Connor arrested for kidnapping." She stormed toward Starla with her fists clenched.

"I think you should calm down." Starla backed up. "Your son is inside, and you don't want to scare him."

"And you need to shut your mouth and stay out of this."

The screen door opened, and Connor stepped outside. He hightailed it down the stairs and stepped in front of Starla.

Starla blew out a breath. She could feel her heart pounding, and her mouth was desert dry. What in the heck was wrong with this woman?

"What's the issue here, Ivy?" Connor demanded. "You knew I was taking Austin. He's staying here with Trudy for a few nights. You need to pull yourself together."

"You didn't even ask me if you could take him for more than one night. I've been to your house several times, but you weren't there. He was supposed to come home today."

"He's not coming home, Ivy." He turned to Starla. "Why don't you go on in? You don't need to be subjected to this bullshit."

He didn't have to ask her twice. She moved up the stairs and into the house as quickly as her legs would carry her.

❧

CONNOR WAITED TO SAY MORE UNTIL STARLA WAS SAFELY INSIDE. He'd asked Trudy and Hialeah to keep Austin busy in the kitchen when he saw Ivy pull up, or rather...when he heard the tires squeal and saw the dust flying.

"Ivy, Austin is staying with me for a while. As you recall, I was given guardianship in the event that anything happened to you. I'm taking full advantage of that."

"Connor." She threw her arms up. "Does it look like anything has happened to me? I'm fine."

"Looks can be deceiving, Ivy. He's not going with you. You've been *hitting him*, for God's sake. What you need to do is take a few days for yourself—see a therapist and find out what the hell is eating at you."

"You can't just keep my son." She glanced up at the window. "I miss him. I *love* him."

"I love him, too, and for that reason, until you pull it together, I'm keeping him. Why don't you take this time and do something fun for yourself? Work on getting your temper under control." He was playing her, so she'd leave. "Now, you know how much I care about the two of you. Let me do this and don't cause any trouble."

"Trouble? I haven't caused any trouble."

He walked up to her and placed his hand on her arm. "Look, I'm worried about you. Let me keep him. Maybe you just need rest. You work so hard and you've been through so much." He tried his best to look sympathetic. "Maybe after you're feeling better, we could take him camping for a weekend, like I mentioned the other day."

She dropped her gaze and used her foot to move a rock on the ground. "Just the three of us?" she questioned.

"Yes." The lie burned his tongue.

"Okay, you're right." Her eyes lit up. "I do need some time to calm down. When will you bring him back?"

"In a few days. Maybe a week." He pasted on a smile. "We need to pick up Toby, Austin misses him."

She stilled and glanced up at the front porch. "Tell him I love him, and you can pick up the cat whenever you want."

"I will," he lied again. He wasn't going to tell Austin anything, but he would pick up the cat.

She stood there for a few more seconds, which felt like forever, and then she turned and walked away, wearing a pink skirt and white sandals, he'd seen her in before. As he watched her, he noticed she had a minor limp, then spotted something on her ankles. What in tarnation? They were both burned, leaving no doubt in Connor's mind about what she'd done. She was worse than he'd ever known, which made him think of Holly. Was it possible? Could Ivy have done something to her that night?

He needed to call Dan and let him know about the burn marks. They should take her in for questioning based on the burns on her legs alone. They could maybe get a warrant to search her house.

Connor stepped inside and heard chatter coming from the kitchen, so he crossed the room and stood at the doorway. All the ladies were at the table, and Austin was sitting on the floor playing with Jimbo. That cat was a little crazy, but he sure could make Austin laugh.

Starla glanced up at him and smiled sympathetically. "You still want to give me a tour? From everything I've seen, I'm totally impressed. This place is stunning."

He nodded and looked down at his godson, wondering what he had been through while living with Ivy. How much had she beat on him? His stomach turned thinking about it.

"You want some coffee, Connor?" Trudy asked. "I have a fresh pot, and these are your favorite cookies—peanut butter and mini-chocolate chips." She got up and walked over to the pot to pour him a cup.

Connor held up his hand. "I need to make a quick phone call to

Sheriff Dan, but yes, I'd love that in a bit. Starla, want to come with me while I make that call, and then I'll show you around?"

Austin stood up. "Can I go out back and play on the jungle gym?"

"Sure, buddy. Go ahead." Connor tried his best to act happy for Austin's sake.

"Miss Trudy, is it okay if I take one more cookie?"

"Sure you can. Take two if you want." She walked over to the counter and held out the plate.

He grabbed them up. "Thank you." He took off through the kitchen door and ran to the jungle gym.

All eyes went to Connor. "When Ivy was here, I noticed she had burn marks on her ankles. I think she's lost her mind. I do think she set that fire, and I firmly believe she was the one following Starla home last night."

Hialeah's eyes widened, and Trudy and Starla nodded, not expressing much surprise.

Connor moved over to the window and watched as Austin laughed and climbed the playhouse in the backyard. "I don't want him coming in here while I'm on the phone."

Hialeah stood. "I'll go keep him company. You know I had her in mind during all this, but I just didn't want to say it out loud. After what happened with Starla and the color matching Ivy's vehicle, I was highly suspicious. Truthfully, I always knew something was off about her."

"I knew in my heart it was her. After everything and what Austin told me." Starla said.

"I guess, deep inside, I did too," Connor stared out the window. "I'm so sorry she did this. I feel responsible. I should have seen this coming."

Trudy shook her head. "Look, I've never liked her—you know that —but even I didn't think she'd do something like this."

Hialeah held open her arms. "Connor, you have nothing to feel guilty about." She embraced him, and then cupped his face as she pulled away. "You're a good man, and you are going to do right by Austin. Just make that phone call, and let's get her put away before she hurts someone else." She dropped her hands, heading out back to Austin.

Connor picked up the phone and dialed. "Hidden Lake Sheriff's Department," a female voice answered. "I need to talk to Sheriff Dan."

16

Two hours after Ivy left Trudy's house, Ivy glanced around her living room and realized what a mess the place was. Even her curtains were torn down. Oh well, who gave a flying shit? It was that bitch's fault that she tore the place apart. Starla needed to get the hell out of town—maybe out of this world. That was a great idea. The stupid woman was trying to steal Connor. "I've worked too hard to let things slip through my fingers," she yelled.

She got rid of Holly and her dear sweet departed husband. Now, she'd get rid of Starla, too. She thought about her mom and dad's old cabin. She could take Starla out there and do away with her. Nobody would ever find her body. It was at least forty-five minutes outside of town, and who would ever go out there, it was out in the boonies? The idea was brilliant. She'd already gotten away with so much, and nobody had ever suspected her. She'd played the grieving widow so well—too well.

And, now, Connor was feeling bad for her. There was no doubt about that. She could tell by the look on his face. She could pretend to take time to herself like he'd asked. When she got back he would have sex with her when they went camping, this time she'd make it happen. She'd bring Austin's own tent. And, she'd pretend to be pregnant after it happened. Yes, she was one smart chick.

Meanwhile, she'd be rid of Starla. Connor wouldn't suspect Ivy, because not a soul would know Ivy was in town. "Yes!" That was yet another smart idea.

She picked up the phone and dialed Connor's cell number.

"Hello, Ivy. What's up?" He sounded concerned when he used that sweet tone of his.

"I thought about what you said, and you're right. I'm going to leave town for a few weeks—that is, if you're sure you're okay with keeping Austin and Toby." I need to get away and get myself together."

"Where are you going, and how can I reach you?"

That right there, was one of the main reasons she loved him.

"I'll be with Debbie Ann. She's been begging me to come for a visit, so I'll be heading out to Nashville and I'll keep my cell phone with me."

"Okay, that sounds good. When are you leaving?" He sounded a little strange. What was that about? Just a second ago, he was being so kind.

"Right now. I've packed everything, and I'm on my way out the door."

"Wow! That's quick. Maybe you should wait until tomorrow morning. You know, just to give yourself a chance to rest up first."

Something seemed off, and Ivy knew it. "Gotta run, Connor. I want to get on the road. I'll be okay. I'm stopping at a hotel, so I won't have to make the drive in one night. Talk to you soon, and please give Austin a kiss for me. I'll see you both when I get back."

"Okay, but be careful. We will come by and get the kitty, but if you get tired, pull over and get a room. I'll pay for it." His voice sounded soft again, maybe he was just worried about her.

She ran through the house and gathered up some clothes, food, and blankets. A rope, a gun, and other supplies went into another bag. She'd have to hide out somewhere on Hialeah's property and wait for the right time to grab Starla. She planned to park her car behind some of those old trees where none of them could see it. Then, when the time was right, she'd grab the bitch. She was as skinny as a toothpick, so that would make it easy to overpower her.

Once she climbed in her car and was driving away, she breathed a sigh of relief. She really should grab Austin because he knew too much. However, two might be a lot harder to handle. Besides, he'd keep his trap shut. She'd beaten him enough he should know what would happen if he didn't. She'd done a good job at scaring the shit out of him.

As Connor drove later to his parent's house, Starla thought about how much she enjoyed getting to know Trudy, even with everything going on. The day grew to be more stressful when they left Austin behind. The poor kid didn't understand everything that was going on, and Connor was doing the best he could to protect him. It had helped when he drove over and picked up the cat, which Ivy left outside. When they took it back to Austin, his face had brightened like the sun.

At least he was safe, though. He was coming out to the cabin for a few hours tomorrow. They'd show him a good time and let him ride the horse. If Ivy was put in jail, would Austin be able to stay with Connor? Or would other family members try to take him? Starla's heart broke just thinking about Austin. His whole little life was about to change.

Starla was still in awe of the way Connor cared for Austin. A lot of single guys wouldn't take the time. She prayed they could stay together. Trudy and Duncan would be good for Austin too, they lived in an amazing home, and would make a great extended family. You could feel the love permeating all around. It must be incredible to be a part of that family. Starla was envious and couldn't help thinking of her own parents. When she thought of them now, it pulled at her heart strings, remembering all the love they shared.

Connor gave Starla a sidelong glance when they pulled up to their destination. "This is it."

His parents' home was much like the other house his brother had, only a smaller version.

"So, you grew up here?" Starla looked around and noticed the wrap around porch and the American flag hanging out front. The yard was fenced, and an old tractor set out front decorated with flowers and plants. It looked like a family home. Neat and tidy, but not overdone. "This is so nice. I bet you loved it."

"Yes, I did. My entire childhood was spent here and, in the treehouse out back. My dad built this place for my mom before any of us kids were born. He taught me everything I know about construction."

Hialeah smiled. "I remember the first time I met your parents. I was new to the area, and they made me feel welcome when they invited me to dinner."

Starla wondered how they'd feel about her. A new girl in town. Would they blame her for Ivy's meltdown? Although, if she did kill Holly, they couldn't blame her for that.

"Do your parents know Ivy well?" Starla asked.

"Oh, yes. They've known her since we were kids. They've tried to be patient with her, but for reasons I never understood, my dad always had issues with her. Well, we best be getting inside." He glanced at his watch. "The attorney will be here in a few minutes."

Connor walked into the house without so much as a knock and waved Hialeah and Starla inside.

"Mama, Daddy. You have company," he yelled out as he wiped his feet on the rug. Starla and Hialeah followed his lead and cleaned their shoes as well. "I'm home!"

Starla glanced around. The place was elegant and welcoming, and the aroma that filled the house felt like home. She'd bet anyone who came inside immediately felt as if they belonged.

"Lord have mercy, this is charming." Starla smiled. "And that scent is heavenly."

A tiny lady walked into the living room, drying her hands on a kitchen towel. She had long, blonde hair tied back in a ponytail with a smile on her face. She didn't look old enough to be Connor's mom, but she was the lady in the picture on his mantle. Her looks and size made it hard to believe she had grown kids

"Connor Zachary Whelan, you do not have to yell. I'm not hard of hearing yet." When she scolded Connor, any doubt about her being his mother went right out the window.

"Well, Mama, I had to let you know we were here." He walked up and embraced her. "Mama, I'd like to introduce you to Starla Moon. She's the one I was telling you about. You know Hialeah, of course."

Hialeah walked up and hugged her. "Hi, Dixie Lee. You never grow a day older."

"Now, that's what you call a good friend." She laughed. "You look amazing, Hialeah. I'm so sorry about that awful fire. But I'm sure happy y'all are safe."

Hialeah nodded. "Thank you. It's still pretty shocking."

Dixie turned to Starla, and her smile touched her eyes. "I can sure see the resemblance between you two. It's so nice to meet you."

Starla stuck out her hand, but Dixie pulled her into a warm hug. "Welcome to our town and our home. I'm so happy to hear that you and your grandmother found each other."

"Thank you. I'm sure happy, too." Starla had to swallow back the tears.

The front door opened, and an older version of Connor walked in. He had on a cowboy hat, tight-fitting jeans, and he was built like a rock. He couldn't be the guy in the photo? Could he.

"Well, looks like I'm fixin' to crash this party." He winked at Dixie and turned toward Connor.

"You gonna introduce me, son?" He arched a brow. "Hi, Hialeah. It's good to see you." He nodded and touched his hat.

"Daddy," Connor said. "I'd like to introduce you to Hialeah's granddaughter, Starla."

Starla could not believe this was Connor's dad. He was much better looking than in the older picture she'd seen. But, she'd been stunned by his mom, too. *Must have good genes*, she thought.

"Nice to meet you, sir." She walked up and extended her hand.

"Sir? How about you just call me Mack?" He pulled off his hat, and his salt-and-pepper hair made him even more handsome.

He shook her hand. "Nice to meet you, Starla." His hands were large and welcoming. "Welcome to our crazy home. I sure hope you've been enjoying this town. Most people come here and never want to leave." His laugh was deep and sincere. "I'm sorry though, to hear about the fire, he glanced over at Hialeah."

"Thank you," Hialeah responded.

"Mr. Morgan should be here soon. Why don't we go in the kitchen and have some coffee and cookies while we wait? I also made some finger sandwiches and punch," Dixie invited.

Connor rubbed his stomach. "Sounds good to me. I can never get enough cookies. We ate some at Trudy's too." He glanced between Hialeah and Starla. "You have to try my mama's cookies and her finger sandwiches. They are always super good."

Starla was surprised when Connor took her hand and guided her toward the kitchen. She saw his parents exchange a glance when they noticed. The look they shared almost appeared like a smile—she could only hope.

Mr. Morgan, the attorney, soon showed up. He was going to get the ball rolling to award Connor temporary custody until they went to court. Child Protective Services had already visited Austin to take pictures of his bruises. Thankfully, the sheriff's department had gotten a warrant and were searching Ivy's home. They confirmed she wasn't there, and they'd found the key Connor had told them about. They'd also found the hairpin that Austin said his mom kept in her closet and had taken it in as evidence. Connor was needed to identify and confirm that it was Holly's. From what they had told him, he was sure it was hers. Starla couldn't stand seeing the pain etched in his eyes and didn't feel comfortable being involved with Holly's case

That was one reason Starla and Hialeah stayed with Connor's parents while he went to the station. He'd told her in private he needed to go alone, and she totally understood. She couldn't come close to imagining how painful the process would be.

While they waited for his return, Connor's parents treated them like family, offering food and asking if there was anything they needed. As warm and welcoming as they were, Starla couldn't help but fidget, thinking about what he must be going through. After a few hours, Connor came walking in. By the look on his face, it was obvious what had happened.

His dad stood. "Well, son. Was it Holly's?" His dad moved closer.

Connor nodded, and tears flooded down his mother's face. "Oh, bless your heart." Unable to say anything more, she went to her son and wrapped her arms around him.

His dad hugged him, too. "Sorry, son. I can't imagine how hard this must be for you." His eyes were laced with tears.

As Connor's shoulders shook, Starla and Hialeah rose to leave and give them some privacy.

"Please don't leave." Connor choked back his tears. "I want y'all to stay."

Starla nodded and felt tears burning her eyes. That horrible woman had killed his wife, which made Starla wonder if, somehow, she'd killed her husband, too.

"The police said the hairpin alone wasn't enough evidence to indict her for killing Holly," Connor whispered. "The fact that it might have traces of blood on it could help. If she had found it in the water the next day, or even the day after, the blood should have been gone," he choked out. "Goddamn her."

His dad frowned. "Ivy has always been short a few dollars. Never did like that girl. She never seemed right."

"I know. I remember the look on your face whenever she would come over with Larry." Connor moved across the room to Starla. "Thank you for staying."

A tear leaked from her eye and trailed down her cheek as she embraced him. "I'm so sorry, Connor. What can I do?"

He wrapped his arms around her. "Just being here with me—means the world." He leaned back and wiped her tears. "Thank you."

Starla wanted to kiss him so bad, but not with his family watching. "Of course. I wouldn't want to be anywhere else." She touched his face.

"Son," Connor's dad said. "Is there anything we can do? We can help with Austin. He's always welcome here." He cleared his throat. "Hialeah and Starla, you're both welcome to spend the night here. Until she's caught, it might be a good idea."

"I'm going to stay with them." Connor glanced between his mom and dad. "I want to make sure they're safe. I don't trust Ivy or what she might try to do and I'm taking my gun." He inhaled. "They haven't been able to get in touch with her friend to see what time she's expecting her. Once she gets there, she'll be picked up and brought back for questioning."

🕊 17 🕊

THEY ARRIVED BACK AT THE CABIN AND CLIMBED OUT OF THE TRUCK just as the sun was going behind the mountain. A slight breeze fluttered the tree branches and the flowery scent of roses settled over the area. The meadows were layered with blooms that shone with yellow, lavender, and shades of orange. Glancing around, Starla noticed at least four trucks lined up by the animal pens.

Hialeah's breath caught. "Oh, my word." Her eyes were misty. "I can't believe this."

Connor placed his arm around her shoulders. "Believe it, because they are here for you."

"Now, this is something," Starla whispered.

The guys were finishing up the barn. They were making trips back and forth to the large trucks, carrying hay and supplies inside. What was left of the old barn was still taped off, but the new barn and two other smaller shelters were standing where the temporary pens had been. The trio moved up to the fence. The barn was amazing and even bigger than the other one.

Hialeah stilled, not moving an inch. "I don't know what to say."

Connor smiled. "Well, then let me just say welcome home, Hialeah. A few of the guys got together and wanted to be sure your animals had shelter and a warm place to sleep. We had everything needed to build this Western style barn and wanted to give it to you. It really didn't take that much with all these guys."

Hialeah rested her hands across her heart. "Oh, this is wonderful." Her voice trembled. "I can't believe it. Oh, Connor, you're a wonderful man. I know this was your idea." She turned toward him and wrapped him in a hug.

"It was nothing." He blushed. "We had all the materials, and some of this was prefab."

"You can't fool me, Connor. I remember hearing about you in high school, always taking care of the underdog. I know how special you are."

This didn't surprise Starla. The way he took pride in being Austin's godfather, the pictures of him as a devoted husband, and, from what she'd seen, he was a wonderful son and brother.

Connor pointed. "Let's go look at your new barn."

IVY HID BEHIND THE TREE, TRYING TO STAY OUT OF SIGHT. CONNOR was walking with both women toward the workers who had been there all afternoon. Crap, it would take something creative to grab Starla without being noticed. Not as dang easy as she thought. She turned and crept back to her little tent and campsite. It was a good thing that damn wolf was gone—hopefully dead. She'd smashed him good. Her car was small enough to be hidden behind the taller trees. Nobody would spot it, that was for darn sure.

Her tent was right behind some bush and one extra-large tree. If things got too strange, she'd just sleep inside her car. Sometimes, the best-laid plans must change a bit.

With Holly, it had been easy. Connor had been nowhere near her when Ivy saw her standing in the water looking up at the stars. Ivy had accidently made a noise as she got into the water and walked toward her. Remembering that night made Ivy proud of what a good job she'd done.

"Oh, Connor. Can you believe what a beautiful night it is? I'm so glad we did this. It's just what I needed." Holly turned to look in his direction. "Ivy, what in tarnation are you doing out here?"

Ivy had the rock in her hand. "Came out here tonight to enjoy the view, too. Larry and I rented a room."

"Oh, isn't it lovely?" She turned back and faced the nighttime sky. "Maybe we could all have some of that delicious angel food cake together."

"Yes. That would be wonderful." She took the rock and slammed it in the back of Holly's head. Holly screamed, which made Ivy angry, so she held her head and hit her again. That was when her hairpin came off in Ivy's hand, but at least she fell into the darkened waters. Ivy swam all the way across to the other side so nobody would see her. And, in the middle of all the commotion, nobody heard a thing. Connor was yelling and splashing around while others were running in the water with him. So, her getaway was easy. She figured she'd best keep that pin since it had been touched. You could never be too careful.

One year later, she got rid of Larry. Nobody had ever suspected what she'd done. She had used the easiest way to kill him and left no trace of her crime. The chemical substances had been easy to get. She had mixed them together, and the fact that it broke down as a natural-occurring compound as it passed through the body, made her task easier than she'd ever imagined. The whole thing had been relatively simple with a little help from instructions she'd found on the Internet. When he was pronounced dead, she had fallen apart in front of everyone, even pretending to pass out. Connor became her protector.

The only thing that still haunted her was when Larry died. He'd glanced into her eyes, and his silence spoke volumes. He knew because she just stood over him, watching as he took his last breath. The guy had always been smart. The way he stared into her eyes left no doubt he knew she had killed him. His last word was Austin.

Shaking off the memory, she got inside her tent. The place was crawling with bugs, so she took a package of crackers and cheese, so they couldn't get it. It was important to keep up her strength, especially since she would have to keep her wits about her.

Just as she finished the last bite of her cracker, she heard several vehicles driving away, and thought they must be done for the night, so she climbed out of the tent and went inside her car. A thrill went through her. Sometime, somehow, when nobody was looking, she would find Starla alone. And Ivy was much bigger and stronger and could kick her ass.

Connor couldn't be with Starla twenty-four-seven and he had Austin and that cat to take care of. Ivy watched a little bird land on the hood of her car, looking for food. She quietly got out and offered the thing some cracker crumbs. At first, it was scared, but soon enough, it got close enough to eat what she'd offered. Ivy reached down, grabbed the bird, and broke its neck. "Fucking pest. I hate birds." She tossed it to the ground.

A few minutes later, she chuckled at how she'd outsmarted the bird. She'd outsmart them all. At that very moment, Connor thought she was headed to Tennessee. Yet, here she was, almost right in the old woman's backyard. After the sounds of the trucks were completely gone, Ivy grabbed her binoculars and walked to a tree where she could hide and look out. There was nothing—no sounds except for the rustling tree branches and birds making their annoying chirps.

She had realized this would be a long afternoon, and that she'd have to be careful what she ate. Not having a bathroom would make this harder than anything else she'd ever done. But there were plenty of trees and she had tissue.

After another hour of seeing nothing, she felt irritable that Connor was still there. Her head slumped, and her eyes felt heavy, so she decided she'd better get some sleep. The tent would keep her warm with the sleeping bag and extra blankets. Once she was inside and comfortable, sleep came fast.

Sometime the next morning, she heard another vehicle and realized she had slept longer than intended. It must be Connor leaving for work. It sounded like it was going up the driveway though. She brushed back her hair, grabbed the binoculars, and ran to her tree. She wasn't sure, but it looked like Trudy's car. "Just great. A family reunion."

She saw Austin dash out of the car and run to Starla, who was sweeping the front porch. Starla put down the broom.

"What the hell is he running to *her* for?" That bitch was trying to steal her son too. She watched as they hugged, and Starla brushed the hair from his eyes.

That was it—she was a dead woman. The sooner she could get Starla away from Connor and Austin, the better.

STARLA RELEASED AUSTIN AND WAVED GOODBYE TO TRUDY, WHO seemed to be in a hurry. "I'm so glad you are here. Thought you might like to ride Sequoia, he's a gentle horse and will go slow."

"Really? I can ride your horse?" Austin's entire face lit up. "Uncle Connor wouldn't let me ride his horse, Dexter."

Starla arched a brow. "Really?"

"He's kind of rough." Austin shuffled his feet.

Just then, Connor walked up and joined them. "Kinda, is putting it mildly, he's thrown me a few times. Remember a few years ago when I broke my arm? I was riding him, and he got moody. So, Sequoia seems like a much better choice, and I don't have to worry about you getting hurt." He motioned to the mare and clicked his tongue so she would come closer. "Let's introduce you two."

Austin pumped his fist in the air and ran to the gate, dragging his uncle Connor. "Awesome!"

Hialeah and Starla both chuckled as they walked to catch up with the guys.

"She's not actually *my* horse," Starla interjected. "Sequoia actually belongs to my grandmother, but she loves it when people ride her."

Hialeah moved up to the enclosure. "Sequoia *is* your horse, in a manner of speaking." She looked over at Starla. "Someday, I'll be gone, and this will all be yours." She opened the fence and waved for Austin to enter.

Starla frowned at the thought. She'd just found her Grandmother. The thought of losing her anytime wasn't something she wanted to think about.

"Wow!" Austin ran inside the gate. "You're so lucky." He stared at Starla. "I've always wanted a horse."

❧

AS THE MORNING RAN INTO AFTERNOON, STARLA ENJOYED SEEING Connor teach Austin to ride. Once they had done that for a few hours, they went to the lake and spent time swimming and enjoying a lazy day. Connor decided to keep Austin with them for the entire day. Never had Starla seen a child so content to be with three adults.

"Miss Starla, Uncle Connor." Austin took a deep breath. "I haven't had a fun day like this since my daddy died and I hardly remember that anymore."

Connor stood and walked over to him. "Well, you can count on many more days like this. I'll see to it." Austin stood and hugged his uncle tight.

Starla had to focus on something else. The last thing she wanted to do was get emotional. She was glad they decided to go ride the horse again. It would help her not to break down and cry.

It wasn't long before her grandmother yelled out that supper was ready.

After Connor helped Austin dismount the horse, they made their way to Starla, but she waved them toward the house. "You guys go on in. I'm going to make sure the animals are in their pens and that they've been fed."

"You sure you don't need my help?" Connor asked.

Austin rubbed his belly. "I'm starving."

"No, I've got it. I love doing this. Besides, you need to get this young man inside, so he can eat."

Connor nodded. "You heard the lady. Let's go wash up, kiddo."

Starla watched as the guys continued toward the cabin. From where she stood, Starla realized how much Austin looked like he could be Connor's son. Everything about him—the way he walked down to the way he held his arms—was the spitting image of Connor. They were adorable together, and there was no missing how much Austin looked up to his godfather. Overwhelmed with contentment, she looked up at the blue sky just as some birds sailed overhead. It was a beautiful day. When she finally tore her gaze from the sky, she noticed the animals were watching her as though they knew it was feeding time.

She couldn't help but think how amazing the people of this town truly were as she went in search of the animal's feed. Hialeah had tried to pay the men who worked tirelessly to rebuild the barn and pens, but neither Connor, nor the other volunteers, would hear of it. They had willingly given of their time and even pitched in to buy new food for all the livestock. Every time she thought of their generosity, she found herself pushing back the tears.

Still lost in thought, Starla sat down on a bale of hay, pondering how different her life was before she ended up here. Most weekends she was pretty lonely and had only a small number of friends who all had their own life, including, Oliver, who was married to a wonderful lady now.

For the first time since her parents passed away, she felt a strong sense of belonging—more so, than she could have ever imagined. While Louisville and Secret Valley River were both beautiful, that is where their similarities ended. It was almost unfair to compare the two. Something in the air of Secret Valley River made a person feel amity. It was as though family lived on every corner.

When her mom and dad were still alive, she felt at home just being with them, no matter where they were. She recalled how her parents always made her feel special, even while they were living in their small trailer. Her mom had worked diligently to keep it clean and tidy during all their adventures. Waking up and having breakfast while watching birds soar through the sky and fish jump out of the lake seemed like a charmed life. Her parents had always told her, don't let adventures pass you by. Be brave and step into the unknown. If only her parents were still alive. She was sure bridges could be mended with her grandmother.

When Starla finally rose from her makeshift seat to grab a hand full of hay, a sharp pain stabbed into her head. "What the heck?" The room was fading when she fell backward onto the ground. Did someone hit her? Then, she saw a familiar face. "Ivy." Everything went black.

CONNOR AND AUSTIN WERE IN THE KITCHEN HELPING SET THE TABLE.

"Boy!" Austin exclaimed. "What smells so good?"

"That is my one-of-a-kind taco casserole." Hialeah grinned. "I sure hope you like it."

Even before they tasted it, Connor knew they would love it. "I don't know about Austin, but if he doesn't like it, I'll eat his portion." He chuckled. "I'm starving."

Hialeah filled two tiny plates. "Here, try it and see if you like it."

After taking the first bite, Connor's eyes closed as he swallowed. The combination of cheese and some other spices he didn't recognize, made his tongue explode with flavor.

"No, Uncle Connor," Austin said with his mouth full. "I'm going to eat every bite." He rubbed his belly, licked his lips, and then stuffed the last few bites in his already-full mouth. "I wish Miss Starla would hurry up." When he swallowed the last bit of his sample, he ran out to the living room and stood by the screen door.

"Why don't you run out and fetch her. Tell her to come on. I can take care of the rest of the animals after dinner." Hialeah laughed.

"Sure thing." Austin took off like a flash, running out the screen door and letting it slam behind him.

Connor shook his head. "I don't think I have to worry about his appetite."

"I think you're right." Hialeah chuckled. "His spirits seem good too considering everything he's been through."

"I think he's relieved to be away from his mother," Connor whispered.

Hialeah looked over at Connor. "My heart breaks for him. I don't even want to think about what he's been through."

A few minutes later, as they puttered around getting the drinks poured, Connor heard Austin yell. It took a minute for him to make out what Austin was saying:

"She took her! Help, Uncle Connor!"

"What?" Connor bolted out of the house and crossed the yard to where Austin stood. "Who took her? What are you talking about?"

"My mama…" He caught his breath. "My mama put Miss Starla into the trunk of her car, and she was bleeding from her head," he cried. "She's going to kill her like she killed Aunt Holly. She told me not to say anything, but I had to disobey her. She'll come back for me, too."

"Don't you worry about that. Go tell Hialeah and stay with her." Connor ran and jumped in his truck that was parked by the old burned down barn. With shaky hands, he started the engine and took off heading towards the driveway, kicking up dust and soot behind him. How the hell had she driven out here without being seen or heard? He clutched the steering wheel and made a sharp U-turn, then glanced at Hialeah, who was standing on the porch with a look of panic written across her face. There was no time to explain, Austin would tell her. He had to find Starla. There was no way he would let anything happen to her.

He watched the loose dirt and gravel fly up behind him when he punched the gas, and the truck slid sideways down the long unpaved road. He was breathing so hard that he felt like his chest was about to explode. Where would Ivy take her? He knew without a shadow of doubt she wouldn't take Starla back to her house. The more he thought, the more his pulse sped up, and his fingers turned white from gripping the steering wheel.

By the time he got out on the main road, he knew he had to calm down and get his wits about him. He needed to think like Ivy. He pulled over and took out his cell from his pants pocket and dialed.

"Sheriff Brown's office," a woman answered.

"I have an emergency. I need to speak to Dan." Connor inhaled, trying to rid himself of his rising panic.

"Hold on, please."

Connor killed the ignition, stepped outside his truck, and paced. He looked down both ways of the road, hoping there were tracks or something to indicate which way Ivy had gone, but there wasn't a thing. "Get on the dang phone," he said out loud to nobody.

"Sheriff Brown, here."

"Dan, it's me, Connor. Ivy has taken Starla. Austin said he saw his mom put Starla in the trunk of the car and she was bleeding from her head."

"Christ almighty. When did this happen?"

"Not more than ten minutes ago. We have to find Starla before something horrible happens."

"I was already issuing a warrant for Ivy, as a matter of fact. Turns out we found some new evidence that could possibly link her to Holly's death. We found Ivy's journal, too."

Connor sucked in his breath as his heart slammed against his rib cage. "We need to find her."

"I'm on my way. Where are you?" Dan asked.

❧ 18 ❧

Ivy wondered if Starla was awake as she continued down the road to her parent's cabin. Connor had only been there once when they were kids, so there was no way he'd even think to come looking at the old place and since nobody knew she was in town, why would he look, unless Austin tells. As far as Connor knew, her parents didn't even own it anymore. Also, nobody was around this time of year—not a neighbor in sight—and her parents hadn't been there in years. Then again, she hadn't seen them in a decade—not since before Austin was born. They wanted nothing to do with either of them, and that was just fine and dandy.

Her mind drifted back to her dad's words. "Ivy, you're just plain evil. You've got the devil in your heart," he would say and glare at her. Her mom was no better. She'd called her the devil's spawn once.

"Fuck you, Mama and Daddy," she yelled and chuckled. "I wish you could see me now. You'd be so proud." She laughed harder. "I've already killed twice, and I'm about to do it again."

She continued driving, glancing out her rearview mirror. Her biggest concern was Austin, even though she had twisted his arm and told him to keep his mouth shut, he could spill. It had always worked, and this time, he stood there in silence, just like he always did. The little coward probably pissed his pants after she told him that she'd come back and teach him a lesson if he told anybody she took Starla.

So, on second thought, she shouldn't worry about him, but they'd know something was wrong when Starla was nowhere to be found. Maybe she should have taken time to go steal her car and get rid of it. Oh well, how in the hell would she have done that? They would just think someone kidnapped her, or she ran off. The truth was, she didn't really give a flying F what they thought. Nobody could prove anything against her.

One of her favorite songs came on the radio when she drove past the empty fields, so she turned up the volume and sang the second verse. *"Got a really good feeling something bad about to happen. Oh, oh, oh."* She had no doubt something bad was gonna happen. That bitch should have never come to this town, and she'd make damn sure Starla never showed her face around these parts again.

When she reached the long dirt road that would lead her to the cabin, she heard Starla crying. "Shut the hell up you little cry baby. Ain't nobody gonna hear you out here!" Ivy pretended to cry. "Wah-wah! Help me."

Finally, she pulled into the old muddy driveway and glanced around. "Perfect place for this bitch to die, but first, I'm going to have a little fun with her. Do you hear me, little bitch girl?" She snorted. "You're going to die today." Only silence, but that was fine with her. Maybe she passed out again.

This area would become Starla's final resting place, and nobody would ever figure it out. Ivy could drag her down to the lake, tie rocks around her hands and feet, and throw her in. Or, she could just bury her. No, she'd throw her in the lake after she made sure the skinny thing was heavy enough to sink forever. The fish and creatures in the lake would eat her before anyone ever found her. Later, she'd tell

Austin that Starla had run off and escaped, she laughed as she slid out of the car.

After she'd looked closely around the cabin, she couldn't help but notice that someone had cleaned the yard. Had her parents been in town? Had they hired a caretaker for the property? With that thought, she knew she'd have to act fast. What if someone was coming around? Damn it. That put a damper on her torture plans. She walked back to the driver's side door and pulled the keys from the ignition.

First things first, she needed to check inside to see what condition the house was in. The minute she opened the front door, a musty smell overwhelmed her, it was like a smack in the face. Nobody had touched anything inside for some time. Glancing around, she noticed how old and run down the place had become. Even the curtains had turned brown and gloomy. Cobwebs hung from the corners of the pine walls. The single stream of light that filtered in the window only illuminated the dust lingering in the air. Her parents told her that they'd held onto this dump because it had been their first home, which sounded like bullshit if you asked her. Who cared about romance anymore? A good roll in the hay was all she'd ever cared about. Although, she'd admit that she wanted more with Connor. She already knew he was better in the sack than Larry because she'd watched him and Holly through an open window once. Oh man, was he built in all the right places. Yes, someday she would have him, and she knew that day was fast approaching.

Well, it was time to get to business, she would knock Starla out cold again if she had to. She opened the trunk to discover Starla's eyes were closed and judging by the blood that was still oozing from her head, maybe she had died after all. There was no movement and no breathing she could see.

"Damn, that's too bad. Now I won't get to torture you."

STARLA TRIED HER BEST TO PLAY DEAD BY BREATHING AS SHALLOW AS possible. She had a plan to knock the crap out of Ivy when the time was right. Ivy didn't know Starla had taken self-defense classes, and even though she was thin, she could kick some serious ass. While Ivy wasn't paying attention, Starla had untied the rope so her hands were loose behind her back—another trick she had learned from her training. It seemed silly to learn how to make someone think they have your hands tied tight, but now, she was glad she'd taken those extra classes. Even through the haze because of the smack in the head, she still stayed one step ahead of Ivy.

"Okay, I'm going to drag your flat ass down to the lake," Ivy said as she tugged on Starla's legs. "Then I'm going to drown you, bitch. No more Connor for you."

Ivy's grip around Starla's leg loosened, bam! Starla kicked her right in the face. The look of shock when she hit the ground was priceless. "Oomph," Starla grunted when she hit her again. She watched Ivy's eyes roll back and blood trickle from her mouth. There was no sympathy in her heart for this evil woman.

"They know you killed Holly, and they will be looking for me!" Starla shouted.

Ivy tried to stand, but her legs were not steady enough to hold her weight. When she reached up to touch her nose, her fingers became sticky with blood. "You fucking bitch. I'm going to kill you." She struggled to move but hit the ground again.

Seemingly at the speed of light, Starla took the rope meant for her and wrapped it around Ivy. Once she had her tied up, Starla picked up the keys from the ground and jumped in the car. Thank goodness, the engine started right away.

With shaking hands and trembling knees, she sped away as fast as she could. She noticed Ivy try to stand as she glanced into the rear-view mirror and drove down the dirt driveway. Even when she hit potholes and the car bounced off the ground, there was no slowing her down. Her heart was beating so hard, she could hardly catch her breath. Good lord, she needed to calm down. The last thing she wanted to do was crash the car. So, she eased off the gas and locked all the doors.

She needed to figure out where the hell she was and find her way home. That wouldn't happen if she panicked.

Adrenaline rushed through her veins as she continued down the dirt road until she came to a paved road. The gas gage showed she had an almost-full tank, so she knew if she kept driving, she'd at least find somewhere to go for help. How long had she been knocked out? If she knew, she could have calculated what time it was. The sun hadn't set, but it was May, so it stayed lighter longer. There was no damn clock anywhere. That would've helped, most cars had them. But hell, she was free. That was the most important thing.

Somewhere there was a house, a town, barn, even a small store where she could be safe and away from Ivy. How does someone get like that? She was bat shit crazy.

As she drove past fields of trees, tears rolled down her cheeks. She'd almost been murdered, just like Holly. Her entire body trembled, and the moisture practically blurred her vision

She kept driving, but there weren't any street signs indicating nearby houses. It wasn't long before the sun set, and she still had no idea where she was, but knew she'd taken a wrong turn. The best thing she could do was go back the other direction. The area had most definitely turned into more wilderness in the last few miles. Just as she was about to turn around, she came to another road heading west. Should she take that, or should she go back the way she came? All she knew was that she didn't want to go back to where she'd left Ivy. The thought alone gave her chills.

After weighing her options, she took the road heading west, but when she turned onto it, she heard a beeping noise. She knew she hadn't run out of gas since she left with a full tank, so she pulled off to the side of the road to figure out where the sound was coming from.

After a few seconds, she could hear that it was coming from the middle compartment.

When Starla opened it, she was pleasantly surprised at what she found. In all the panic, she hadn't thought to look for a cell phone. The screen flashed, displaying Connor's name and number, so she answered.

"Hello, Connor," she cried. "I managed to get away from Ivy and took her car, but now I'm lost. She was going to kill me."

"Take a breath, sweetheart. Do you see any landmarks or street signs nearby?"

"I turned down a road going west but it's nearly deserted. All I can see are trees and bushes."

"Okay, keep driving. Does it look like this phone has a good charge? Is there anything to charge it with?"

"I don't see a charger, but it has almost a full battery and decent signal."

"That's great, so you must be somewhere not too far. Now put the phone on the passenger's seat and turn on speaker phone. Tell me anything and everything you see. Are you okay? Are you hurt?"

"I've got a pretty nice bump on my head, but it's nothing serious. More than anything, I feel shaken."

"We will make sure you get looked at as soon as you're back. What are you seeing, Starla?"

"I'm still only seeing trees that seem to have some kind of green fruit growing on them and it's getting darker. Wait…I see a wooden sign. It says, "no trespassing" in big orange letters."

"That's good. If someone went to the trouble to put that sign there, maybe there's a road leading to a house."

"Okay." She slowed down but saw nothing. "There's no road that I can see. Just more fencing and trees."

"Then keep going and drive slowly." He spoke calmly. "I'm glad you are okay. I was so worried."

"Me too. I thought my number was up until I got out of the ropes. She didn't tie me up very well."

"You did a good job getting away." He sighed. "Now we just need to get you home. Where did Ivy take you, can you describe the area?"

"Some old cabin by a lake."

"An old cabin by a lake..." He repeated. "Shit, I bet that's her parents' place. I went there a few times when we were kids. I'm going to head that way, it's off Hidden lake drive. Starla, can you find your way back to that place? But don't turn down the road to her parents' place."

"Yes, I know right where I turned, and I won't turn down that dirt road."

"Stay on the main road, okay? They need to get street signs out in that area. I need to call Dan and tell him where you are and what happened with Ivy. I'm sure he knows where that cabin is. I'll call you right back."

"Okay, I will keep driving slow. Just make sure I get back home to my grandmother's house," she whispered, tears filling her eyes.

"You're a brave woman, Starla Moon," Connor told her. "I'm in awe of you."

"Thank you, Connor. Is Austin okay?"

"He'll be fine. He was just worried about you. We all were."

When she hung up, her heart had finally started slowing down with the sun. It wasn't long before the phone rang again.

"Starla, I'm on the road now. Look for my headlights. I'll be going slow."

They spent the next ten minutes talking about Ivy. The truth was, Starla knew deep in her heart something wasn't right with her when she came out to the house and threatened her to stay away from Connor. To murder Holly and then her own husband... what caused someone to become so deranged?

"I see headlights." Starla exclaimed. "Is that you, Connor?"

"Yes, I see you. Pull the car over so you can come with me. Let's get you out of her car and get you home. The police are on their way out to Ivy's parents and they'll take the car in for evidence."

He didn't have to ask her twice. When she'd edged the car over to the side of the road, she flung the door open and ran to him, practically jumping into his warm and welcoming arms. She was safe. Starla had never been someone who needed a man. However, in that moment, she needed *this* man.

Before she could say anything, he held up his finger. "Let me get you something." He came back with a heavy wool blanket. "Here, let's get you inside the truck. I have some bottled water for you, and I'll turn on the heater."

He lifted her into the truck, and she slid across the seat. Moving quickly, he went around the cab, climbed in the driver's side, and then started the engine.

"Here," he said as he switched on the heater, "get closer to me." He wrapped his big warm arms around her cold body.

"Oh, Connor." She laid her head on his shoulder. "I thought I'd never see you again."

"I was so worried." He studied her face. "I know this may sound odd, but I feel like I've known you all my life." He kissed her forehead and brushed the hair out of her face.

"It isn't odd, because I feel the same." She squeezed his arm. "Should we go now, or do we need to wait for the sheriff?"

"No, we can go. I called my brother while I was on my way to meet you and he offered to take care of Austin. The poor kid has been through so much. They will take good care of him."

"Thank goodness he has you and your family."

Connor nodded as he put the car in gear and pulled back onto the road. "I agree. I'm wondering if Larry's family will want custody of him since Ivy won't be in the picture, but they've been in poor health for quite some time. I don't think they could handle raising a little boy."

"Where do they live?"

"In Memphis, Tennessee in senior housing, so if they took Austin in, they'd have to move."

"What about Ivy's parents?" Starla tried not to sound worried.

"No, they won't want him. They rid themselves of Ivy when she turned eighteen."

"It would be interesting to know why."

"Agreed," Connor said.

About thirty minutes later when they drove down the dirt road that led to her grandmother's, they met two cop cars and a few vehicles she didn't recognize. Connor pulled up as close to the front as he could, and Starla saw her grandmother's hand go up to her mouth. There was no doubt she was crying. Never had Starla been so glad to see anyone.

Hialeah ran toward her, and Starla did the same.

"Oh, my beautiful granddaughter." She wrapped Starla in a tight embrace. "I was so afraid I had lost you." A sob escaped from her as she clung to Starla even tighter.

Starla couldn't hold back the tears. "I'm so glad to be home with you, Grandmother."

While they hugged and cried, she saw Connor approach one of the sheriff's deputies. Two more big guys stepped out on the porch, and one hugged Connor and shook his hand.

Starla turned her attention back to her grandmother. "I left her tied up at what is apparently her parents' cabin. It's a long story, and I'll fill you in, but right now, I think they should be concerned about Ivy trying to take Austin if she gets free."

Hialeah shook her head. "No, they already caught her. She was found walking down the road on foot like nothing had happened."

"What?" Starla shook her head. "I'm not surprised that she escaped from the ropes, but the fact that she walked down the street like nothing had happened? In plain sight, no less?"

"Of course, she tried to tell the arresting cops *you* had kidnapped *her*, tied her up, and stolen her car, but they knew better. Austin watched her put you in the trunk. Plus, they found some incriminating evidence at her house when they executed the search warrant for Holly's murder."

"I can't believe she thought people would believe that." Starla touched the back of her head where Ivy had hit her. "She did a pretty good job of knocking me out."

"Let's get you inside and look at that bump."

Just then, Connor strolled over. "Maybe we should take you to the hospital."

"I really don't want to go. I'm so glad to be home." She glanced between the two of them.

"Maybe I can get the doc to come out here and look you over," Connor said. "I'd feel better if he just took a peek."

"Okay. Thank you, Connor."

"The Sheriff will want to take your statement as soon as possible. Are you up to that?"

"Yes, but I need to change my clothes and get some water first," Starla explained.

"Of course," Connor agreed. "We'll all give you some time to get your bearings."

Hialeah wrapped her arms around Starla. "Let's get you inside."

✴ 19 ✴

THE NEXT MORNING, CONNOR WALKED INTO THE SHERIFF'S OFFICE AND up to Marlene. "Hey, M, is Dan around? You look as lovely as ever." He winked and watched her touch her salt and pepper hair.

"Sure, go on into his office, you charmer." Her brown eyes sparked with laughter. "He's getting some paperwork done. He's expecting you."

Connor nodded and still couldn't believe his sixth-grade teacher traded in her chalk board for law enforcement. He twisted his way down the hallway to Dan's door which was open.

"Hey Dan, how goes it?" Connor asked.

"Well, you might say it's been a crazy ass morning. Shut the door and come in."

Connor closed the door and took a seat in front of Dan's desk. "So, where do we stand?"

"Well, Ivy said she ain't talking until you see her. I know that isn't something you want to do, being we know damn well she killed Holly." Dan winced. "Sorry, pal. I shouldn't have blurted that out like that."

Connor shook it off. "I will see her. I will do my best not to murder her, but I want her locked up for life."

"Now, Connor. I don't want you to do anything that would get you in trouble. I am not asking you to put yourself in that situation."

"You don't have to ask, Dan. I want her ass locked up. She killed my wife and tried to kill Starla and look what she's done to Austin. I don't want her to hurt anyone ever again. So," he exhaled. "Let's do this."

"Okay, are you sure? We could wait and hold her and that way you'd have a few days."

"Nope." Connor stiffened his shoulders. "Let's do this now. The sooner the better. I'm just thankful you caught her."

"Well, you know what they say. It takes a devil to catch a devil."

Connor laughed. "You my friend are no devil."

"Oh, you never know. Look how Ivy fooled so many people. Poor Larry. She wrote about how she murdered him. Right now, I can't go into it, but it makes me sick."

Dan stood and grabbed the clipboard on the wall. "Follow me and I'll bring her into the interrogation room. We will have cameras on and hopefully she'll pour her wicked guts out."

Connor sat at the table while they got Ivy. He took a deep breath and let it out. It would take everything he had to stay calm. He picked up the glass of water and took a long sip. What should he say to her? How could he even look into the face of the person who had killed the love of his life?

The door opened, and Dan led Ivy in.

"Oh, Connor. I knew you'd come to rescue me. They are accusing me of horrible things. Someone is trying to frame me, and I think it's that Starla woman. I knew she hated me." She sat down and took his hand.

By sheer force he played along. "Ivy, I know you did it, but I also know you did it for me because you wanted to be with me." He raised her hand to his lips and kissed it, but bile rose in his throat.

"Connor, I didn't do it. I swear." Tears dripped down her face.

"I know you did it. I didn't realize how much you cared. Starla is gone. Austin and I are going to wait for you. We will get the best attorney and I know you will be set free."

Ivy studied his face. "You sent Starla away?"

"Of course. After I heard what you did. You did it all for me and for love. How could I not?" He rubbed her hand. "If only you would have told me. We could have run away together. Somewhere nobody would know us." He stared into her evil eyes and acted sad.

She glanced around and leaned over the table. "Can you bail me out of here? I can't talk right now since they have cameras." She pointed.

"I'm already working on getting you out. I also made Dan turn off those damn cameras. You can come to my house and we can be a family. You know how much you've always meant to me, you and Austin are my life. I won't let anyone ever hurt you." He kissed her hand again.

Ivy leaned closer. "Everything I did, was for you. I always wanted you since we were in high school. It wasn't hard to get rid of Larry, but it was hard with Holly. I did care about her. But not as much as I did for you." Once again tears dripped down her cheeks. "I never loved Larry, it was always you. It was so difficult to wait and get rid of him, but I had to at least give it a year after Holly was gone. But for us, I had to make it look good."

He wanted to smash her face so bad, but he kept his cool. Never had he imagined hitting a woman, but right here and right now, he clenched his fist and shook inside with the desire to take her out. He started to tremble.

"Don't you see, Connor. That's why I wanted Starla gone. She was trying to steal you away from me and Austin."

He stood and knocked the chair backwards. "I can't do this anymore." He glared at her. "I think you've said enough to spend the rest of your life in prison."

"What? No. Connor, you can't say that or do that. We are a family."

Dan opened the door and looked between Connor and Ivy. "We got enough to lock her up for life and then some." Connor nodded and walked out the door, hearing her scream and yell as he walked down the hall and out of her life forever. It was over.

✦ 2 0 ✦

THREE WEEKS LATER, ON A CALM EVENING AT THE END OF MAY, Starla stood, staring at her reflection in the mirror. So much had happened in such a short amount of time. Oliver and Thea had come and gone, and Starla's doctor had removed her lump. Her car was back and running great. The greatest news was the doctor discovered the growth was extraordinarily tiny and had continued to shrink even more in the days prior to the removal. There was no medical explanation as to why or how this happened. Maybe, as the doctor mentioned, it seemed to be more scar tissue than cancer.

She had followed the health plan and advice of her grandmother. Maybe there was something to, eating all organic and healthy food. At least this time around, she didn't have to do chemotherapy again or radiation. The thought of losing her hair for the third time put shivers down her spine. To change the direction of her thoughts, she focused on the mirror once more and spun around in her new dress.

"I do love it," she whispered, "but does the color work? Is it too simple?"

It wasn't just the dress she was unsure of. She'd never been to a high school dance. Truthfully, she couldn't remember the last time she danced. What if she made a fool of herself? Maybe there wouldn't be any *real* dancing. They would chaperone his niece, not act like two teens trying to keep up with all the moves.

No matter how hard she wanted not to think about it, her mind drifted to the last few weeks and the hearing. Things had changed drastically. Ivy was found guilty not just for abduction with the intent to kill, but for two counts of first degree murder. The evidence against her in Holly's case was overwhelming. Connor had gotten her to admit to everything. Not to mention they found her journals that had all the information in how she'd murdered both Holly and Larry. Because of the terms in the plea deal the prosecution offered, Ivy finally admitted to murdering both, Holly and Larry. Even after everything she'd done, Connor didn't want her to die, and the only way to get the death penalty off the table was for her to confess. Because she had given the prosecution her testimony and her crazy behavior, she would be spending her life in a mental hospital.

Starla agreed that Ivy shouldn't face the death penalty and was relieved that the court had given her another option. Austin might have felt like her death was his fault. The thought alone caused her to shiver. But there was to be no more bad thoughts. Right now, all she wanted to do was think about her date with Connor. She smiled.

"Hello." Her grandmother's voice came through the door. "Can I come in and take a peek?"

"Of course, you can come in! I love the dress, but I'm not sure if this color works for me." As she turned toward her grandmother, she studied her approving smile.

"Oh, sweetie, you look precious."

"Precious?" Starla tilted her head. "Not sure if that's the reaction I was going for." She laughed.

"Well, you are going to be around high school children. I think you look gorgeous, but I have something that would look great on you. Let me get it for you."

Starla once again looked at the green dress. With its raw-edge appliqués layered over a shimmering linen-blend material and the rounded neck with Baroque-inspired filigree, the dress was feminine and showed off her waist. Okay, so it *did* look good.

A few minutes later, her grandmother waltzed back in the room holding a box. "My mother gave this to me when I got married, and now I want you to have it." She handed the dark velvet box to Starla.

With ease, Starla opened it. "Oh, my heavens. This is beautiful." She swallowed back emotions.

"It's a real pearl necklace surrounded by small, but genuine, diamonds. They'll go nicely with that dress."

"I've never had anything so elegant." Starla ran her fingers across the pearls and diamonds.

"Let me help you put it on." Her grandmother's voice quivered.

With her grandmother's help, Starla slipped it on as unshed tears welled up in her eyes. "Thank you so much. It's perfect."

"It's like it was made for you." Hialeah turned Starla around. "You look stunning."

The moment was broken as a knock on the door resonated through the house. "I bet that's your date." Hialeah winked. "I'll go let that young man in. Come out when you're ready."

Starla had no clue why her stomach felt jittery. Even though she and Connor had spent almost every day together since they met, they had yet to go on a *date*, date. She didn't know how to explain it, but she felt like she'd always known Connor. They hadn't done much since that one afternoon, but that was mainly because Austin now lived with Connor. But Austin was with Connor's brother and sister-in-law tonight, so they had the whole evening to go out.

"Starla, your handsome date is waiting for you." Her grandmother's voice outside the bedroom door, pulled her from her thoughts.

"Okay, I'm ready." After one last glance in the mirror, she grabbed her wrap from the bed, her pocket book from the night stand, and took a deep breath. Tonight, was a night to celebrate. Connor had Austin and Starla was cancer-free. Those were happy things.

The minute she stepped out into the living room, her throat became dry and the pounding in her chest went into overdrive. Oh, holy wow, her heart would never be the same. She inhaled, and had tiny, tingling sensations running through her veins. It was like she was breathing in electricity.

A sudden gust of wind swept in through the windows, and she heard the low rumble of thunder in the distance, but that didn't stop Connor from gazing into her eyes. "You look incredible." He swallowed hard and inspected her dress with what appeared to be absolute approval.

"You clean up pretty nice yourself." She scanned him from top to bottom and loved the black leather vest with the white shirt opened in the front. She took in how his black jeans fit tightly, showing off his narrow hips, and his boots matched his Stetson cowboy hat.

Hialeah walked back into the living room with a camera in her hand. "Okay, you two, stand close. I want to take a few pictures and don't give me a hard time," she ordered.

After about six pictures, Connor took Starla's hand. "Okay, we best be taking off. I can't leave Megan alone too long at the dance or her daddy will come hunt me down and shoot me.

When Starla hugged Hialeah, she saw the sparkle of happiness in her grandmother's eyes. "You both have a great evening." She hugged Connor as well.

The night air was crisp when they stepped out on the front porch. Starla gazed up at the partially cloudy evening that promised rain. The sun was sinking down behind the mountains. There were streaks of orange and pink that shimmered across the sky like a painting.

Connor opened the truck door. "Here you go, little lady." When she was inside, he closed the door, walked around, and hiked himself up into his seat. "Well, ma'am, are you ready for a night of chaperoning teenagers?"

"I am." Starla chuckled as he started the engine.

Once they arrived at the high school and parked, Starla took in her surroundings and was impressed with the size of the place. She had expected a much smaller school. The lawn was manicured, and trees were scattered about. Outdoor stairs led to the front of the brick building. A few girls in different colored dresses and guys in jeans and formal shirts stood in the courtyard laughing. There were a few couples holding hands and some taking selfies.

"This is a really lovely high school," Starla said.

"It is, isn't it? Even though it's been around for many years, they've kept it up nicely." He took out his keys. "There are quite a few kids in this town."

"Did you and..." She paused.

He nodded. "She was a cheerleader and I was a jock." He climbed out of the truck and opened the door for Starla. Connor placed his hand on the small of her back as they climbed the stairs. A few seconds later they walked down a hallway, until they reached a set of opened double doors.

"Wow," Starla uttered as they stepped inside. "This is enchanting."

Connor nodded. "It's nice. They always go all out for these big school events."

Starla looked up at the glowing golden stars and moons that hung from the ceiling. Somehow, they had made it look like clouds were hovering above them and even had little twinkling lights inside. Never had she imagined a high school event could be so elegant.

"Uncle Connor," Megan called out while she rushed toward them. She was pulling a guy who was obviously her date behind her. "Hi." She glanced between Connor and Starla. "I'd like you to meet Eli. Eli, this is my Uncle Connor and his girlfriend, Miss Starla."

Starla almost corrected her, but she let it slide. "Nice to meet you, Eli."

Connor stepped forward and stuck out his hand. "Hi, Eli, you intend showing my niece a good time tonight, I take it?"

"Yes, sir, I mean, Connor... sir." Eli shifted from one foot to the other. "I'm happy you came so Megan could be my date."

Megan's entire face lit up. "Thank you, Uncle Connor and Miss Starla." She hugged her uncle and surprised Starla when she hugged her, too. "You look amazing in that dress, by the way," Megan whispered as they embraced.

"Thank you, Megan. You look beautiful, too." Megan's dress was a gorgeous shade of blue that matched the color of her eyes. Her hair was pulled to one side and held in place with a beautiful hair comb. "That color is perfect on you."

"Thank you. There is punch and snacks on the far side of the wall. We already had some. It's really good." She paused and stared at Connor. "Is it okay if we go hang with Emma and Paul? We will stay inside."

"Sure." Connor winked. "I better not see any funny business." He laughed.

Megan's cheeks flushed as she nodded. "Okay, Uncle Connor." She took Eli's hand and they dashed in the other direction, but not before Megan called out her uncle's name, one last time as she signed I love you. By the look on his face it was obvious the gesture made Connor's heart melt. How could a girl not fall in love with him? He was kind and gentle, yet all man.

"Your niece is adorable." Starla touched his arm as he looked deeply into her eyes.

"Thank you." He put his hand on her back again, leading her across the room to the punch and the snacks.

After a few minutes of comfortable silence and listening to the ambient laughter, Starla took a sip of the raspberry punch Connor handed her.

"This is wonderful." She took a second sip and couldn't stop herself from licking her lips. When she glanced at Connor, he was staring at her mouth with a look of desire etched on his face.

He moved closer. "Have I told you how sexy you are?" His voice was deep and raspy.

"I'm not sure you've used those exact words." Heat crawled up her neck.

The soft flow of music fell over the room and the lights flickered across the wall. Connor reached out, took the cup out of her hand, and set it on a nearby table.

Without a word, he swept her toward the dance floor and then stilled. His gaze raked over her as he pulled her close. Her heart raced when she inhaled his woodsy and manly scent. Now she knew what it would be like to drown, because she was drowning in desire,

The warmth that started at her neck grew inside her the minute he wrapped her in his arms. The way they moved in sync made her heart thump to the beat of the music. There was no need for words to express what they were feeling. Yet, they were determined to maintain a mature front for the kids. With each slow song that came on, Starla's insides were on fire and there was no doubt Connor knew.

When the night came to an end, Starla was happy that it was over. Her heart couldn't have taken another hour of restraint. Her body was hot and the chill in the air did nothing to extinguish the flames.

Connor helped Starla into the truck. "You can sit next to me if you want," he said with a grin. Then moving extra close, he helped her with the seat belt. "Megan can sit next to the window." His breath whispered against her cheek.

Starla grinned. "Thank you for tonight."

"You're welcome and thank you for coming with me." His eyes glided across her face and landed on her lips.

A few minutes later he moved around the truck and slid inside. Once he closed the door, she noticed that he studied his niece while she talked to Eli. Connor was obviously taking his role seriously.

Megan started running toward them, dragging Eli with her. Connor held up his finger to Starla, then stepped out of the truck, so she rolled down the window to hear what was going on.

When Megan reached her uncle, she held up her hand and wiggled her finger, which glittered with an oversized ring. "I'm going steady, Uncle Connor. Look Eli gave me his class ring." She was so excited she jumped into his arms.

"Congratulations, sweetie." He gave her a giant hug. "I hate to burst your bubble, but a little word to the wise…" He released her from their embrace, but still held her at arm's-length as he glanced down. "Tell your mom first." He chuckled. "Let *her* tell your daddy."

Megan's eyes twinkled. "Oh, I will. I'm going to hide this ring if Daddy's still awake." She glanced at her finger as she held the ring to her heart.

"If he's still awake." Connor cracked up. "Oh, he'll be awake, alright. Now, let's get you home before he sends out a search team."

Connor reached out and shook Eli's hand. "Congratulations, young man. I take it you'll be good to my niece."

The guy gulped and nodded. "Yes, sir. I will be very good to her." His face flushed.

"You better never hurt her. Or you'll deal with me."

"Uncle Connor." Megan touched his arm. "Eli would never do that."

"He better not. You have a good night now, Eli." He shook Eli's hand once more.

Poor Eli looked like he was ready to run away until Megan smiled. She watched as he got that puppy dog, in-love look on his face, and it was then Starla knew the kid was crazy for Megan. It was so adorable.

As soon as Connor and Megan climbed inside the truck, they took off. Judging by the dreamy look on Megan's face, Starla knew she was head-over-heels for the guy. She reminisced back to when she had thought she'd been in love like that, but her high school romance ended in total heartbreak. Eli didn't seem like the kind of boy who would break a girl's heart, at least she hoped he wasn't. From what she could see, he was dedicated to Megan.

Both of Megan's parents stepped outside onto the porch right as they pulled in the driveway. While Duncan had a serious look on his face, Trudy was smiling from ear to ear.

Before she got out of the car, Megan surprised Starla again when she gave her another hug. "Thank you both for coming with me tonight." She took off the ring, slipped it into her tiny purse, and looked over at Connor. "Thank you, Uncle Connor."

"You're welcome, sweet pea. Now, go tell your parents what a wonderful time you had and that I'll pick up Austin before noon tomorrow."

Megan nodded before she dashed out of the truck up the stairs to her parents. Duncan waved goodbye as he turned and guided his daughter inside. Trudy lingered behind, mouthed "thank you", and blew a kiss.

They were mostly quiet during the ride through town. Starla was more than a little disappointed he was taking her back to her grandmother's. When they drove by the water she noticed how the glow from the moon reflected on the lake. All threats of the rain and storm were gone. It turned out to be such a beautiful night.

"I'd like to stop off at the lake and take a walk with you, if that's okay. Are you in a hurry to get home?" Connor asked.

"Not at all."

He parked near the water and shut off the engine. "I love this place at night. It's one of the reasons I could never leave here." Connor pulled out the keys and looked at Starla. "Have I told you how utterly stunning you look tonight?" he asked.

"A few times, actually." She reached for his hand. "But I don't mind hearing it again."

He gently pulled her closer. "Hello, you beautiful woman." Connor grinned.

"Hey," Starla whispered. She felt her heart race and her palms started to sweat the moment he touched her. For the first time, she noticed a small scar on Connor's upper lip. "What happened?" She reached up and ran her finger gently across the faded mark.

"I fell off my bike when I was five and busted my lip." He inched closer and held her gaze. "You smell like coconut and vanilla—good enough to eat."

Waiting for him to kiss her was becoming unbearable. "Connor," she whispered, but before she could form another word, his warm lips melted across her cool mouth. Oh, the taste was like berry pie with a hint of cream, and the sensation sent a current through her.

He inched back ever so slightly. "Yes, beautiful," he whispered into her lips, causing even more electricity to course through her veins. She moved her mouth back over his, parting it ever so slightly with her tongue.

After a few more seconds, Connor pulled back and cleared his throat. "Darlin', if we don't stop this and take a walk, I won't be able to get out of the truck."

Starla nodded and gave him a tiny grin. "I guess we better take a walk, then."

After he inhaled deeply, he opened the door for her and helped her out of the truck. The cool night breeze made her shiver, bringing back memories of the first night she arrived here. There was something about this place that took hold of her heartstrings and hadn't let go.

"I love it here." Starla gazed up at the trees and then out toward the moon-filled lake.

Connor nodded. "Me too. I want to show you one of my favorite spots." His voice was gentle as he took her hand and led her down the path to a wooden bridge. The way it crossed over the water was so lovely, and the only sounds were from their feet crunching on the gravel and a few birds chirping to each other. Every now and again, Starla could hear melodies from the windchimes hanging in the storefronts. It made everything even more in synchronicity.

Once they made it to the middle of the bridge, Connor stopped and pointed. "Look at the water."

Gazing down, she saw the largest golden fish she'd ever seen swimming just beneath the surface.

"What kind of fish is that? It's beautiful."

"They're called Butterfly Koi, but the amazing thing, is that they are native to Indonesia. No one knows how they got here."

"I've never seen anything like them. They're downright haunting."

Connor chuckled. "They sure are. Some people believe they are ghosts because of the way they glow."

Starla bent down further to get a closer look and noticed the fish seemed to know they were there. "They look like they're just hanging out here. They don't seem to want to go anywhere else."

"For good reason." Connor took her hand and crossed over the bridge. On the other side was a stand with a shovel stuffed inside of some pellet food. "They're waiting for us to feed them." He pulled out the shovel and filled two small bags. "Now we can give them their nightly treat."

"Do you always do this?" Starla asked as they walked back to the middle of the bridge.

"No, I haven't come out here in a long time." He became quiet and looked out over the water.

"I'm sorry, Connor. Is this what you did with Holly?"

When he turned to face her, his eyes were filled with sadness. "Yes. I wish it would stop hurting. I thought it would be okay to come here, and I want to be able to do this again, but it just hurts so much."

"You spent a big portion of your life with her. The pain might not ever go away. You can only make peace with it." Starla understood more than she would like to admit. She still felt the pain of losing her parents after all these years.

"I'm trying." He pulled her close and wrapped his arms around her, the bags still in his hands. "I want to move on."

"Wanting to be ready and being ready aren't the same thing." She inhaled. "And I might not be the best person to take that gamble with."

Connor set the bags down and placed his hands on her shoulders. "Why would you say that?" He stared into her eyes intently, as if he was searching for an answer.

"I've had cancer three times, and I'm leaving town soon. I have to get back to work."

"You're still going back to Louisville?" He appeared surprised.

"I need to get back to my catering business. Oliver can't run it alone."

Connor backed up a few steps and studied her expression. "I guess I let myself believe you were sticking around." His jaw tightened, and he looked back out at the lake. "I'm not worried about you having cancer, Starla. You've beat it three times, and this last time was without chemotherapy. You got the all-clear."

"But there will always be that threat," she softly said and moved closer to him.

"We better get you home," he said, abruptly taking her hand and starting toward the truck.

"Wait, Connor." The air suddenly felt frosty. "What about the fish? Aren't they waiting to be fed?"

He squinted and frowned, then begrudgingly picked the bags back up. "Okay, let's feed the fish," he said curtly.

"I had a wonderful time tonight. I wish I could stay in this town a little longer, but I've been gone too long as it is. Almost a full month."

His face softened. "I'm sorry. I understand you have to get back. I just don't want you to go."

"I don't want to go, either. I want more time. But we have over a week left until I have to leave." She stepped closer to him. "Can't we enjoy ourselves? It's not like I'll never return. I'm not that far away."

Connor slipped his arms around her and pulled her even closer. "You're right." He sighed. "I just don't think I knew how much I wanted more time with you until tonight."

Starla looked up into his denim-blue eyes and tried to swallow the lump in her throat. "What do you mean?"

"I want more, Starla—way more." He leaned down, only stopping when his lips were close to hers. "I want to be with you as much as possible. I want you to stay here and be a part of my town, my life, my world. I know we haven't known each other long, but when I'm with you, everything feels… *right*."

Starla nodded. "I think so, too."

"You could start up a catering business here, you know. We don't have one, and there are some empty storefronts on Hidden Valley Lane and Secret Valley Road." His pleading eyes melted her heart. "Rachel Ann is our local realtor. She could show you the properties. Would you be willing to at least look at the spaces and think about it?"

"I will, but I can't make any promises. I made a commitment to Oliver when we launched our business and he just got married."

"Okay, I do understand, but I would bet that Oliver would want you to follow your heart. I can call Rachel Ann tomorrow and see if she will meet with you, if that's okay?"

"Yes, that's fine." Starla chuckled and smacked his arm.

"What?" He grinned back at her.

"You are very persuasive, Mr. Whelan."

"You ain't seen nothing yet, Miss Starla Moon Holloway." He picked her up and swung her around.

The rest of the evening, they sat on the bridge under the moonlight, holding hands and watching the reflection of the night sky twinkle on the water. While they held hands, Connor skimmed his thumb across the backs of her fingers, sending sparks through her. How could something so simple do so much?

Every now and again, they'd both chuckle at a deep-croaking frog.

After a while, Connor pulled her closer and wrapped his arms around her tightly. "I don't want the night to end." He spoke in a quiet tone. "Can you stay with me tonight?"

"I didn't bring anything to wear." She looked down at her dress. "I don't think I'll want to wear this home tomorrow."

"I have some jeans and shirts in the spare room upstairs. There might even be some night gowns up there."

"Oh, okay. Are you sure that's not going to bother you?" She leaned her head on his shoulder. "I'd love to spend the night, but I don't want to make things harder for you."

"No, the clothes belonged to my sister. I was supposed to donate them for her, but I shoved them away instead and never got around to dropping them off after that." He stood. "Let's get going." He reached out for her hand and pulled her up.

When they arrived at his house and entered the front door, he held up his finger. "I have to go feed the cats. Would you like something to drink? I have iced tea, hot tea, and of course, coffee or fresh bottled water."

"I'll get some water while you feed the kitties. Would you like some?"

"I'll take some iced tea, if you don't mind."

"Not at all. I'll meet you back out here in the living room." She swallowed, feeling her heart pound.

"Sounds good. There are also some tea cookies my mom made. You'll see them on a covered plate on the counter."

"Sounds great." She made her way toward the kitchen while Connor walked to the mud room.

The minute she stepped into the kitchen, the sweet scent of spices permeated the air. The cookies had to be super fresh. The smell of vanilla made her mouth water. "Yum," she said quietly to herself.

Sweets were something she didn't have much of anymore, so this would be a big treat. She walked over, gathered them from the covered platter, and placed them on a small plate she found in the cabinet. It was amazing at how clean Connor kept his house. When she opened the icebox, she noticed how spotless everything was. Few bachelors were this neat. Of course, she would be the one to notice these things, the woman who could let nothing be out of order. When she pulled out the iced tea and poured a glass for Connor, she decided to have some. It smelled delicious and there were slices of lemon and lime floating inside.

Connor was standing by the window when Starla came out with

the cookies and tea. The lights were dim, and the fireplace was lit, which caused the shadows from the flames to flicker across the wall, creating a sensual ambience. He turned to face her, and their gazes locked. His eyes were so intense, and she realized for the first time they resembled a glowing blue moon. As if in slow motion, Connor moved toward her and took the tray out of her hand, then placed it on the chest used for a coffee table.

Her heart fell into a slow but steady rhythm. Their desire for one another was so palpable it was as if it hovered all around them, filling the room with passion and craving.

Nothing was said, but plenty was understood. Connor stepped closer to her, his lips hovering just inches from hers. She pressed against him, enjoying the feel of his breath and the scent of his musky fragrance.

With ease, he wrapped his arms around her and unzipped her dress with the gentlest touch she'd ever felt. There was no misunderstanding what was about to happen, and she wanted it with every bit of her heart.

The minute the dress hit the floor, she remembered she was only wearing a pair of white panties and a bra to match—there was no slip.

His eyes scanned over every inch of her. "Starla." His voice dropped until it was practically inaudible. "You are breathtakingly gorgeous." His fingers trailed down her neck, and then she felt them slide slowly down her arms and hands.

Starla couldn't stand the anticipation—her insides were ready to explode. She reached up, grabbed the front of his shirt, and started taking it off, one button at a time. Not once did they take their eyes off each other. It wasn't long before Connor gathered her up in his arms and she wrapped her legs around him. With a swift move, he grabbed a throw from the back of the couch and carried her in front of the fireplace.

He put down the blanket and laid her on top. Starla watched as he retrieved their ice tea and placed it nearby on the floor. When he glanced at her, she felt her entire body shiver. It wasn't until he slipped off his pants that her heart thumped like a native drum.

Never had she seen anyone so beautiful. He eased next to her and stared at her breasts. What would happen when he saw the scars? What if they turned him off? He slid his hand up her back toward the clasp and was about to remove it when she caught his fingers.

"Wait, I need to tell you something before you do that." Her voice tremored. "I have a few scars, and they're not pretty."

He gave her a small smile. "Would you like to see mine? I have more than a few."

He gently moved her hand away from his and unclasped her bra. She closed her eyes when it fell to the floor, leaving her bare and exposed. There was no way she could handle seeing the disappointment in his eyes.

"Oh, Starla," He turned her face toward him. "Open your eyes. You are perfect." He placed his lips on hers, giving her a kiss filled with hope and promises. Then, with a whisper of a touch, he gently ran his fingers across her scars, touching each one.

"I'm sorry." She inched away, recoiling from his gaze.

"Starla, let me love every part of you. You should be proud," he said as he pointed to the scars. "They tell the story of the battle you fought through the fire and pain, and the fact is, you won."

Her eyes filled with tears. "We don't know that for sure," she murmured.

"Yes, we do. You've won, and you are my hero." He pulled her up so she was sitting, topless, in front of him. She started to cover her breasts, but he held her hands. "You are beautiful just the way you are. I love everything about you."

That did it. Tears streamed down her cheeks as she reached up and cupped his face. "I love everything about you, too."

He ran his thumb under her eyes, wiping away her tears. Then, he guided her backwards on the blanket. It was as if the flames from the fireplace flickered in his eyes when he slid off her panties. Never had she let a man examine her in the manner she was allowing him. Without looking away from her, he stood and pulled off his pants. He was the most perfect man she'd ever seen. Even with the scars on his leg and chest, he was flawless. When he settled down next to her, he pulled her back into his arms.

The heat from his skin made her feel the overpowering urge to make love with him, and she didn't want to slow down—she wanted him *now*. In a move that surprised even herself, she took his hand and showed him what she wanted. It was instantly clear that she wouldn't have to beg or tell him anything. The flames had already been ignited.

❧ 21 ❧

THE MORNING LIGHT FILTERING THROUGH THE CURTAINS WOKE STARLA. She wasn't sure what time it was, nor did she know when they'd finally fallen asleep. She'd never made love with a man three times in one night before. If she were being honest, she had always thought sex was overrated. But what she experienced with Connor, made her know if anything, it was underrated. He knew what he was doing and made sure she was over the moon before he would stop. The sound of his breathing told her he was still asleep, so she took his shirt, slipped it on, and snuck out of the room. The shower was calling her name.

Once she entered the bathroom, she hung his shirt on the wall rack, turned on the water, and stepped into the oversized shower. The showerhead was gigantic, and the water came down in a pulsating motion that warmed her to the bone. The entire enclosure was so large that a person could have a small party inside and still have room for more, which made her wonder how often Connor invited women to join him.

Why was she feeling so sad? As she took the liquid soap and

lathered it down her body, for reasons she didn't understand, she cried. Before she could collect herself, a set of arms wrapped around her.

"Did I do something wrong?" Connor's voice was gentle. "Did I hurt you or make you feel bad?"

"Are you kidding me." She turned to face him and gave a tiny smile. "You did everything perfectly and the truth is, I had never experienced an Orgasm before last night."

He tilted his head in question and lifted her chin. "I don't understand, you never had that experience before?"

"No, never. I'm happy and I feel good. I think I'm just overwhelmed with all these emotions. I've never felt so many, this strong at once before."

"Starla, I'm falling for you, but I'm scared, too." He paused and took a deep breath. "I never thought I could have these types of feelings again, and you're leaving." He pulled her closer to him. "Please don't leave. Please stay here."

The sincerity in his eyes and the sound of his voice melted her heart into a big puddle, and all her strength went right down the drain. "I need time to think—to see where I fit in."

"But, you said you'd look at those properties. Will you still go?"

She was feeling pressured and didn't know how to tell him but would need to figure it out. Her business with Oliver meant the world to her. Could she just walk away? Did she even want to? She had said she'd at least *look* at the places…

She nodded. "Yes, I'll still look."

"In the meantime," he said as he backed her against the shower wall, "let's see if I can sway you with another kind of temptation and help you catch up on a few things."

"I think you play dirty." Starla giggled.

"Oh, yes I do. Let me show you some really dirty tricks." He groaned and went down to his knees.

CONNOR HELD STARLA'S HAND AS THEY WALKED UP TO THE EMPTY storefront. All he wanted was for her to stay, but he knew he shouldn't pressure her, she had hinted that he was doing that. She had a life back in Louisville, and as much as he wanted her here with him, he wouldn't ask her again. The fact was, she knew how he felt, and now the ball was in her court. Her hint came through loud and clear on the ride over.

After spending a few minutes standing in front of the empty space, Starla started looking around.

"I do really love it here. It's so different from what I'm used to, and the people are so friendly. I can see why nobody wants to leave and just look at this view." She waved toward the lake. "Who wouldn't want to be here daily. It's so tempting."

"Hello." Connor heard Rachel Ann greet them as she approached. "Sorry I'm late." Jesus, the woman's choice of clothing was wild. She wore leopard-print pants with a short crop top that showed off her waist.

Connor almost laughed when he saw Starla's eyes widen.

"I was on a date and had to leave him early and he still wanted more." She smiled at Starla and winked at Connor.

"Well, bless my heart, Connor. You just keep getting more handsome. How is that possible?" She gave him a big hug, and then turned to Starla.

"I'm Rachel Ann, and you must be Starla. I heard the story about how your car broke down and then everything that happened with that awful girl, Ivy. I even heard that you'd found your grandmother, completely by chance. You've been through a lot." She held out her hand. "Some awful and some downright good. It's so nice to meet you."

Starla smiled and took her hand. "It's nice to meet you, too."

"Well, let's get ourselves in this place so I can show you around." She stuck the key inside the lock to the glass door and turned it, opening the door so the three of them could enter the space.

Just after they'd stepped inside, Connor felt Starla's body go completely slack and caught her right before she hit the ground.

"What the hell?" He held Starla in his arms, but she was nonresponsive. "Call 9-1-1. Starla, honey, wake up."

Rachel Ann dialed on her phone. "Can we get an ambulance, this is Rachel Ann. I'm with a female who has passed out over at the old Rusty Nail. Yes, please hurry. She's breathing right, Connor?"

"Yes, but something's not right. She's out cold." Connor tried to wake her again. "Starla, can you hear me?"

"She's breathing, but she's not conscious." It was like she was sleeping. His stomach turned when he wondered if the cancer had come back. Rachel Ann hung up and stood next to Connor, who remained on the floor, holding Starla.

"Is she pregnant?" She arched her brow.

"No, that would be impossible. She has been fighting cancer, though," he said without thinking.

"Oh, no." Unshed tears coated her lashes. "How serious?"

"She's had breast cancer three times, but her doctors thought she'd beat it this time."

"Sounds just like what happened with my Harry," she said and touched Starla's face. "They told him it was gone, and then the next thing we knew, it had spread through his body. That's one of the reasons we moved here. We wanted to spend whatever time he had left in peace and with nature."

The mention of nature made Connor wonder about Hialeah and the springs. "Did you ever try any of the hot springs or see Hialeah to treat his cancer?"

"No, you know how Harry was. He didn't want to do anything other than what those doctors in the city told him to." She wiped away a tear. "They pumped his body full of chemotherapy, and after a while, he decided he wanted to stop doing that. After he pulled the plug on his treatment, the cancer spread everywhere. He thought he had won for four short months. Then the nausea came back."

Just as they heard the siren, Starla's eyes fluttered. "It's okay, sweetheart. The ambulance is here." Connor brushed the hair out of her face. "We are going to get you all fixed up."

"Connor? What happened?" Starla opened her eyes, looking confused.

"You passed out, so we called for help."

Before he could say anything more, three big paramedics came inside carrying bags, a machine, and a stretcher.

Connor kissed her forehead and stood, giving them room. One was his football buddy from high school, Foster, who was moving toward her and nodded.

"Hey, Connor. So, what is going on?" He hooked her up to a monitor. "What's your name, sweetie?" he asked.

"Starla Holloway. I don't know what happened. From what Connor told me, I guess I passed out." A worried expression crossed her face. "I've had cancer in the past, but my last tests came back negative for cancerous cells."

Connor spoke up. "She just slumped down out of the blue and I caught her."

"Bless her heart. We were so worried." Rachel Ann gave a tiny grin.

"I'm so sorry to have caused all this trouble. I think I'm okay." She glanced between Rachel Ann and Connor.

"We still need to take you in so you can get checked out by a doctor." Foster winked and gave her his one-of-a-kind charming smile, just like he had in high school when he'd wanted to pick up a girl.

Starla's cheeks flushed. "Okay, but I am feeling much better now."

Foster turned to the other two paramedics. "Well, boys, let's get this beautiful lady in the ambulance and take her to the hospital." The tall guy with the stretcher, who wore a name tag that read Rob, brought it right next to her. "Let's get her on here."

"I can stand." Starla moved, but Foster shook his head."

"No, that's our job." On the count of three, they all lifted her onto the gurney. "Connor, do you want to follow us?" Foster asked.

"Yes." He nodded and gave Starla the best smile he could achieve. "Rachel Ann, is there any way you could go out to Hialeah's place and let her know what's going on? She doesn't have a phone. Do you know where she lives?"

"Of course, honey, I've been out to see her many times. I was fixin' to ask you if you wanted me to do that, anyway. You know, she really needs to get a landline hooked up out there."

"She does," Connor agreed.

"Don't worry, sugar. I'll make the trip out there right now."

"Thank you," Connor said and sailed out the door.

Heading through town past the church, he pulled into Valley Lake Hospital behind the ambulance. It had never been a busy place, so he knew Starla would get the best, top-priority care. Worry plagued his mind. What if the cancer had come back, or what if they'd made a mistake and it actually spread? His stomach turned. Starla was right when she said there would always be cause to worry.

After he parked, he rushed through the glass doors toward the emergency room. Nobody was in the waiting area—not one soul, he dashed up to the front desk. Terry, the receptionist, still looked sixteen. Her red hair was still frizzy, and she still wore what appeared to be the same glasses perched on the end of her nose. "Terry, where is Starla?"

Glancing up, she smiled. "Hi, Connor, she's in room twelve. She's our only patient right now, so she's getting the best care possible and our undivided attention." Terry hit a button and the doors buzzed right before they opened. "Go on back. I know you guys have been seeing each other."

"Thanks." He took off down the hall, following the numbers to the right. Times like this he was sure glad he lived in a small town.

Once he rounded the corner, he saw the room. Nobody was with her that minute, so he rushed to the side of her bed.

"Hey," he said and made sure to smile.

Nervously, she glanced up. "Hi Connor." Her lip trembled.

The sounds of the door opening, and the squeaking wheels of a wheelchair being rolled in the room caused them both to look in the same direction.

It was an older nurse with a big grin. "Okay, we are taking you down for some tests." She smiled at Connor and almost melted his heart. "You might have a long wait." Her name tag read Sharon—a big lady with gray hair.

"That's okay. I need to pick up Austin, anyway." He looked at Starla. "I'll come right back as soon as I'm done, okay?"

Starla nodded when he leaned over and kissed her cheek. "Take good care of her," he said to the nurse. "I'm Connor by the way and it's nice to meet you." He watched her cheeks turn rosy."

22

STARLA AND THE NURSE WATCHED CONNOR STRUT OUT OF THE ROOM.

Sharon smiled. "Well, goodness gracious. I've heard about this man, but I've only seen him from a distance." After she helped Starla into the wheelchair, Sharon pushed her out of the room.

"He's even better up close and personal," Starla said.

"I can see that." Sharon laughed. "We are going to be running a lot of tests, so you should try to relax. Everything is going to be just fine." She glanced down at Starla and gave her a big, confident smile.

Starla wished she could believe that, but she'd never fainted out of the blue before, unless she was doing chemotherapy. So why would this happen now? The only thing that made sense was that the cancer must have come back, and it was probably bad.

Three hours later, Starla was finally back in her room. They had run every test known to man and checked every part of her body. She was exhausted, but at least this way they'd have the results right away. Her stomach turned while she waited for what she knew had to be bad news.

Just as she closed her eyes, she heard footsteps and saw Connor and Austin entering the room.

Connor smiled, and Austin rushed to her bedside. "Hi, Miss Starla. Do you feel better yet?"

She nodded and took his little hand in hers. "I am doing okay." She brushed his brown curls from his eyes. "But you being here makes me feel so much better."

His eyes sparkled. "It does?" He was precious.

"Of course, it does."

His eyes filled with unshed tears. "I like it when I make people feel better instead of getting on someone's nerves."

Starla's heart broke and she fell even more in love with him. The poor little guy didn't know how special he was. "You would *never* get on my nerves." She motioned for him to come closer and gave him a soft kiss on his cheek.

"Austin." Connor touched his arm. "Why don't you go right down the hall and buy yourself a soda and some kind of treat. I want to talk to Miss Starla about boring adult stuff. Can you do that, son?"

"Yeah, I saw the vending machines when we came in." He gave Connor a small smile.

"Okay, you stay there and don't wander off, okay?"

Connor handed him a bunch of change. "Not too many sweets, now."

Austin nodded and practically ran out of the room.

"We are going to have to work on that boy's low self-esteem. But given the way he was treated, it's no wonder why he thinks the way he does. He still has nightmares." Connor pulled up a chair and moved it closer to Starla.

"It might take some time to really figure out everything he's been through," she said.

Just as Connor had settled down in his chair, the doctor walked in. His white hair matched his jacket, and he had a look of seriousness in his gray eyes. Starla wanted to stand up and yell but refrained.

Connor turned toward her. "Do you want me to stay or leave?"

"Please stay," she pleaded. She felt like her nerves were bolting through her veins.

"Hi." The doctor nodded to Connor and moved to stand at the end of Starla's bed. He glanced between Starla and Connor, then he looked down at the clipboard and flipped through some pages.

"Well, it appears that you, young lady, haven't been drinking enough fluids and that can be serious."

"Wait, that's it? There is no cancer?" Starla blurted out.

"Nothing. Everything came back clean." He stared into her eyes, and Starla knew he was telling the truth.

"You really didn't see anything?" She gulped air and felt dizzy again. "Why did I faint? Was it just because I was low on fluids?"

"Starla, you've been under a lot of stress." He patted her foot. "You were kidnapped, for starters, and the only abnormality in your bloodwork indicated that you are severely dehydrated. You need to drink plenty of water and make sure you are getting enough rest, but other than that, you have a clean bill of health."

"I *have* been through a lot lately, and that hasn't been helped by the fact that I don't like drinking water," she explained.

Connor smiled. "That's great news, doc." He moved closer to Starla and took her hand. "When can she come home?"

"I would say she'll be cleared to go home sometime tomorrow. We want to get you hydrated and you need to rest, so let us get all your electrolytes in balance. Then, my dear, you can be discharged."

"Thank you." Starla couldn't help but smile. "I'll make sure to drink plenty of water and get a lot of rest."

The doctor smiled. "Good. Make sure she does that," he said as he looked over at Connor.

"Oh, you can bank on that," Connor said.

Taking a deep breath Starla collected her emotions. "Nothing there?" Gratitude blossomed through her heart. "I have no cancer?"

"We will send all the tests to your doctors, but we couldn't find a thing." He patted her foot and left the room but turned back. 'Starla, your readings do all look wonderful."

"Wow. Thank you, Doctor."

Connor ran his hand down his face as the doctor left the room. "This is great news. I admit, you gave me a scare."

"I'm sorry." She motioned for him to lean closer so she could give him a tender kiss. "Am I forgiven now?" She smiled.

"Oh, yes, ma'am." He lightly brushed his tongue across her bottom lip.

"Maybe you should go check on Austin. I don't want him thinking he was getting on our nerves."

"Okay." He kissed her again. "I'll go check on him and bring him back."

As she watched Connor walk away, she realized there was no way she could accurately put into words how happy she was in that moment.

The next day, Starla was released before noon, and she was sure glad about that. Even though she had only been in the hospital for a short time, she'd already lost track of how many people visited her. Never had she imagined so many folks taking an interest in her health. She received a lot of flowers and did not know where she was going to put all of them. Her grandmother had stayed for a long time, but she eventually needed to get home so she could tend to Shadow. He was still a little weak even after all this time, but he was doing much better than before.

Starla sat in the truck between Connor and Austin, and her heart melted when Austin reached over to hold her hand.

"Miss Starla, I'm so glad you're all better and you don't have cancer." He gazed up at her with his big, brown eyes. "I was mighty worried."

Oh, my heavens, Austin was becoming just as charming as Connor —maybe more so. "Thank you, Austin. Just having you with me has made me feel so much better."

His smile widened.

"Hey, now. Don't y'all forget I'm here." Connor chuckled. "I hope, I helped some, too."

Starla leaned over to Connor and rested her head on his shoulder. "You helped a lot." She smiled and felt like she was home. In the city, she'd never felt like she belonged—not once. But right here and now, she was exactly where she wanted to be. How in the world would she ever leave these two? She couldn't even begin to think about saying goodbye to her grandmother and the rest of the wonderful people who had become so endearing to her. That's why she'd made a call to Oliver, but she wasn't sure about the outcome.

Connor pulled into Logan's Grill. "Now, I'm treating you both to a wonderful lunch." He parked the truck and stared at a short heavy man walking with a tall blonde.

"Who's that?" Starla asked.

"That's the mayor, and I think that's his new lady friend." He shook his head. "Be prepared for a lot of chatter when we walk in."

"Why?" Starla saw Austin cock his head like he wondered what was going on, too.

"Well, the ink on his divorce papers ain't even dry yet." He turned off the engine and pulled out the keys.

"Uncle Connor, what kind of ink takes that long to dry? My ink is dry right away. I could loan him my pen."

Connor cracked up and ruffled Austin's hair. "That's mighty kind of you, Austin, but that was just a metaphor."

"Oh." Austin stared at Connor. "What's a metaphor?"

Starla smiled and explained. "It's just a saying, like: "We are all shadows on the wall of time" is an example. See, we aren't really shadows, so that means it's a metaphor."

Connor nodded and smiled.

"What does it mean, Miss Starla?"

"Well, I take it to mean that we are all merely passing through this world for a short time, we are all the same. We all cast shadows on the wall if we stand in the right spot. No shadow is brighter or more colorful than the next."

Connor touched her arm. "Now, I'm impressed."

"I'm confused." Austin scrunched up his nose and they all laughed.

ॐ

A FEW MINUTES LATER, THEY WALKED INTO LOGAN'S GRILL, AND SURE enough, there was no missing the hushed whispers and people looking out the window toward where the Mayor and his lady were standing outside of what must be his car, showing off their new *friendship*.

Connor shook his head. "Oh boy, I bet the town is going to have a special meeting about this."

Just then, Logan came up. "Well, look who we have here." He glanced at Austin and Starla. "This is the way I like to start my day. A beautiful woman and," he leaned down and touched Austin's nose, "A real-life cowboy. What more could a guy ask for?"

"I am a real-life cowboy." Austin grinned. "I can ride a horse and everything."

"You can?" Logan arched his shoulders. "Then I think I better get y'all the best seat in the house. It's reserved for real cowboys only. Follow me." He picked up the menus and Connor had to grin when he noticed how Starla's eyes twinkled with laughter.

And, indeed, they got the best seats in the whole joint. Austin was proudly walking tall with his brown curly hair hanging around his face and his cowboy boots on. Connor couldn't help but feel that his life was complete with Austin and Starla by his side. If only she'd stay.

Starla and Austin were coloring together on the placemat when Connor noticed Ella and Dedra's heads appeared fused together as they spoke in whispers. Were they talking about them or the mayor? It didn't matter. They were two gossipy busybodies, anyway.

Starla glanced up at him and took his breath away. There was only one way to describe how he felt about her—he was in love, plain and simple. He couldn't take his eyes off her and he adored how much she cared for Austin. Then the waitress approached the table, pulling his mind back to food, and she pulled a pencil from behind her ear to take their order. Her name was Raylene, and she had been a waitress there since he was a little boy. She was chubby and cute as heck with her snow-white hair and piercing green eyes.

"What can I get for y'all this morning?" She smiled and looked around the table.

Starla made a face. "We haven't even looked at these menus. I'm sorry."

"You know what I want, Raylene," Connor said.

"I sure do. You want the Grand Slam with extra pancakes. How about we get Austin the Jr. Grand Slam?"

Austin looked up from coloring. "Does that come with pancakes and it's okay if we have breakfast for lunch?"

"It sure is. And, it comes with big pancakes." Raylene smiled. "And hot chocolate with extra marshmallows, too."

"That sounds great, thank you." Austin went back to coloring.

"And how about for you, Starla, breakfast or lunch?" Raylene smiled at her warmly.

"I'll have the same thing Connor is having." She licked her lips, and Connor had to shift around in his seat. Lord, the things that woman did to him.

"Well, y'all made that really easy on me." She winked and took their menus. "Any coffee for you two?"

They both nodded as they watched how careful Austin was coloring, staying inside the lines. A few minutes later, Raylene was back with their coffee, hot chocolate, and orange juice.

"Thank you," Connor said and Starla followed suit when Raylene placed their drinks on the table.

"Connor, how'd the waitress know my name?" Starla seemed perplexed.

"Darlin, everyone knows your name, now. You're somewhat of a celebrity around here." Connor wanted to bite his tongue off when the words left his mouth. Her fame stemmed mainly from her involvement in bringing down Ivy, but that wasn't something he would ever say in front of Austin.

"Famous? Why in the world would *I* be famous?" She chuckled.

"You beat cancer," he said quickly even though he knew it was a partial lie.

"And because you helped the cops arrest my mama," Austin said matter-of-factly without taking his eyes off his coloring. "Also, because Uncle Connor is in love with you and nobody thought he'd ever fall in love again," he added without missing a beat as he continued to color.

Connor felt his face flush and changed the subject. "Wow, this coffee is really good." He blew on the cup and took his first sip.

"Really?" Starla chuckled. "Well, I hope you two handsome men don't mind if I step outside and make a quick call. I need to call Oliver. I'll be right back."

Connor's heart sank, and all he could do was nod. One minute he was feeling as happy as a clam, and the next minute he felt like his heart sank into the pits of hell. Now that the cancer was gone, she'd be returning to work, and the city, even sooner. He tried to hide his disappointment, but Austin was already staring at him.

"Are you okay, Uncle Connor?" Austin studied his face.

"Yes, and no." He decided to be honest. "I'm going to miss the dickens out of Starla."

"Why?" He stopped coloring. "Is she going somewhere?"

"Yes, son. She has to go home. She runs a business in the city, and they need her back." Connor watched Austin's eyes fill with tears.

"I don't want her to leave." He looked out the window and Connor's heart broke when he saw the pained look on his face. He hadn't thought about how attached Austin was getting to Starla.

"We'll go see her and she'll come to see us. But she has to get back to work."

"Why? We need her. I need her and so do you."

Before Connor had to answer, Raylene came over and topped off his coffee.

"Where is Starla?" Raylene asked. "Is she coming back?"

"Yes, here she comes now." He nodded his head toward her. "She had to make a call."

"Ah," Raylene said and then moved to the next table.

Immediately after Starla sat back down next to Connor, Austin stared at her. "Please don't leave us, Miss Starla."

Connor felt like a heel. He had already asked her twice. What if she thought he'd put Austin up to saying that? It wasn't fair to her.

"I explained it to you, son," Connor said. "She has to get back to work." He gave Starla an apologetic look.

Her smile was sweet and soft. "Austin, honey." She tried to take his hand.

"No." He put his hands over his ears "I don't want to hear anything." Tears traveled down his flushed cheeks.

Starla leaned over and gently moved his hands away from his ears and cupped his face. "I have a surprise for you," she whispered.

"I don't want a surprise." He shook his head.

Connor had to correct him. "Now, Austin. You don't talk to adults like that," he scolded.

More tears rolled down his face.

"Well, if you'd both listen, I was about to tell you I'm not going anywhere."

"What?" they both said in unison.

"I called Oliver from the hospital and I talked with him again just now. I wanted to know if he would be able to buy me out but had to wait on a transfer to go through before he could determine how much he could offer. I only wanted back what I put in, but he wouldn't hear of it. He has a friend who is a commercial agent and he told Oliver what the business was worth in the current market. He's buying me out at half market value in payments to me. They are drafting a contract and will send it to me to sign online. It should be ready tomorrow. There was no way I could leave my two favorite guys."

Connor couldn't help himself. He stood up, pulled her up with him, and swung her around as he whooped and hollered. "She's not leaving! She's staying here, which I think means she's my girl."

Austin got up and joined the fun. "She's my girl, too." He pumped his fist in the air.

The entire place whistled and clapped with them. Living in a small town could be a pain, but all the love and support from so many familiar faces made him realize there was no place on earth he'd rather be than in Secret Valley River.

Starla's cheeks were cherry red as Raylene came up to the table carrying a tray loaded with all the food. "Well, now, y'all better save some room for dessert. This is a day to celebrate." She laughed.

"It sure is, Raylene." Connor embraced Austin and Starla. "This is a big day." When he laughed, joy filled his heart.

§

LATER THAT SEPTEMBER, ON A COOL, BRISK DAY, STARLA STEPPED outside and waved to Tracy, a new friend and the owner of the local coffee house. Starla noticed how long her legs were and how very tall she looked in her ski pants and white shirt. Her short, spiked hair was chestnut brown, and she was cute as heck. Somehow, she just looked like a coffee house owner. Starla smiled. "How's it going? Are you close to opening?"

Tracy called out, "Getting there. We should be open before Halloween."

Starla strolled down the street and joined her.

"The town is so excited to have a local catering service for all the weddings and parties. It's going to be great. In the past, we all tried to pitch in, but a real, professional catering service, we are not."

"Well, Ria has been great. She's been calling up some of her seasonal workers to see if they would like a full-time job. Ria said some of them are fantastic cooks." Starla was so thankful for her friend.

Tracy nodded. "I've eaten there plenty of times, so I would bet they are."

Just then, they both turned and looked down the road when they heard the sound of a Harley.

"Well." Tracy smiled. "You're one lucky woman. It looks like your boyfriend is back to hang out with you again. I'll go make you both a cup of coffee. Tell him it's waiting inside when he wants it." She winked and walked back into her shop.

Starla would never tire of hearing people call Connor her boyfriend. The entire town knew they were together and had been supportive of their relationship. While she waited for him, she glanced out at the lake and felt her heart soar. She was lucky to live in this wonderful town with all her new friends and grandma and have a boyfriend who was kind, sexy and, fun to look at. When he finally pulled up, he turned off his engine and pulled off his helmet. There was no way not to stare at the way he swaggered toward her. She was in love, and there was no doubt about it. The minute he was close enough, he leaned down and gave her what was supposed to be a small kiss, but his lips lingered.

"Just a reminder, darlin'. You do remember, we have the house to ourselves tonight." He winked. "I've ordered dinner to be delivered and Austin is leaving with my brother, fishing and camping before it gets too cold." He wore a sexy smile.

"I did remember that, actually," she said and arched a brow. "Anything you have in mind besides food?" She blushed.

He laughed. "You might say that."

"Tracy has two cups of coffee waiting for us if you want to go down and grab them."

"Oh, she must have read my mind. It's been a good day. Stopped by and visited with the Owen's. They are happy campers in their new home and that puts me in a mighty fine mood." He leaned down, kissed her cheek, and walked down the road.

Starla turned around to go inside when her cell phone played her Grandma Judy's song. How strange? Her grandma never called her. "Hello, Grandma."

"Is this Starla Moon?" the lady asked.

"Yes, this is she, and you are calling from my grandma's phone." She felt her heart sink.

"Don't worry, she's fine. My name is Terry, and I'm from Adult Home Care. Your grandma has been asking for you."

"For me? She asked me not to come see her anymore, but I was going to pick her up and transfer her here in October, anyway. I spoke to Debbie from the administration office and set it all up."

"Oh, I heard about that. However, she's asking for you now."

Starla almost lost her breath. "Okay." She swallowed her tears.

"Starla? This is grandma. How are you, dear?"

Starla could barely keep from sobbing. "I'm good, Grandma. I miss you."

"When are you coming to take me home?" Her grandma sounded sad.

"I was going to be there in two weeks to pick you up and bring you here."

"I want to go home now. I don't know anyone here. Please, can you come and get me right away?"

Starla sucked in her breath again and couldn't believe the change. "Let me check with Whispering Pines here. If I can get you in sooner, I can come tomorrow."

"Okay, dear, I miss you so much. It feels like it's been forever. I love you, Starla."

"I love you too, Grandma. I'll make it work. See you tomorrow."

"Promise?" her grandmother lightly said.

"Yes, Grandma. I promise." The phone went dead, and Starla

started to cry. "Oh, Grandma," she whispered and placed a hand over her heart.

"Starla?" She heard Connor's voice. She could see the worry etched across his face when she looked up at him. Her tears wouldn't stop, there was no way. "What's wrong?" he asked and stepped closer, setting both cups down on the small table.

"My grandma from Louisville called. She wants me to come and get her tomorrow. She said she misses me, and she sounded so alert and normal. I need to call Whispering Pines to see if they can take her earlier than we originally planned. I hope she remembers me tomorrow." Connor touched her cheek. "Do you think she could get up in my truck? We could pick up all her stuff and bring her home."

"She asked to come home, and I want to bring her here. She was there for me when my parents were both gone. I always felt loved. Until she forgot me."

"Well, it sounds like she remembered today, and that is great news."

Starla nodded. "I feel like I'm in a dream. I found you, Hialeah, I'm cancer free, and I have Austin in my life. Now, my grandma just told me she misses me."

"Well." Connor swallowed hard. "I came here today because I had something to ask you. I hope my timing is okay, but if it's not, I'll do a repeat when it is." At that, he sunk down to one knee, and the only sound she heard was the pounding of her own heart. "Starla Moon Holloway, I know we haven't known each other all that long, but I love you. I want to spend the rest of my life loving you and raising Austin together. I was wondering if you would do me the honor of becoming my wife? Will you marry me?" His eyes were clouded with tears.

She put her hand over her mouth and all she could do was nod.

"Is that a yes?"

She nodded again and choked out. "Yes."

EPILOGUE

Starla stood gazing into the bedroom mirror at Hialeah's house. She wore a leather Native American wedding dress with white fringe. She and Connor were getting married out near the lake by Jerry Wolfe, a Cherokee pastor who seemed like a great friend to her grandmother and was doing this as a favor. Connor had agreed to the plans, seeming happy the wedding would be simple. His family had been understanding as well. They had designed their own ceremony and although it wasn't traditional Native American or any other formality in any sense, they had loved the ideas and the clothing they chose. Starla inhaled a deep breath and placed her hand across her heart.

She couldn't believe how much she looked like an Indian bride. "I am an Indian bride," she whispered.

The beads in her hair were turquoise, which matched her belt. Her entire outfit was amazing. Hialeah had worn it on her wedding day, which made it even more special to Starla. Hialeah had said it would bring the couple good luck and great times. After a few minutes of standing in front of the mirror, there was a light knock on the door.

Come in," she responded. The door opened to Thea and Oliver. Tears laced both sets of eyes.

"Look at you," Oliver said as he walked over to embrace her. "You look stunning."

"I've never seen a more beautiful bride," Thea said, taking her turn hugging her.

"I still can't believe I'm getting married." Starla gazed between the two, loving their casual way of dressing.

Oliver wore a white shirt and grey pants, his blue eyes sparkling with happiness. Thea looked beautiful in a light blue dress that showed off her Italian skin, her dark hair flowing over her shoulders.

Starla cleared her throat. "A few months ago, I didn't even think I'd ever be able to get married. Yet, here I am. I still can't believe it."

Just as Thea released her, there was another knock at the door. Hialeah poked her head in.

"It's time." Her smile reached her eyes. "You are beyond stunning." She waved for them to follow.

"Thank you, Grandmother."

Oliver touched Starla's arm. It's my pleasure to present you to the love of your life."

Thea nodded. "And my pleasure to be your bridesmaid."

"I had to put a little tradition in there, and I wanted you both as close to my side as possible."

"We wouldn't want it any other way." Oliver said as he held up his arm, and Starla threaded hers through it.

Ten minutes later, they exited Oliver's car down by the lake. People were seated in chairs under a canopy for shade. The wedding was small but included Connor's family and a few people from the town. They were heading to the lodge afterwards for the reception. Ria had set up the entire shindig, and there was no saying no to her. Starla watched Thea gracefully march down the aisle, looking elegant.

Still, Starla didn't see Connor until she got to the edge of the second set of chairs. Everything faded, and the only face she saw was his. His shirt was the same color as her turquoise belt. He wore black slacks, and his eyes shone with joy. God, she loved this man. Never in a million years had she dreamed that such a person would become her husband.

Two Native Americans played the "Lakota Love Song", which sent chills throughout her body as she walked to the side of her forever husband. Oliver put her hand in Connor's, and a small tear slid down Starla's cheek. With a whispering-soft touch, Connor wiped it away.

They turned and faced Pastor Wolfe. He held a feather in his hand.

"Father in heaven," he said, glancing between them. "These two have come here today as two people, but with one life in front of them." He touched them lightly on the head with the feather. "Bless this union." They held hands. "You will feel no rain—for each of you will be the shelter from the cold and the storm." He turned to look at the drummer and nodded. Softly, they played as he continued speaking. "Let happiness rain in your home and all around you. Smile often and laugh together. Be playful and joyful, and you will sing in harmony. Remember to focus on what is right between you, not what is wrong. Let the moon shine its love on you, and the breath of your love will soothe any fear."

The words touched Starla's heart deeply as the music began to play again.

Pastor Wolfe touched them with the feather on their shoulders. "Share the band of gold that will seal the journey ahead of you." He touched the rings with the feather and the couple exchanged them.

Starla could hear sniffles all around her. Her eyes overflowed with tears of pure joy at the vows exchanged between them.

Pastor Wolfe finally said, "You are now husband and wife. Celebrate today and every day for as long as you both shall live. And as you kiss each other, remember to do this often and every night before you close your eyes to sleep."

On that beautiful fall day, September Twenty sixth, while the multicolored leaves scattered across the lawn and birds harmonized in the trees. Connor and Starla sealed their union with a kiss, becoming husband and wife, in love and best friends forever.

Two years later

STARLA LOOKED AROUND THE LIVING ROOM AT CONNOR'S PARENTS' home. It was filled with her family and friends. Sometimes, she still needed to pinch herself to remind her she wasn't dreaming. Today Connor's sister, Paige, was there, and she was a doting auntie. She had gone through her own hell and split up with her college boyfriend and was home to mend her broken heart. She'd arrived last night.

Connor waltzed in. "Hey, sweetie. Where did you put the pull ups?"

"I think we forgot them in the car."

Ria grinned and answered for Starla. "We were busy talking about Sandy and how well she is running things at Moon's Catering. I just love that name, by the way."

"I think you're right. We were so busy running our mouths we totally forgot. Here, you take Carrie Ann and I'll run out and get them. I don't want to wake her, she finally got tired and is napping"

"No, let me have Carrie Ann," Dixie said. "I want to hold my granddaughter. She's growing up so fast." She smiled at Starla. "I can't get enough of this precious girl and she was telling me she wuved me." Dixie chuckled.

Connor handed his mother, Carrie Ann and stood and watched her cradle her granddaughter in a way only a grandma could. Then he strolled out the door, but not before he'd turned and winked at his wife. Starla went to stand. "Well, I sure do need to do something. I'll go check in the kitchen."

"Now, you sit there, and don't you move," Dixie scolded. "You look like you're ready to pop."

"I feel like it, too. Even though I'm only six months." Starla ran her hand over her belly and felt the baby kick. "Oh, he's a strong one." She chuckled. "He wants out of there." The front door opened, and Starla's grandmother walked in holding Connor's hand. Duncan was trailing close behind.

"Hi, Grandma," Starla said, holding her breath as she waited to see if her grandma would remember her today.

"Well, look at you." Her grandma's sweet face told her everything she needed to know. It was a great day. Her Grandma sat down and embraced her. "I sure wish this little one would make its way into the world." She pulled back and touched Starla's tummy.

"Soon, Grandma. He'll be here soon." Starla smiled and squeezed her hand.

Hialeah and Mack walked in the room, each carrying a tray of sandwiches, and Austin followed holding the lemonade. Mack glanced at his wife holding their granddaughter. "As I live and breathe, I don't think I've ever seen anything so precious." He set the food down on the coffee table and moved over to his wife. "Hard to believe our granddaughter is edging toward eighteen months."

Starla placed her hand across her belly. "I need to get her potty trained before this one gets here. We are pretty close, but not there yet."

"We are doing great, little lady." Connor grinned. "She's asking to go plotty now." They all chuckled.

Austin set the lemonade down and glanced around the room. He was so tall and handsome now. "I'll get the glasses and ice."

Connor stood. "I'll help you, son."

"Okay, Dad." Austin waited. "I was thinking maybe we could bring out some of Grandma Dixie's cookies."

"I think that's a great idea," Duncan said. "I'll be in charge of that." He laughed. "By the way, I invited an old friend of yours, sis." He winked at Paige.

"Who?" She tilted her head. "I already invited Mary Ann, she'll be here later. She had to work."

"Nope." He started walking away. "I invited Spencer. You remember him, don't you?" He chuckled.

"You did what!" Paige rose with her hands on her hips, glaring at her brother and trailing behind him. "You can't just do that, Duncan. I haven't spoken to him since all my big brothers," she waved around, "made him start avoiding me and he stood me up for the prom. You do remember that don't you."

Starla winced. "Uh, oh. I think Duncan is in the dog house," she said lightly.

Starla loved the interaction between this family, and any day the family would be complete. The adoption would be final or, so she hoped. She and Connor had gone through a long procedure, and since she was pregnant, the attorney said he'd call when everything was done. "Mom." Austin turned to her. "You want some milk instead?"

She nodded. "That sounds wonderful." She blew a kiss to him, and his face lit up. She loved him just as much as she would if she'd given birth to him. In a sense, she had given birth to him, but in her heart instead. It had been such a shock when she'd got pregnant, she didn't think she could ever have children, but much to everyone's surprise, including her doctor's, she and Connor had conceived Carrie Ann and were thrilled. Now, here she was, knocked up again and ready to pop. Everything in her life had been a miracle since she'd followed the old wooden sign, "Highway to Heaven." Starla couldn't help but think about how much she loved Connor, he had taught her so many things about making love. No wonder she got pregnant, they rarely missed a day.

Ria leaned over the side of the couch. "Earth to Starla. You look like you're lost in another world."

"No." Her cheeks heated. "The only world I live in is right here." She patted her grandma's hand and smiled at Hialeah.

How blessed could a girl be to have two wonderful grandmas and this fabulous family. She glanced around, not to mention, all the best friends she could ask for and be cancer free. The phone rang, and her attention fixed on Duncan as he ran out of the kitchen and picked it up in the dining room. "That better be my wife saying she's on her way, she's got my cell phone."

Paige had her hands on her hips, standing behind him. It appeared she was going to beat him to a pulp. Starla laughed inside. "Give Trudy a break," Dixie said. "That poor girl has so much on her plate, she needs a semi to carry it around for her."

Duncan waved her off. "Hello? Yes, they are both here." He brought the phone to Starla in the living room. "It's your attorney. Let me get Connor."

"Hello?" Starla noticed that Paige was relaxed and attentive now too.

"Hi there, Starla. Is Connor around? Can he pick up the other line or put it on speaker phone?"

Connor came barging into the room. "What's up?"

"The attorney is on the phone and he wants you to pick up the other line or put it on speaker phone."

A few seconds later, Connor was by Starla's side. "Okay, I'm here."

"Well, I wanted to let you both know that everything is final. Austin is now legally your son."

Starla glanced up and saw Austin holding a glass of milk, tears rimming his eyes. He was so afraid the judge would say no. "Can you repeat that to Austin?" Starla requested.

"I sure can." She patted the seat next to her and Austin sat down. "Okay, here." She turned off speaker phone and handed it to her son.

"Hello, this is Austin. They are?" He swallowed hard. "And nobody can ever change it?" He paused. "Thank you, sir." A tear trailed down his cheek. He held the phone in his hand and glanced between Starla and Connor. "You're my mom and dad, and nobody can ever take me away."

With Connor's help, Starla stood and faced Austin. "You are my son, always and forever. I love you." She pulled him into a big hug and Connor joined in.

As they embraced, she couldn't help but notice there wasn't a dry eye in the room. Even her grandma seemed to understand what was going on. It was one of the happiest days of her life. One beautiful son, a daughter, and another son on the way. That was the day Starla Moon knew that magic lived in that little town of Secret Valley River. Magic was all around her.

Just then, the doorbell rang, and Austin ran to answer it and flung it open. A young man with blond curly hair and dark almost black eyes stood there. "Hi, I'm Spencer and I'm here to see Paige. Is she around?"

"Oh yeah. She's here. Come on in."

Spencer stepped in the door and Starla watched as Paige walked over.

"Hi, Paige," he said with a smile and twin dimple's that lit up his face.

"Well, four years later, you decide to show up. That clock has run out, wouldn't you say. After all, you left me hanging on prom night, with my new dress, shoes, and hairstyle. If you're here to pay me back, give the money to my parents, they paid for it all." She turned and walked out of the room the same way she had entered.

He stood there with a look that was determined, held up his finger. "That didn't go well, but I'm going to make a wrong, right" He headed in the direction she had gone.

THE END

Turn the page for a sneak preview of
The Beauty of Heartbreak
Secret Valley River Series #2
Coming Soon from Satin Romance

Don't miss out on your next favorite book!

Join the Satin Romance mailing list
www.satinromance.com/mail.html

THE BEAUTY OF HEARTBREAK

CHAPTER ONE

PAIGE STOOD OUT BACK, STARING AT HER PARENTS' GARDEN, FEELING her insides boil. That's something she'd never do—grow a damn garden. For what purpose, when you could go to the store or farmer's market and buy all the vegetables you needed? She bent over and put her hands on her knees, trying to catch her breath. Angry wasn't the right word to describe how she felt. She was still reeling from having her childhood sweetheart show up, all because her oldest brother, Duncan, had invited him. What in God's name was he thinking? After growing up with six brothers, she had learned to be tough as steel. They had taught her to fight, play basketball, and to fish, catching as many or more, than they did.

However, the last thing she needed was to run into her old boyfriend after just breaking it off with Danny, her fiancé. Her family didn't even know she'd gotten engaged last year. Why? Simple, her overbearing brothers, would have come and given him the third degree and then some. Her eldest brother, Duncan, knew that her childhood sweetheart, Spencer Rawley, had stood her up on prom night. So why the hell would Duncan do something like that? How dare he invite him over. After ten years, she still was not one step closer to finding out why he'd stood her up, but she'd never forgotten it.

She was home after spending ten years in school. After all her hard work and all that time studying and going non-stop, her fiancé had decided she shouldn't be a doctor. Was he insane? He'd told her that he wanted her to be a stay-at-home mom. Right. No one spends four years getting a bachelor's degree, four years in medical school, and two years (so far) in Residency just to throw it all way. What the hell was this, 1952?

She'd thought they were going to be doctors together and have this wonderful life living in the city. He'd known that was her dream when he met her. After she dumped him, she had placed her hand on the bible and swore off men for life. That was her final answer and she was firm in her conviction.

"Hello, Paige. I heard you were back in town, and I wanted to see you—that's why I came over." His voice was soft and kind just like she remembered.

"Okay, you've seen me. Now you can leave," she said without looking at him.

"Are you going to stay mad forever?" he replied. "It's been ten years."

"Yes. As a matter of fact, I might be mad for my entire life."

"Paige, can you at least look at me? I've grown up. Changed. I'm sorry. You wouldn't answer any of my letters, and I've sent one every year since you've been gone. The last few came back to me."

"I was engaged, and he didn't like that you kept writing."

"From what I hear, that's over now and he has no say."

"That's none of your business, Spencer. Go away," she snapped. "We were having a family moment, and you interrupted that." She finally turned and stared into his dark eyes. "Starla and Connor just adopted Austin. Can you please just go away? We want to celebrate."

The hurt on his face squeezed her heart. "Sure. I'll leave, but I hope we can at least be friends. I've missed you."

"Go away, Spencer. Right now, is not a good time for me to decide who I'm going to be friends with."

"Alright," he said, studying her. "You looked fantastic, by the way. Your hair is blonder, and I like how you cut it, shows off your beautiful green eyes."

He paused staring at her for a minute too long, then turned and left around the side of the house. She heard his Harley start, and the crunching of gravel beneath the tires told her he was gone.

"Shit, shit, shit," she said out loud. Her stomach was in knots. If she did have a conversation with him, Paige wondered if he'd at least explain why he'd stood her up and had broken her heart all those years ago. Maybe there'd been a reason. However, there was *no* excuse why he hadn't called to let her know he wasn't coming. It was still the most painful night in her twenty-eight years of life.

They had gone steady since the seventh grade, and she had been in love with him. The fact that he'd never called her afterwards had made it easier for her to go away to college. She thought about that night and how she'd waited for him with such excitement. Even though they had been so young, she'd honestly thought they'd be together forever. That whole event was deep-rooted in her memory.

May 6, 2010

A knock on her bedroom door made Paige jump. "It's me, honey. Open up, I want to see your dress."

"Okay, Mama." She went to the door and slowly opened it. "Ta-da!" She spun around, then smiled at her mom.

"Oh, Paige, you look beautiful. Spencer is going to fall down to his knees." She put her hand across her heart, and her eyes filled with unshed tears.

"Mama, don't cry. I'm not getting married. I'll be home by midnight!" Paige hugged her. "Thank you for buying all this. You and Daddy did so much. My hair, new shoes, everything is wonderful."

"Well, my darlin' daughter, you deserve the best." She swallowed hard. "You've made such wonderful grades and look at the university you were accepted into. We couldn't be prouder. Our daughter is going off to become a doctor."

Paige smiled. "It's going to be hard work, and, and..." Her lip trembled. "I'm going to miss you and Daddy."

Her mom nodded. "We will miss you, too. I have every faith that you will do amazing things."

"I'm going to work hard." Paige walked over and stared out the window. "He should be here anytime," she said, then looked at her clock and realized he was late. "More than likely he had to get gas. He always waits until the last minute," she laughed.

"Well, her mama smiled, "why don't we go down and show your daddy, and by that time he'll be here."

But it never happened. An hour went by, and then another. Paige called his house, but nobody answered.

She thought his car might have broken down and wanted to go look for him. But just as they were walking out the door, the phone rang. Paige was sure it was Spencer, and she flew to pick it up.

"Spencer, where are you?" she asked, winded.

"It's not Spencer, it's Mary Ann." Her best friend's voice sounded sad.

"We were just on our way out to look for Spencer. We think maybe his car broke down."

"No, he's not coming to pick you up. He left town and won't be back for a week."

"What? Why didn't he call me?"

"Nobody knows why. Even Timmy didn't know, and he normally knows everything about Spencer."

After Paige hung up, her dad offered to take her to the prom, but there was no way she wanted to go. By eleven, she knew he wasn't going to call, so she changed out of her dress and took her hair down. Her mom and dad looked as sad and sorry as she felt.

"I have a good mind to go kill that boy," her daddy said.

"Now, Mack, I'm sure something must have happened for him to go out of town."

"And he doesn't know how to use a phone?"

"Paige," her dad said, interrupting her sad memory.

"Yes? What is it, Daddy?"

"We just got notified that something has happened to one of your brother's. Hunter was on a helicopter, and it went down. You need to come in."

THANK YOU FOR READING

Did you enjoy this book?

We invite you to leave a review at your favorite book site, such as Goodreads, Amazon, Barnes & Noble, etc.

DID YOU KNOW THAT LEAVING A REVIEW...

- Helps other readers find books they may enjoy.
- Gives you a chance to let your voice be heard.
- Gives authors recognition for their hard work.
- Doesn't have to be long. A sentence or two about why you liked the book will do.

ABOUT THE AUTHOR

Brenda Ashworth Barry's first book was a memoir titled, Healing the Voices Within, which was never published, but sponsored on a local TV station and flew off the shelves at her Healing Center in Redding California.

Her most recent work is a seven-part saga of star-crossed lovers separated by the war in Vietnam, entitled Seasons of Love and War. Brenda worked for over five years to bring the six-part Saga alive.

Brenda lives in Roseburg, Oregon, by the Umpqua River, and has raised four children three birth children and one adopted, born in her heart. Her husband, who was in the military for 21 years, gave her help and encouragement while writing her novel. When she's not writing she can normally be found walking the trails with her husband and their little dachshund, or in their RV enjoying nature.

www.brendaashworthbarry.com
brendabarry.blogspot.com
brendabarryashworth.wordpress.com

f facebook.com/Seasons-of-Love-and-War-Author-Page-411210412247684

𝕏 twitter.com/sunsetsky52